# BLACK
# MAGIC ROSE

## BOOK 1 OF
## THE ALLIANCE

## JORDAN K. ROSE

Lyn –
Such a pleasure
to meet you and
your mom @
RomFest 2014

Jordan K Rose

Jordan K. Rose, Publisher
PO Box 714
West Kingston, RI 02892

The Vampire Hand Guide: Tips, Myths & Advice
Jordan K. Rose

ISBN: 978-0-9894175-8-7

Cover Art:
*Phatpuppyart.com*
Claudia McKinney

Editors:
Judith Roth
Jane Haertel

Copyright
Kimberley A. Dias
All rights reserved

Jordan K. Rose Publishing December 2013

*For my parents who always encouraged me try new things.*
*Without you I'd have never believed I could do this.*

# CHAPTER ONE

"Dr. MacDuff to the ER! Stat! Dr. MacDuff to the ER! Stat!" The overhead page sounded for the third time in less than ten minutes. First calling Osgar, then Meg, now Dr. MacDuff. Whatever was happening in that ER must have been traumatic if they needed the head of security then the Director of Nursing and finally the Chief Medical Officer.

The young lab tech sitting across the desk from Sofia flinched and glanced toward the door, then he fidgeted in his chair. Tears welled in his eyes.

"Patrick, though you've been doing fine in this interview, I want to remind you this is just a job, not a gladiator challenge. No need to cry."

He swiped the tear away. "You don't understand. Cader is the most secure hospital in Rhode Island. I need to be here. And I'll devote myself to this place. Forever." He folded his hands as if praying to the hiring gods. "This is where I belong."

He was right. Cader House Hospital was the most stable hospital and the oldest and the smallest and the only one Sofia knew of whose entire staff was currently comprised of werewolves and vampires and her. Who'd have thought little Wooddale could be so exciting?

"Ms. Engle, when can I start?" Patrick slid his certification across the desk. "And here's my reference list. Charlie knows me and Donald Cooper, your lab manager, is a friend of my family. He'll vouch for me. He'll tell you he wants me here." He grabbed Sofia's hand. "When can I start?"

There wasn't any reason why she wouldn't hire him based on the interview. He was certainly eager, and clearly, this was where he wanted to be. "Patrick, let me check your references. I'll call you by the end of the week."

"End of the week? Can't you finish them today? I can call Charlie and Donald now. They can tell you I'm really a good worker, and I'll do anything needed."

"What else is going on, Patrick?" Recruitment had been a very easy task at Cader. Applicants were literally banging the door down to get into the place. However, Cader did have some very discriminating practices.

For example, you practically had to be superhuman to survive working here.

"I know Dr. MacDuff wants you to hire more humans, but Charlie said you'd still consider me." Patrick bit his lip.

It was true. Dr. MacDuff wanted to change the hiring practices and bring on more humans. This was the major goal of Sofia's employment and her second biggest challenge. Dr. MacDuff's love of humans spawned the theory that vampires and werewolves should be able to work side by side for extended periods with humans without any unfortunate mishaps.

"Yes, well. I have to hire the best person for the job, human or otherwise." She could barely believe she'd heard herself say those words. Female or otherwise. Black or otherwise. Those were classifications she was familiar with. Human or otherwise was an altogether different perspective.

"I was a patient here once." Patrick stared toward the door. "Got good care, too."

"I'm glad to hear you had a good experience." Sofia knew all too well how good the care was at Cader. It was only days before she'd been recruited to work here that she'd been taken to the ER by ambulance. She'd managed to thwart the burglar but not without sustaining a concussion and several bruised ribs.

The memory of that night made her pulse quicken. Until that attack in her own home, she'd always felt safe.

Patrick picked up the phone on Sofia's desk. "Just call Donald, Ms. Engle. He'll tell you he wants me to start tonight. I swear." He shoved the phone toward Sofia.

She kept her attention on Patrick, ignoring the phone he'd placed less than three inches from her face. The young werewolf sighed and replaced the receiver in its cradle, then sagged into the chair.

Being the only human employee here was so far not only a new experience, but odd to say the least. She'd never had a job where she lived with the weird feeling that everyone thought she smelled way too good.

"I need to be here. Please, Ms. Engle. It's not safe for me anywhere else." Staring down at the desk with shoulders slumped, he mumbled, "My family's gone. Bas Dubh killed them all. I'll be dead by nightfall if you don't help me." He lifted his head and tears streamed from his sad blue eyes.

If there's one thing Sofia was not, it was a hard-ass. In spite of what every employee and manager in the world thought of every Human Resources professional, Sofia was not mean.

And she certainly wouldn't be responsible for anyone's death, not at the hands of another human or Bas Dubh.

"Okay. Wait in the lobby down the hall. I'll see what I can do." She handed him a tissue. "And stop crying. This is a job interview. There's no crying in job interviews."

Less than an hour later Patrick's references were complete, he'd filled out all the employment paperwork, and was downstairs in the ER waiting to be seen for his employment health screening. His new residence was listed as Cader House and his training would begin in the evening.

Sofia had wrapped up her day and was headed for the door in hopes of avoiding Dr. MacDuff, who'd been paged down to the ER once again. No such luck. And their argument from early that morning continued. "But Dr..."

"No."

"But..."

"Sofia, no. If you want to avoid having a guard, then reconsider my offer of housing here at Cader." Dr. MacDuff stopped walking to level a stern gaze at her.

"No," she answered without a second's hesitation.

"Then that's the last I'll say about this." Dr. MacDuff walked away, leaving Sofia standing in the hospital's lobby, coat hanging open, handbag and lunch box slung over her shoulder, keys in hand.

She glanced toward the man waiting to the right of the entrance, and although his stone-faced expression never changed, she knew he was laughing at her.

"Well, it's not the last I'll say about it." She zipped past the guard's desk, trailing after Dr. MacDuff, ignoring Jamieson's warnings to let it go.

"You can't win this one, Sofia," the old guard whispered before reaching for the ringing red phone on his desk. "Not with everything that's happening."

"Dr. MacDuff, I absolutely refuse to allow this. You can't force me to accept a bodyguard I don't want or need. I don't like or trust him. He's scary and mean and *dead*." Not to mention he had a reputation for being a cold-blooded killer who didn't bother to ask questions first, later, or ever. She'd heard he thought of only one thing. Kill. Kill. Kill.

"That's a bit discriminatory, wouldn't you say?" Dr. MacDuff asked, tossing a casual glance her way.

Sofia frowned and peered back into the lobby.

The dead guy loomed in the entranceway. His broad shoulders and height nearly filled the entire space. He stared in her direction. Black hair hung in his face and stubble shadowed his chin and cheeks. But she could still see his dark eyes tracking her every move like a panther stalking Bambi. She ducked into the security office, knowing full and well he'd heard her. They all seemed to have supersonic hearing. It made her nuts.

Dr. MacDuff leaned around her and checked the lobby. "He appears alive to me, lass." The doctor sighed and shook his head as he walked to the back of the room.

Sofia followed him to the far wall where he punched in his security code on the panel hidden just inside a fake closet door, another of Cader's many tricks and secrets. "I suggest you decide what you want to do. If you're going home, Dragomir is going with you. If you're not, then you're coming to the Lower Level with me." The back wall of the closet rose to reveal a stairwell.

She shook her head at yet another attempt to get her to move to Cader. She hated the Lower Level. *They* slept down there. Sofia bit her lip. They wouldn't be asleep now. They'd be awake like *him*. She glanced toward the door.

"Dragomir is like me," Dr. MacDuff said. "You forget."

"I only forget because you don't act like *him*. You act...human," she said. Three weeks in and Sofia continued to struggle with acclimating to the vampires. Though she knew she needed to, and had agreed to be available to staff on all shifts, she had not been able to develop a comfort level with the night staff.

The wolves covered the hospital during the day and early evening. The vampires worked the late evening and night shifts. Sofia preferred to work days, basically only the sunlight hours, which was getting to be difficult as autumn rolled toward winter.

She'd managed to legitimately avoid working the later shift because with the recruitment and new hires, so much kept happening during the day. Thanks to Bas Dubh's tactics, she'd been up to her eyeballs getting frightened new recruits processed and ready for orientation. The nighttime assaults had increased since she'd started, and that meant more recruits came to Cader for refuge. She simply hadn't had the stamina to work past sunset.

Then, two nights ago she'd had her first opportunity to spend some time on the floors with the staff. She'd gotten the once-over from a vampire named Carl and hadn't been able to shake the creepy feeling since. His gaze raked across her like someone rubbed freezing gel over her body. She shivered just thinking about that night.

"Dragomir didn't have to do *that*," she said. The memory of Dragomir's actions played in her mind. Her stomach turned as she remembered his hand shoving through Carl's skin and into his chest. As if it was happening all over again, the sound of squishing muscles and breaking bones echoed in her ears. She swallowed back the bile rising in her throat.

Dr. MacDuff sighed. "I'll agree he responded very quickly. But he did make a clear point."

Sofia gaped at Dr. MacDuff. "The violence is outrageous!"

"Aye. You've told me."

"Yes! And you agreed not to let these...these..." She waved her hand in the direction of the dead guy. "...vampires and wolves use death as an option for addressing behavior." She slung her bag back up onto her shoulder. "I developed a progressive discipline process for those types of issues."

"Aye. I know."

Her voice rose. "But you haven't done anything about him! You think he's safe for me!" She threw her hands in the air.

"Aye." Dr. MacDuff patted her shoulder. "He is, lass. He doesn't need corrective action. He handled that situation just as I would have."

And this was Sofia's number one biggest challenge—the bizarre belief that death was the appropriate response to every performance, behavior, or personality problem. She was fairly certain it was this perspective that gave Dr. MacDuff the odd belief Dragomir was appropriate.

Sofia hadn't been able to make a case to get rid of the brute in spite of sending several well-written emails, including reference material about violence in the workplace, impact on morale, and her own fear of the monster. Both Dr. MacDuff and Fergus, the president and werewolf alpha, responded with, "We'll take your requests and all the accompanying information into consideration." Then two seconds later a second email would arrive. "We determined the appropriate outcome is to leave everything as is. Thank you."

She'd taken to yelling and hissing, banging her fist on the desk and finally giving up in complete and utter frustration. It was like talking to a wall. Or yelling at one.

"My counsel on this issue doesn't seem to have any impact," she huffed.

Dr. MacDuff merely offered a slight nod.

Though Sofia had known about vampires most of her life, she'd only ever known two—Dr. MacDuff and Noelle Duluth, Cader's Director of Nursing. As Sofia grew up, they visited her parents now and again, but their condition was never a topic of discussion, so Sofia never thought twice about them. Nor did she consider that as her parents aged they did not.

Dr. MacDuff still had the dark curly hair and youthful skin of a man in his late twenties in spite of being hundreds of years older.

The wolves, though they hadn't really accepted her, treated Sofia like she was accustomed to being treated. They liked her when they felt she'd done what they wanted and didn't like her when she disagreed with them. For the most part, they were completely ambivalent toward her. It was the same way that every other employee in any organization felt about Human Resources, and very familiar.

On the other hand, with the vampires she felt like she had a giant spotlight shining over her head. She literally *felt* them looking at her. It was as though their gazes held temperatures. Some were cold or downright frigid. Others were warm. Sometimes she'd swear someone was touching her, but she'd turn to find no one near her, just a vampire down the hall.

Dr. MacDuff smiled, and his green eyes sparkled against his pale skin. When he touched her cheek, his hand was warm.

*He's fed.* She recoiled at the thought.

"He will no' hurt you. No matter what you've heard or believe. I trust Dragomir with my own life. I'm absolutely certain he will safeguard yours as well." He unrolled his sleeves and pulled two cuff links from his pocket. Black dragons on ivory backgrounds. The Cader House crest. He wore them every night.

"How can you be so sure? He's like an animal."

As soon as the words came out of her mouth, Sofia stopped, knowing she was caught in a sticky situation.

Dr. MacDuff raised his eyebrows. "An animal? More savage than say Donald or Meg or Fergus? What about Osgar? Is Dragomir wilder than a werewolf?"

She shook her head, never taking her eyes off his hands as he cuffed his sleeves. "You know what I mean."

His fingers worked the cuff links with such speed she hardly had time to process the movements.

"Nay, I don't." Dr. MacDuff placed his hands on her shoulders and held her gaze. "You feel safer with werewolves than with a vampire who has sworn a blood oath to me? I'm at a loss, child. I've no idea how to comfort you. But I will not risk your safety. You can come down to meet with The Alliance or go home. Either way, Dragomir will be present."

Meet with The Alliance? Nope. Sofia did not want to do that.

She sighed. "What if he just follows me and then leaves?"

"Absolutely not. Have you so quickly forgotten the break-in and the brush fire behind your house? What about the blown-out tires on the drive home?" Dr. MacDuff stepped toward the entrance to the Lower Lever. "I haven't. Those were not coincidental."

"I could get an alarm," she offered for the four hundredth time.

"By the time anyone responded, you'd be dead." He didn't budge.

In two months her entire life had completely changed. She'd become an adult orphan, moved back home to her parents' house, lost her long-time job at what she thought was a stable company, and been recruited to Cader. She'd had to finally accept that not only did vampires exist, but werewolves did too, and together they ran the hospital as a front for The Alliance, the organization tasked with maintaining balance in the supernatural community. Cader's chief vampire was her dad's best friend who just happened to be a bit overprotective.

"Bas Dubh is on the move. We are at war, Sofia." Dr. MacDuff's gaze hardened. "I never should have…" He touched her chin. "What's done is done. Now I must ensure your safety. Kiernan knows you work here. If I don't send a guard, he'll come for you."

Sofia scowled at the floor. There was nothing in the world like being a prisoner in your own life. She couldn't argue. She'd completed enough workers' comp reports to know Kiernan didn't play nice. And if Dr. MacDuff hadn't sent Bernie, Cader's electrician, to install motion detectors at her house the day of the brushfire, she'd probably be renting a room at the local motel.

"And if he takes you, it won't be to help decrease the amount of workplace violence in his organization." Dr. MacDuff had a way of tying everything to Sofia's number one personal agenda. She'd never worked in a place where it was not only perfectly acceptable but encouraged to beat the hell out of new staff during the training period. She could not allow it to continue.

"Can't Osgar come home with me?"

"Osgar needs to train the new recruits. He cannot spend all his time guarding you."

"He's monitoring *all* the trainers?" Sofia asked, stressing *all*. She'd already had a run-in with Rick, Osgar's second in command. He clearly disagreed with her definition of acceptable training practices.

"I'm sure he is."

She'd managed to convince Dr. MacDuff to assign Osgar to her for day duty. If she'd thought quick enough, she'd have suggested that simply being at Cader during the day was enough and that Osgar could guard her at night. Instead, she thought she'd save herself from being guarded by another werewolf, a very pleasant, very young man who talked her ear off, making it completely impossible for her to get any work done.

Dr. MacDuff gave her what she wanted. Osgar by day. And then got what he wanted and assigned her Dragomir by night.

Sofia sucked in her cheeks and glanced into the lobby. The dead man faced the exit. His black leather duster covered all but his boots and a couple inches of his jeans.

"As much as I enjoy spending time with you, Sofia, I do have a meeting to attend. Are you coming or going?" He stepped toward the stairwell.

"Dr. MacDuff…"

"Sofia." One word and his tone said it all.

# CHAPTER TWO

Sofia's Camry bounced along her unpaved driveway. She knew the half-mile ride well and easily maneuvered around the potholes and ridges. She'd lived in the chalet-style home most of her life. It officially became hers a couple months back when her mom died.

She pulled into her usual spot directly across from the porch and pushed the gearshift into park before taking a deep breath. She'd managed to get past *him* without having to speak. But now she'd be very clear on her expectations and what *he* was allowed to do.

A truck pulled in beside her, dwarfing the Camry with tires four feet tall, a truck bed that had to be six feet long, and an engine compartment that could easily house the Camry. Rays of light shot into the woods, illuminating a twenty-foot area.

*Why does every vampire have to drive something ridiculous? Porsches, Hummers, jet airplanes. Can't even one of them drive a normal vehicle?*

She huffed, pulled her gold cross from beneath her blouse to lie exposed on her chest, and reached for the handle. The door opened before she touched the lever.

"There is absolutely no need for you to have any contact with me," she snapped without turning to face him. "I can open my..."

The door closed.

Sofia threw open the door. "That was rude." She pulled her handbag and lunch box from the car. "You will stay outside. You have no need to come in. You can simply do that thing you do and sniff around to figure out if anyone has been on the property. I'll wait here." She slammed the door and leaned back against the car, arms folded across her chest.

Dragomir didn't move.

She waited, tapped her foot, and refused to look at him, knowing he was staring at her. More easily than with any other vampire, she could always tell when he was watching her. It was one of the many things about him she did not like. Other vampires didn't make it so obvious they were looking. But Dragomir made no secret of it. He let his gaze linger as though he was trying to stare right through her, and even though she never felt threatened by him, she didn't like it when they made eye contact.

She avoided his eyes as if he was Medusa, and she might turn to stone looking at him. Only she knew she wouldn't turn to stone. She had more of a jelly sort of reaction to his gaze. Whenever she met his stare, she felt like she was falling down a deep, bottomless pool, one that left her helpless and exposed.

Her body did things she didn't appreciate. Her arms turned to rubber, making her drop things. Her stomach flipped and her legs barely held her up, causing her to trip in front of him. She was not a klutz, had always been agile and graceful, played sports, took dance lessons, never had any problem controlling her limbs before. She absolutely did not like this sudden lack of poise.

"Well? Are you going to just stand there all night?" She glared up at him, trying to focus on his chin, but his lips drew her attention. For a quick second, the red lines parted just enough to show a sliver of white teeth, then they closed and it was as though he vanished.

He practically disappeared into the night, a silent shadow. If it wasn't for his scent, she'd have sworn she was standing alone.

But she could smell him, a combination of leather and something woodsy, like pine or fresh air or the crisp scent of autumn. And the faintest hint of soap.

She inhaled. It always flummoxed her, the soap scent. What was it? Irish Spring? No. But what? She inhaled again.

*Distracting. That's what.*

"Well? How long are we going to stand here?" she demanded. Her bags slid down her arm.

"I did not want to disturb you," he answered, his voice so low it rumbled. His scent wafted around her as he stepped closer. Her stomach knotted.

"Disturb me? What are you talking about?" she growled, straightening her back and realizing her bags were no longer in her hands.

He sniffed. Once, twice, three times. "You smelled something. Maybe Jankin is teaching you how to scent. If so, I did not want to disturb your practice." His deep Romanian accent made the words roll together. He held her bags in front of her.

Sofia's cheeks heated, and she was damn glad for the darkness. She swallowed and snatched the bags from his hands, returning them to her shoulder.

"What? No. I wasn't doing whatever, scenting." She waved her hand in front of her face and her bags slid back down her arm. "How long before you complete your task, and I can go in the house?" Her bags dangled at her wrist and she shifted them to her other shoulder.

"My task was complete before I opened your door." He stepped closer and she couldn't resist the urge to look up at him, past his mouth, into his dark eyes. He rested one hand on the top of the Camry, and his body shielded hers from the cool night breeze.

It was happening. Her arms and legs were melting into jelly. She had to get away from him before she ended up in a puddle on the ground. "Fine." She turned and marched up the steps, triggering the sensor that turned on the porch light. She unlocked the door and slipped inside.

"Just so there's no question," she said through a crack in the doorway. "You are not welcome in my home." She slammed the door, locking both locks behind her.

It was true. A vampire couldn't enter a personal dwelling without an invitation. She made sure every vampire, with the exception of Dr. MacDuff, knew they did not have an invitation. And even allowing Dr. MacDuff in was a huge concession.

Finally alone, Sofia followed her usual routine, changing her clothes, cleaning out her lunch box, and preparing dinner. She had planned to grill a steak, which meant she'd have to go outside.

She flicked on the deck light and stared out into the backyard. She couldn't see him, of course. Finding him would be like plucking a single snowflake from a snowball.

She pushed the slider open and walked to the grill, throwing side-glances over her shoulders as she went. Where was he? She hated that *they* could sneak up on her with no warning at all. She turned on the grill and went back in the house.

When she returned to cook the steak, she smelled that mix of leather and soap. She closed her eyes and inhaled. He certainly did smell clean and manly. Nothing wrong with that, *if* he were a man *and* alive.

She threw the steak on the grill and stomped back into the house, glaring in the direction of his scent.

With one wall made almost entirely of glass, the chalet-style home her parents loved made it nearly impossible to find a place to relax without feeling like eyes were on her. After dinner she organized the bookcase, dusted, vacuumed, and finally decided to take a bath. There was only one window in the bathroom, and it had curtains and blinds, both of which she pulled tight.

After that, she snuggled up in bed wearing her fleece jammies. She rarely wore this much clothing to sleep, but she wasn't risking exciting "the guard."

"Cool, comfortable, and dead or hot and sweaty, but alive. I'll deal with the sweat," she said, straightening the blanket.

She lay in bed wondering what the vampire outside her house was doing and whether he was staring into her room watching her. Frustrated, she rolled over and pulled the blanket up over her head, willing herself to sleep.

Nearly an hour later she was still awake and annoyed. Giving up on sleeping, she grabbed a book and her itty-bitty book light. But before she'd read more than a page, she was sound asleep.

\*\*\*\*\*

Dragomir Petrescu watched. He listened. He inhaled. Nothing. No one. Not even a small animal stirred in the woods.

The night was so quiet he heard Sofia breathing inside her bedroom. Even, relaxed respirations. She slept.

*Good.*

He'd agreed to help Jankin because they'd been friends for more than six hundred years. When he received the call, the doctor told him it was a top priority and that he'd trust no one else for the job. The worry in Jankin's voice brought Dragomir from the front lines in Italy where Bas Dubh was attempting to build a stronghold near Rome, using the multitude of tourists to fortify its army.

Dragomir smirked. He'd been duped. His old friend had played quite a trick. He admired Jankin's skill. Telling Dragomir the job was very dangerous and only a master vampire of his caliber would be mentally prepared to handle this adversary was genius.

He shook his head. His own arrogance had been his downfall. He should have known nothing that exciting could possibly occur in Wooddale. And now, he was stuck. He'd agreed to take the assignment, sight unseen.

A man of his word, he would never renege on his promise, in spite of his fierce desire to see Kiernan MacDonald dead. He was sure Jankin had bet on this, and it jerked his chain something fierce.

The recent uptick in attacks on innocents angered Dragomir. If Rome hadn't been in the same situation, Dragomir would have noticed the trend occurring in New England, and he'd have come on his own, though he'd have gone where the action was, not come to one of the sleepiest towns in the region.

Since joining The Alliance in 1412, Dragomir had fought in many wars and lost many an ally on the battlefield or in the pursuit of Kiernan. The damn vampire hid behind his army, never fighting his own battles, but letting the members of Bas Dubh do it for him.

The ravages of war haunted his memory. There was no escaping the echoes of the screaming men and women, those who died and those who lost someone in the fight.

War taught Dragomir that all issues were black and white. Good versus evil. Light versus dark. And letting your mind wander to what ifs was the same as questioning your entire reason for existing. Pointless and confusing.

It was Jankin who understood Dragomir. He'd been the only one to offer his hand to the warrior, the only one to thank him for his sacrifice. Jankin was one of a very small group Dragomir trusted, even cared for.

So here he sat at—he glanced at his watch—0321, in a tree in the backyard of one Sofia Maria Engle, the unwilling, angry woman in need of guarding.

Half Italian, half Scottish, one hundred percent American. Only child, born to parents later in life. Age twenty-five, father died. Age twenty-six, mother died. Has a passport but has never left the country. Under the delusion that "human resources practices" can be applied to vampires and werewolves.

Dragomir chuckled. He'd had to research the term "human resources," having never heard of it. Leave it to humans to count themselves among their own resources, and then design a job for someone to hold their hands. He shook his head.

It wasn't the actual profession he liked. He had no use for namby-pamby "support" of employees. Subordinates should do as they were told, whatever was asked of them without complaint, and be happy to have a job. They should be even happier to have a master to ensure their safety.

He did however like the idea of "human resources." Vampires needed human resources. He'd never formally considered humans as resources, but they certainly were. And quite necessary at that.

He drummed his fingers on the branch and sighed. He estimated the temperature at about thirty-eight degrees, wind at about eight knots. Clear skies. Dry, not a hint of humidity in the air. *Small blessing.*

At the very least it wasn't raining.

Sofia moaned. His fingers froze. He listened. The sound of fabric brushing fabric came to him. She yawned, and then her breathing returned to the slow, even respirations of a sleeping woman.

0344. No change in weather. No disturbances in the area. No reason for a vampire to sit in a tree.

He jumped to the ground without rustling a leaf. After a leisurely stroll of the perimeter, he found himself under Sofia's window again.

Jankin had to have known this would be the world's most boring assignment. How could he have possibly believed she needed a guard the likes of Dragomir? Surely Osgar or any one of Cader's security team could handle brushfires and a silly female with lofty ideas for making everyone hold hands and get along. Maybe there was intelligence to lead Jankin to believe Sofia needed the attention of one of the most highly skilled vampires in The Alliance's ranks. Intelligence he'd neglected to share.

The simple idea that he had been a friend of her family would not have caused any interest in her on Kiernan's part. Unless Bas Dubh thought she was Jankin's. His own descendant.

Dragomir raised an eyebrow.

There had been rumors. Nothing confirmed. Could it be true?

He scaled the wall, pulling himself onto the roof, then walked to the peak. Tossing his leather duster aside, he scanned the property once again. Nothing.

After securing his weapons, with bat-like precision he dropped over the edge of the roof to hang upside down outside Sofia's window.

She lay curled in a little ball, hardly any part of her visible with all the pillows and blankets tucked around her. A tiny light illuminated the left side of her face. Shiny black hair, auburn highlights. Creamy skin. Freckled, small, upturned nose. Eyelashes long enough to brush her cheeks.

She certainly resembled Jankin with the same almond-shaped green eyes and thick black hair as his.

She stretched and moaned, then snuggled further into her cocoon of blankets.

He inhaled. Her scent wafted in the air stronger than he'd expected.

*How's that?*

Intrigued, he studied the room.

Carpeted floor. Sand-colored walls. One chair with blanket, far corner. Plant—Peace Lily to right of chair.

Bathroom at the rear, towels hanging on hooks. Hairbrush on counter. Four lotion bottles lining wall. Glass shower stall. Tub with jets.

Black bra, panties, and stockings folded on bureau. Suit hung on hanger over door. Shoes placed beneath.

Two lamps—one on each nightstand. Queen-sized bed. Four, five, six, seven, eight pillows.

He shook his head.

Southern wall: fifty percent glass.

Northern wall: bathroom, closet—walk-in.

Eastern wall: two smaller windows—bed placed between.

Western wall: door, stairwell.

His eyes darted back to the eastern wall. A window was cracked.

He inhaled. Sweet. Flowery.

Dragomir rolled the aroma across his tongue, tasting her essence, memorizing her scent. Her fragrance, soft and sweet, hinted of flowers. Just a mild breath of something floral.

He smacked his lips, focusing on the one aspect.

*Green. Clean. Gardenia?*

He sucked his tongue.

*No. And not dahlia or jasmine.*

He inhaled.

*What is that?*

He worked his way toward the edge of the roof, inhaling and focusing with each movement.

*Petunia?*

Sniff.

*No.*

When he reached the window, he chuckled.

Sofia had pushed the window up a quarter inch, allowing her scent to flow into the night air, a sweet invitation. But she'd tried to safeguard the opening. Rosary beads hung from the window lock, the crucifix dangled in the opening.

Dragomir tapped the cross and watched it swing.

*Silly girl. Jankin has a great deal to teach you.*

He inhaled, filling his lungs with the sweet, intoxicating berry-scented air. He enjoyed the aroma, but the floral undertone continued to elude him.

*Rose?*

Sniff. Sniff.

*No. Too sweet.*

"What the hell are you doing?"

Dragomir's head snapped up. He flipped onto the roof, landing in a crouch, fangs descended, a knife in each hand.

"Planning to kill me?" Osgar asked. He stood at the edge of the woods, grinning like he'd just caught the biggest fish of his life.

"Your skills have improved," Dragomir said, replacing the knives into the sheaths strapped to his forearms and regarding the werewolf he'd grown to think of as a son and friend.

The wolf had matured in the past six years and not just physically. At just under six feet three inches, he now stood almost eye-to-eye with Dragomir, and his movements, even in a relaxed state, were graceful with an edge of savage power. With Dragomir's guidance, Osgar had developed from the skinny teenager into a rugged leader, moving up the ranks of his pack to become an alpha. Dragomir took pride in this.

It was Dragomir who taught Osgar the ways of the sword and to be cunning, ruthless if need be to outsmart and outwit the other wolves. Dragomir swore to ensure Osgar's knowledge of strategy and skill. It was a pact every master made with his wolf—teach them all they need to know to become the strongest, most powerful in their pack, protect them, discipline them.

It was a fair exchange. During the day the wolves protected their masters. The symbiotic relationship was necessary for both groups.

Dragomir picked up his coat and, noting the brightening horizon, wondered how long Osgar had watched him. "She has slept the morning hours without incident. No one has breached the perimeter." He dropped to the ground, slipping into the coat when he landed.

"No one but me has breached the perimeter. Or really, no one but me has let you know he's breached the perimeter." Osgar's grin widened. "Still hasn't let you in the house?"

"No." Until that moment Dragomir hadn't been bothered by the lack of access, but now the limitation was an annoyance.

"It's a shame. It's warm and cozy in there," Osgar said, walking toward the front door. "Beats being out here in the cold. Not that it bothers you, I'm sure, vampire and all."

"She has secured the house." Dragomir was pleased with this. In spite of the fact that she refused to allow him access, he admired her efforts to keep herself safe. "She's locked every door and made other adjustments." He laughed to himself and glanced toward the window.

"You know her locks won't keep me out," Osgar called over his shoulder.

"You would break in?" Dragomir's eye twitched. His jaw tensed. Though Osgar was bound to him, Dragomir would not hesitate to deal with him should he become a threat to Sofia.

"No, of course not. No need." Osgar turned around and jangled a key as he walked backward toward the porch. "She likes me." He winked. "The whole living thing, you know."

Dragomir felt it, the twist of the proverbial knife in his gut.

"I leave. Safe day," he said, and with vampire speed he returned to Cader, hearing the lock turn and Osgar laugh as he stepped over the threshold.

# CHAPTER THREE

Sofia's nose twitched. She rubbed it. Something tickled. She rubbed her nose again. This time whatever touched her moved up her cheek.

*Spider!*

Her eyes flew open. She swiped at her cheeks and bolted upright, shaking her hair to get rid of the critter.

It scooted along her neck.

She screamed and jumped out of bed, batting at her neck, raking her hands through her hair, and jumping up and down. From the corner of her eye, she saw the truck parked in the driveway.

"Oh, no," she said aloud. "He's still here?"

Where? Where could he be? Not in the house. She'd told him he wasn't welcome. Outside? The bright sunlight made that seem impossible. According to Osgar, vampires really did burn in sunlight. Was he under the truck?

She bent to the windowsill to peer under the behemoth vehicle, but couldn't see a thing. She stared out the window, searching for upturned ground or leaves or something to indicate he was hiding in a hole.

*Stupid vampire.*

The bed creaked.

*In the house? How?*

She spun around.

"Your...your..." Osgar couldn't get the words out. He lay on the bed, clutching his stomach and laughing. Tears streamed down his face. He barely made a sound, he was laughing so hard. "Your face."

Sofia glared at him. His sandy-blond hair was a wild mess, as usual. His typically tanned face was bright red. He looked as though his face might pop if he kept laughing.

"You thought it was a bug." He held up a neon green pipe cleaner.

"Why did you do that?" she asked, reaching to snatch it from his hand and missing. "Get your feet off the bed." She swatted at his work boots.

He jerked away, still laughing. "It's eleven in the morning. You need to get up and go to work."

"Eleven! Why'd you let me sleep so late?" Sofia ran around the bed, leaving Osgar reclined, waving the pipe cleaner at her.

"I think I'll keep this." He tucked it into the pocket of his flannel shirt. "Your face was priceless. I've never seen anyone freak out like that. The jumping and arm flailing, I loved it." He bounced around on the bed doing a ridiculous imitation of her.

"Why'd you let me sleep so late? You know I need to go to work," she called from the bathroom. And why hadn't she set her alarm? Because she was too focused on Dragomir hanging around her property to remember to set it. She couldn't let him get to her this way.

If she'd been able to fall asleep at a decent hour, she'd never have slept so late. But knowing that damn vampire was outside her house kept her awake, wondering what the hell he was doing and if he'd try to come in while she slept.

"You can just go in for noon," he answered. "We have plenty of time."

"I don't have plenty of time," she said before shoving the toothbrush into her mouth and lamenting the fact that now she'd be stuck at Cader until eight. Somehow, she needed to find a way out of the hospital before *he* rose.

"I'll take the back road. We'll be right on time. Your reaction to that pipe cleaner…" He snorted. "I thought you were going to knock yourself out." He laughed again. Sofia heard him blow his nose.

"I'll drive myself." She pulled her clothes into the bathroom and shut the door. "How'd you get here?" she called. "No motorcycle?"

He shook his head. "I walked. Cader's not that far when you cut through the woods, which we could do."

"I'll drive myself," she said again and pulled on her skirt. After tucking in her blouse she opened the door. "Where is he?" She motioned toward the window as she brushed her hair, pulling it up into a bun.

"Back at Cader, I'm sure. Why?" He smiled.

"Why's his truck still here?" She frowned. "I don't want him leaving his stuff at my house, not even in the yard."

"Why don't you like him?" He rolled onto his right side to face her, resting his head on his hand. His blue eyes sparkled, still wet from laughing.

"He's dead. That's why." She went back into the bathroom to apply her makeup. *And he does that* thing *to me.*

"So what? Jankin's dead, and you seem to like him just fine," he called. "And Noelle, too."

The truth was she did like Dr. MacDuff, and Noelle was nice enough. She couldn't explain it, but she never felt nervous or like she was part of a walking menu when she was near them. Plus, her arms and legs remained intact and capable of normal use when she was with them. As overbearing as Dr. MacDuff was, and he could be very overbearing, she liked him, trusted him. She felt the same way about Noelle. She genuinely cared for both of them. Why, she didn't understand.

"Dr. MacDuff is my boss. I have to like him," she said.

"No. Actually, Fergus is your boss," Osgar said.

She stuck her head out of the bathroom and frowned.

"Fergus is the president, and you report to the president." Osgar nodded.

"Ultimately, everyone reports to Dr. MacDuff as he is the founder of Cader House and the head of the American branch of The Alliance. That makes him everyone's boss, including mine."

He shook his head. "Whatever. Why don't you call him Jankin? It's ridiculous that you call him Dr. MacDuff. That would be like me calling Fergus, Mr. McFie."

It was a good question. And Sofia believed she had a good reason.

"I do not like to mix my business life with my personal life," she answered from the bathroom.

"Well, you might as well get over that, girl. Your business life is your personal life." He appeared in the doorway.

"Not if I can help it. You're a mess." His hair needed a comb. His face needed a shave. His clothes needed an iron. His boots were unlaced. He looked like he'd just rolled out of bed. "How can you possibly go to work looking like that? Don't you think patients will notice?"

He grinned. "I think you like me."

"What?" She pushed past him. "Let's go. I just need to pack my lunch and grab something for breakfast."

"You think I'm cute, don't you?" he asked as he followed her down the stairs, boots clomping the entire way.

"You're all right. You're a slob, but you're okay," she answered, tossing a container with a salad into her lunch box and grabbing a yogurt and a handful of strawberries.

"You like me. You like me." He rocked back and forth, heel to toe. "I knew it. I'm irresistible."

Sofia didn't bother to look at him. He'd been flirting and taunting her for two of the three weeks she'd known him. It took him the first week of semiprofessional behavior to wear down her defenses enough to speak with him about anything other than work. According to Dr. MacDuff, that week was a record length of time for Osgar to behave in such a professional manner.

"Get out." She held open the door, sighing at him as he walked by, grinning.

"You think I'm hot," he whispered.

She shook her head, locked the door, and walked to her car. Though he was handsome, and Sofia had watched many a nurse flirt with him at work, she had grown to think of him more as a brother than anything else. Even that idea disturbed her.

"So again I ask, why is his truck still here?" she asked, unwilling to hide her annoyance.

"His truck? Are you kidding? This is my truck." Osgar opened the door and climbed into the cab. "He would never own anything this cool." He revved the engine and cranked the radio. Lights came on above the windshield.

"What happened to your motorcycle?" She was used to him riding on one of those bikes with giant handlebars and an engine much louder than it needed to be.

"The chopper's at Cader. I'm getting it ready for winter." He nodded toward her Camry. "Let's go. Since you insist on traveling the regular roads you're going to be late."

*****

Emails continued to pop up in Sofia's inbox, and although she was tempted to open each one, she forced herself to face Charlie and try to remain focused on his long and drawn out story. But some ten minutes into the conversation, he'd lost her and now she sat in her office staring blankly at him, waiting for his lips to stop moving.

"And then he had us jumping from the top of the building. He actually had us up on the roof of the hospital, jumping to the ground. I didn't think I could do it. Three stories up, you know. I thought I'd break my leg. I didn't want to do it, but I did. He said we didn't have a choice. If we didn't jump, he was going to push us. I jumped. And look, I'm fine. You know, he did push Louis. He just walked right up to him and pushed him. Didn't even give Louis a chance to change his mind. Just pushed him. He fell, you know."

At the word *pushed* Sofia perked up, yanking herself from the near comatose state Charlie's blathering had induced. Her mouth dropped open.

"Pushed? Did you say that Osgar pushed Louis off the roof?" she asked, the Human Resources professional taking control.

"Not Osgar. Rick. It was incredible. I mean, he's fast. Louis couldn't have stopped him, if he'd tried. The guy's like…fast." Charlie's head bobbed up and down. "It was like nothing I've ever seen before. He came up behind him…" Charlie stood up, turned the chair around, and stepped back. "…like this." He crouched and then pounced on the chair, shoving it forward to fall on its side.

"Louis shot off the roof like a ball coming out of a cannon." He picked up the chair. "It was so cool."

Sofia scribbled her notes as quickly as she could. "Is he all right? Louis, that is."

"Oh, yeah. He's fine. Well, now he's fine. He did break both his ankles landing like that. I mean, Rick told us what to do and how to twist and maneuver so that our bodies absorbed the shock and we didn't break anything." Charlie sprung into the air, twisted, and landed on the opposite side of the room. "But Louis wasn't ready when Rick pushed him."

She gasped. "Both ankles! Has he been admitted to Cader?"

*Worker's Comp. Lawsuits. Abuse. Hostile work environment. What the hell is wrong with Rick? I have to speak to Fergus.*

"He was sleeping down below when I came to work this morning," Charlie said.

His walkie-talkie crackled. "Charlie? Where are you? We need you to bring Mrs. Jackson down to x-ray."

"I gotta go. I'll talk to you later, Sofia." He jumped up and ran toward the door, pulling the two-way radio from his pocket. "I'm coming."

Rick worked for Osgar. Sofia dialed Osgar's pager number, well aware he was somewhere in the hospital. She had managed to argue her way out of spending each day with Osgar glued to her hip by promising not to leave the building, which meant he couldn't leave either.

The phone rang and the caller ID listed, "Security."

"Osgar, do you know what Rick did last night?" she asked, picking up the phone.

"No 'hello, how's your day going?'" he asked.

Sofia heard him moving and mumbling directions to someone.

"No. Did you hear my question?"

"Yes. I do know what Rick did last night," he answered, and then said something to someone else.

"So you know he shoved Louis off the roof?" she asked.

"Well, I'm not sure 'shoved' is the correct word. But I do know he was teaching the new recruits jumping and landing skills last night."

"It has been reported that he pushed, and 'pushed' is the correct word, Louis off the roof."

"Who reported that?" Sofia heard something brush against the phone and then Osgar came back. "Well? Who?"

"I want to speak with Louis," she said.

"Do you? You're sure about that?" he asked.

"Yes. I'm sure. It's my job to investigate claims of this nature," she answered. This was the first actual investigation she'd performed at Cader.

It wasn't, however, the first investigation she'd ever performed. She'd conducted plenty of them at her other jobs. She'd get a statement from Louis, then speak to Rick. She may need to suspend Rick pending completion of the investigation. She knew that wouldn't go over well. But she'd discuss it with Fergus and Dr. MacDuff.

"Come on down," Osgar said.

"Is Louis still at Cader?" she asked.

"Yep. He's just finished eating. If I were you, I'd hurry," he said.

Sofia heard the laughter in his voice and glanced toward the window. To the west the horizon was lit with a peachy pink glow. To the east darkness blanketed the sky. Soon, *they* would rise.

"Is he on the second floor?" she asked, voice filled with hope.

"No. He's still in the Lower Level. I don't want you to be surprised when you get down here," Osgar said.

"Surprised by what? Is Louis all right?"

"Louis is fine, aren't you?"

Sofia heard a voice say, "Yes, sir. Ready to have another go at it."

"Osgar, surprised by what?" Sofia asked. "And don't get him worked up. I want to speak to him without your interference."

"I will not interfere in the least. I'll meet you at the stairwell. I don't think you know the code, do you?" Osgar asked, referring to the security access code.

"No. I don't have one. Surprised by what?" she asked again.

"Hey there, Drag. How'd you sleep?" Osgar said.

Sofia's heart thumped when she heard *his* voice.

"Same as always."

"So, like The Dead, you mean?" Osgar chuckled.

# CHAPTER FOUR

Fluorescent lights flickered overhead as Sofia followed Osgar down the stairs, through the corridor, and into the security office. A bank of TV screens lined one wall. Lights flickered across a panel below them. Osgar stopped in front of a computer and tapped a few keys on the keyboard before turning back to Sofia.

"This is where the action is monitored," he said. "There are cameras at all the access points, outside the building, and on all the units within the building. We see all." He wagged his eyebrows.

Sofia looked around. Three men she'd never met before sat behind computers, and although not one of them looked up, she had the very distinct feeling they were watching her.

"Marvin, Jefferson, and Bart," Osgar said, pointing to each of them.

Bart nodded, Marvin waved, and Jefferson's eyes met hers for a brief second before his glance moved across her like freezing rain. And she knew immediately he was the vampire.

"This is Sofia," Osgar said.

Two nods and another ice-cold glance, only this time it lingered. She shivered.

"They're studying the Rhode Island crime reports. There's been an uptick in attacks at the malls, carjackings, muggings, and the like. A number of the victims were knocked unconscious and don't remember what happened. Most likely they were fed from or wolf bitten. We'll track them for changes in behavior or disappearances," Osgar explained.

Sofia nodded. "The malls? Why the malls?"

"Lots of people gathered in one spot and parking garages where women walk alone. Bas Dubh can hide easily enough between cars, attack, and escape virtually unnoticed. It's a perfect place for new vampires to practice honing their skills," Osgar explained. "And with the holidays coming, it's bound to get worse."

Sofia remembered the news report from the night before. A man had jumped from the top of the four-story parking garage, killing himself. It had been the third suicide at the mall in as many months.

"What about the jumpers?" she asked.

"We think they might have been attacked by wolves and the shock or horror of the experience sent them over the edge." Osgar scratched his chin. "Literally."

"The paper said the man from the other night had long-standing financial problems. His family believed he jumped because he was going to lose his house," Sofia said.

"It helps to have the right people in the right places." He smiled.

"What do you mean?"

"The Alliance has members embedded in the police force, at the local papers, and now with the medical examiner's office. We'll know the real story about the guy who jumped yesterday when The Board convenes tonight," Osgar answered.

"So, the paper guy made up the story? How did you get the family to agree to it?"

Before Osgar could answer, Jefferson was across the room, standing between him and Sofia.

"I'd be happy to answer that question for you," he said. Deep within his brown eyes something glowed, lighting his eyes like crystals.

Sofia gasped as she felt him. His presence closed in around her, trying to force her compliance. "Stop that!" She turned away from him, lost her balance, and landed on the floor.

Osgar grabbed Jefferson, and hooking his arm beneath the vampire's chin, trapped him in a headlock. The vampire choked and clawed at Osgar's arm.

From her position on the floor, Sofia saw the door fly open, and the room was suddenly cramped. Dr. MacDuff came to Sofia. Fergus and Meg stood in front of them like a barrier between Sofia and Jefferson. Sofia leaned to the right and saw Osgar and Jefferson dangling in the air, held off the floor by Dragomir.

"Sofia, look at me." Dr. MacDuff knelt beside her.

She pulled her eyes from the scene in front of her to focus on the doctor. Her mind was fuzzy. Something was wrong. She shook her head.

"How are you feeling?" He held her wrist, fingers poised over her pulse.

*Warm.* She glanced at his hand. "Did you feed before you slept?"

A gentle smile crossed his mouth.

"No. I fed when I rose," he answered.

He gazed at her face, and she felt him, a gentle brush of his presence beside her, near her, not trying to claim or possess her, just existing with her.

"It's only now sunset. How could you feed?" she asked, her voice sounding smaller than it should.

"Master vampires rise early, and sometimes we don't sleep at all." He helped her to her feet. "I think you'll be fine." He turned around to face the situation behind them.

"You can let him go," Osgar said, still holding Jefferson in a headlock.

"What is he doing awake before nightfall?" Dragomir asked, his hand wedged beneath Osgar's arm, fingers digging into Jefferson's neck.

"I'd say passing out from lack of oxygen, if he was a wolf. But as a fairly new vamp, I'll assume he's trying to figure out how he'll feed with a broken neck," Osgar answered, releasing Jefferson's neck and dropping to the floor before stepping away from the two vampires.

"Why is he awake?" Sofia asked, peering at them from behind Dr. MacDuff, Fergus, and Meg. A buzz of energy flowed between Meg and Fergus.

Fergus, the alpha for the wolf pack, and Meg, his wife, seemed to have a connection of sorts, something Sofia didn't quite understand. When Osgar stepped closer, she felt the pull of energy from him. The three of them were somehow connected.

"I awakened him early to assist with the study of the last three nights," Dr. MacDuff answered. "I did not realize you would be so tempting to him."

Jefferson's eyes bulged. His jaw dropped. His fangs, shorter, stubbier than Sofia expected, descended.

"He's killing him," she said.

"No. He's already dead, remember?" Osgar said and grinned. "Although, you are rendering him utterly useless for the rest of the night."

Osgar clasped his hand on Dragomir's shoulder. "You should let him go."

Dragomir stared at Jefferson, not responding to Osgar. Silence filled the room. Bones cracked, and Sofia's attention was drawn back to Jefferson's neck.

"Stop it!" Sofia rushed past Dr. MacDuff, Meg, and Fergus and pushed Osgar aside. "Let go of him!" She reached up and pulled on Dragomir's arm. Having no impact, she positioned herself between him and Jefferson and pounded on Dragomir's chest. "Let go!" Still no change.

Dragomir stared past her at the young vampire, his dark blue eyes, glowing brighter than anything Sofia'd ever imagined, as if two sapphires sat in his eye sockets.

"Dr. MacDuff, stop him. This is outrageous. The amount of workplace violence that occurs in this organization is unacceptable!" Sofia gaped at the doctor.

"Dragomir, I think you've made your point," Dr. MacDuff said.

"There is no point. My job is to protect her. I've seen his desires. He would take her, given the chance." Dragomir glared at Jefferson.

The weaker vampire cringed. His body trembled.

Dr. MacDuff stepped beside the vampires, facing Jefferson. The longer he stared at him, the more his eyes glowed. He nodded. "He would have her. Do as you must."

Dragomir stepped around Sofia and dropped his arm, lowering Jefferson so that the barely conscious vampire slouched onto the floor. Without loosening his grip, he dragged Jefferson to the door.

"Wait!" Sofia ran to block him. "What must he do? Where are you going?"

With a swipe of his arm, Dragomir moved Sofia aside and continued toward the door.

Sofia grabbed his hand, clinging to him. She dug in her heels, unsuccessfully trying to stop him. "No! Where are you going? What is he going to do?" she called toward Dr. MacDuff.

"Woman, step aside," Dragomir ordered, shaking his wrist in an attempt to dislodge her.

"I will not," she snapped. "Let him go," she barked at Dragomir as she shifted her weight to shove against his body.

It was like trying to move a cement wall. Every place her body touched was hard.

"I do not take orders from you," he said and continued walking without any indication that she was impeding his progress.

"As the Human Resources…"

"We are not human," Dragomir interrupted, reaching the door.

"I mean as the Employee Relations Manager, it's my duty to insist we give him an opportunity to explain his actions." Sofia clung to Dragomir, pulling herself in front of him. One hand crested his shoulder and one held his waist. She wedged her feet in the doorway and leaned against him, forcing Dragomir to stop walking or break her legs.

"Every employee deserves the chance to be heard before being…dealt with," she huffed.

With her cheek pressed to Dragomir's chest she could hear his heart beating. Strong, steady beats pounded against her skin. His body was warm and she knew what that meant. Her nose scrunched.

His scent enveloped her. Leather and the musky scent of the woods and soap. She inhaled. Something stirred inside her, starting in her belly and spreading to her chest and limbs. Warm and tingly. Her legs buckled.

Her arms became rubbery. She dug her fingers into him, feeling the firm muscles of his shoulder. His skin twitched under her hand at his waist. His shirt bunched in her fists as she held on, trying not to slide down his body.

"Oh!" Her legs gave way. The sound of ripping fabric filled the room.

Dragomir dropped Jefferson and caught Sofia as she tumbled downward, ripping his shirt from his chest. He placed her back on her feet and stared down at her without any hint of expression on his face.

She held the left shoulder of his shirt in one hand and the waist portion of the right side in her other. The fabric covering his right shoulder remained connected along the sleeves, which were protected by his leather coat. Only the back of his shirt remained tucked into his jeans.

Sofia looked down at the cotton shirt in her trembling hands, swallowed, and sighed.

"Well," was all she said. She couldn't bear the idea of looking at him or anyone else for that matter. Her performance was completely out of the realm of professionalism.

She nodded at her hand.

"I apologize for ruining your, uh, shirt," she began, not looking up at Dragomir. "However, I was trying to…well, stop you. And you weren't responding. It, um, was not my intention to…do this…"

She motioned to the shirt in her hand. "I'm happy to replace the shirt… for you." She tucked the fabric up over his shoulder and under the coat without allowing her gaze to wander above his neck. Then she attempted to button a couple buttons but found them missing.

"I would like to give Jefferson an opportunity to explain himself," she said, turning to the vampire on the floor as she straightened her own clothes.

Jefferson's eyes shifted from her to Dragomir. His neck held the imprint of Dragomir's fingers, and giant bruises had formed on his skin. It was obvious he also had several broken bones. His head flopped to the side.

"Oh, my God!" She'd never seen anything like it. He should have been dead, but he wasn't. He blinked at her.

"Dr. MacDuff, do something. Help him." She knelt to touch his neck.

Jefferson reached for Sofia. His tongue darted out, barely far enough to lick his lips. His eyes blazed and Sofia felt that strange pressure descend around her again. He curled back his lips as though jutting his fangs at her.

A growl sounded behind Sofia, and before she registered what she'd heard, Dragomir was crouched beside her, his hand pinning Jefferson to the floor by his neck.

"Stop that!" Sofia swatted at Dragomir. "There is no need..."

Dr. MacDuff pulled Sofia to her feet. "There is a need to protect you. Jefferson would hurt you in his current state. Dragomir, take him to the cells. Noelle will see to his recovery."

Dragomir dragged Jefferson out of the room before Sofia could intervene.

"He's not going to kill him, is he? Jefferson should be given an opportunity to explain himself before he's...punished." Sofia pointed after them. "And death is an awfully harsh punishment for a workplace incident," she yelled toward the door.

"He will be held in a cell where Noelle will help him recover. It will take a couple nights, but then you will be able to speak with him. With a guard, of course," Dr. MacDuff said.

"I don't agree with the..."

"We will not debate this point," Dr. MacDuff said.

She knew better than to argue. The last argument landed her with Dragomir. She might as well not push her luck.

"What has brought you to the Lower Level after sunset?" he asked. "I will tell you I am pleased to see you here, notwithstanding this incident. Maybe you're coming around."

Sofia shook her head. "I have work to do. It seems that one of the new werewolves was assaulted by Rick last night during a training exercise, and I've come to investigate the situation."

"Is that so," Fergus said. "What happened?" He sat at the desk Jefferson had vacated and tapped at the keyboard of the computer in front of him.

Meg and Osgar had both seated themselves at other computers and were busy at work.

"It's been reported that Rick pushed Louis off the roof, causing him to break both his ankles. I plan to speak with Louis and then Rick," Sofia answered, retrieving her notepad and pen from a nearby table.

"Hmm. That's interesting. Osgar, how's Louis?" Fergus asked.

"Fine. Ankles are back at one hundred percent. He's waiting to speak with Sofia so he can get back to training." Osgar stood up and smiled. "You about ready?"

"Before you go, Sofia…" Fergus turned from the computer. "Has anyone explained the training to you and the wolf's ability to heal?" Fergus sat back in his chair and faced Sofia. His red hair was cut short. A beard covered his face with sideburns that merged into his hair. Brown irises sparkled in his deep-set eyes.

"No. But I'm not sure that shoving someone…"

"Pushing. Pushed was the word Charlie used," Osgar corrected.

"Yes, pushed." Sofia tucked her notepad under her arm. The difference between shove and push was neither here nor there in this situation, and she wasn't interested in arguing the point. "I don't see how pushing someone off a roof can be considered acceptable behavior."

"Part of the training to ensure that wolves can make high jumps and land without hurting themselves is forcing a jump," Fergus said.

"They're all tested on a jump. Some of them are tested multiple times," Meg said. "The born wolves naturally jump without needing the help. Changed wolves are usually hesitant and need the encouragement."

"Are you saying that pushing someone off a roof is encouraging? It's abusive and mean and completely unacceptable," Sofia said.

"He's fine. You'll see when you meet with him. He's ready to try again," Osgar said.

"Fine? How can he be fine? He broke both his ankles. It's outrageous that you'd expect him to jump again tonight," she said. "And even more outrageous that you're forcing someone who is naturally inhibited to perform a task."

"He's been practicing the jump for a week," Osgar said. "It's not like he didn't know what was coming."

"A week? You've been shoving him off the roof for a week?"

"Pushing, and not me. Rick. But yes, a week. He's afraid of heights or something so he's just not getting it." Osgar turned to Fergus. "I'm a little concerned. We may need to make an adjustment. It's been the same outcome every night with no improvement. He may not have the wherewithal to accomplish this."

Fergus nodded. "You're thinking quarantine at base camp?"

"Yeah. That might be…"

"What?" Sofia's voice echoed in the room. "You've been pushing him off the roof every night for a week, causing him to break both ankles every night, and you're thinking he's not smart enough to figure out how not to break his ankles? Are you crazy? What is wrong with you?"

"You're overreacting. He's a werewolf," Osgar said, eyes wide and shaking his head. "Preternatural, remember? We heal with the shift. Don't you know anything?"

"Yes, obviously I understand how you physically heal. However, don't you think torturing someone is a bit cruel?"

"Torturing him? He'll never learn to fight, if he can't jump. And he has to learn to fight," Osgar said.

"Why does he have to fight? You're going to force him to do something he's not capable of or doesn't want to do. Why?"

"It's fight or die. I guess you're right. He can choose." Osgar walked toward the door. "Come on. We can go ask him now. It would be a heck of a lot easier if he'd just choose to die."

# CHAPTER FIVE

"Wow. You really did a number on this guy." Noelle cut Jefferson's shirt off to get a better look at his injuries. "Several crushed vertebrae in his neck." She probed his shoulders. "Two broken clavicles." She ran her hand along his chest and down his abdomen. "Two, three broken ribs." She drew a sheet up over his chest.

Jefferson writhed beneath the silver straps wrapped around his wrists and draped across his abdomen. "Bet you're wishing you weren't a vampire now. You can't possibly feel very good. She inserted a needle into Jefferson's arm, taping it into place.

He grimaced and tried to jerk his hands free.

"Sorry. No other way to get the blood in. You're obviously not swallowing anything tonight." Noelle hung a bag of O positive.

Dragomir draped yet another length of silver across Jefferson's abdomen, then made sure his wrists were secured.

Jefferson hissed and whimpered.

"Seriously, Dragomir, I think this is a bit of overkill." Noelle used a towel to remove the second, third, and fourth straps of silver from atop the sheet covering Jefferson's skin. "He's not going anywhere. He's locked down here with me. He can't even hold his own head up, and he's already covered with one layer of restraint." She tossed the silver onto a nearby table. "The prisoner is secure." She saluted.

Dragomir grumbled and glared at Jefferson as he removed the protective gloves and replaced them on the hook above the box of silver restraints.

"You should be fine in a couple nights," Noelle told Jefferson. "Just don't piss off Attila, here." She thumbed toward Dragomir.

"You jest, but he tried to kill Sofia Engle." Dragomir clenched his jaw. Was he slipping? How was this new vampire able to gain access to Sofia? He should have known her whereabouts from the moment he rose, not let even a single minute pass where he was not monitoring her safety.

But amazingly he had not sensed her in the Lower Level. He snarled at his own failing. His typical vampire ability to recognize an individual's aura seemed to elude him where Sofia was concerned.

He'd noticed this challenge the very first night he'd taken the assignment. She managed to exit the building without his knowledge. If not for old Jamieson, he never would have caught up to her before she left the parking lot.

Noelle's surgical scissors clanged against a metal basin as she slammed her instruments onto the tray. "Oh." Her blue eyes widened for a second, but in a flash, the look of surprise on her face vanished. "Well, we'll just deal with him right now."

"That is not an option. He's to recover." Dragomir clasped Noelle's wrist as she raised a scalpel above Jefferson. He pried the knife from her hand and tossed it into the metal basin.

Dragomir thought it was a fluke, hunger, distraction due to his own interest in the local attacks. But by night two, when he stood in the doorway above, watching Sofia as she tried to convince Jankin she did not need him, he knew a strategic change for managing her was in order. From across the lobby he smelled her fruity-florally scent as though he'd buried his face into her chest, yet try hard as he did, he was completely incapable of sensing even one little fizzle of her energy.

"I don't believe this. Are we really following new rules set forth by a human?" Noelle stared from Jefferson to Dragomir. "In all the years I've known that woman...since she was a baby...that's how long, I never thought she'd have this much influence."

Lost in his concerns about Sofia's safety, Dragomir barely focused on the tirade Noelle unleashed as she paced back and forth.

He wasn't entirely certain if Sofia was a fluke or if this loss of vampiric sense, a skill he'd honed for more than eight hundred years, was permanent. Was this some sort of vampire dementia? Did this happen to every vampire at his age?

If he was not able to see, hear, touch, or smell Sofia, he could not be certain she was near. He could recognize everyone else from afar just by the fact that they existed. Everyone gave off a certain energy, an aura specific to each individual human, vampire, werewolf and the like. But with Sofia there was a void. As if she didn't exist until she appeared in front of him.

Stubbornly and unwilling to accept defeat, he opened his senses intending to find her.

He knew every presence on the Lower Level—Meg, Fergus, and Jankin remained in the security room with the two other wolves assigned a security detail. In the conference room members of The Board gathered. Six of them were already present. In another conference room he located Rick. Sofia was nowhere to be found.

Clearly, there was something odd with the Employee Relations Manager. Could the legend be true? Could Jankin's child have been conceived after he was made vampire? Was that the reason for Sofia's lack of energy? Was she some sort of mixed breed? A vampire-human?

Noelle faced Dragomir wearing the most perplexed looked he'd ever seen. "Why wasn't he dealt with? Why are we recovering him?"

Those were very good questions. Good enough to force Dragomir to give up his futile attempt to find Sofia. And though Dragomir knew the answers, he couldn't for the life of him understand them. Jefferson had attacked Sofia or at the very least made a clear threat of attack. His thoughts were of seducing her and drinking from her until there was not a drop of blood left in her body.

Dragomir ran his hand through his hair, holding it back from his face. He sighed, unable to comprehend Sofia's thinking. "The woman wants him to be given the chance to explain his actions before he is punished."

"What's to explain? He's a fledgling with bloodlust." Noelle shook her head. "I knew this new employee relations position was a mistake." She tossed the wrappers from the IV and bandages into the trash bin. "I hope I'm not going to be expected to waste precious Alliance supplies and time caring for the likes of this guy. You know what will happen. He'll just do it again. Now that he has her on his mind, he won't be able to forget about her. He'll be completely obsessed." She jammed the table against the wall. "How many chances does this behavior get? Hmm?"

Noelle echoed the feelings of most of the leaders at Cader House. The idea of progressive discipline and allowing employees the opportunity to improve over time had not been well received. This was an organization of warriors. They were accustomed to dealing with bad behavior in a swift, decisive manner. The basic theory being—if you were dumb enough or devious enough to do it, you deserved to die for it.

Noelle released her long blond hair from the giant clip holding it into a tight twist. "And to think I used sterile technique on this guy." She glared at Jefferson. "We're watching you. She may not understand, but we know what you're up to." Her fangs descended.

Dragomir admired her. He'd fought beside her in Greece in 1848. She was strong, proud, and cunning. She knew the problems that lay ahead of them with Jefferson. He'd keep Noelle as an ally, though he'd trust Sofia's safety to no one but himself. He realized now that even Jankin did not see the dangers surrounding her.

Jankin thought Bas Dubh was his biggest worry. But Sofia was going to get herself killed on her own and probably right at Cader. Her ridiculous idea of Employee Relations applying to vampires and werewolves had just moved into the number one spot on the list of reasons to be concerned for her safety.

"Hey, what happened to your shirt?" Noelle nodded, one brow arched. "Did this guy actually put up a fight?"

Dragomir glanced down. His shirt hung from his waistband and the left side of his chest was exposed. A light florally scent lingered on his coat. His shoulder even carried her sweet clean scent. He couldn't help but subtly inhale the fragrance.

"What? Do you have BO? That would be a first." Noelle sniffed toward Dragomir. "Vampire BO. Ha. Maybe Sofia can write a new policy on vampire bathing." She grinned with fanged delight.

He shrugged out of his coat and ripped the remainder of the shirt from his body. "*She* happened to my shirt. The woman has no idea what she's dealing with." He tossed the shredded shirt into the trash before slipping back into his duster. "I go."

"Ah, yes. Duty calls. Go guard your charge before she ends up getting herself killed by another fledgling or possibly bitten by a werewolf or maybe trips and falls out of the building or…" She grinned. "I think you may have met your match in this one, Dragomir." She barely concealed her laughter.

Dragomir left the infirmary to the sound of Noelle talking to herself about how "the fine and noble, mighty and powerful Dragomir has come to Cader House to face his newest opponent, the all-powerful Employee Relations Manager." Her laughter followed him up the stairs.

He once again sent out his vampire senses searching for Sofia.

# CHAPTER SIX

Louis smiled as he paced back and forth in the conference room. He even did a couple jumping jacks to demonstrate his good physical condition. After escorting Louis from his hospital bed Osgar had left him alone with Sofia.

"Louis, you are allowed to speak freely. I don't want you to have any fear of repercussions from Rick or anyone else."

"Really, I feel fine, Ms. Engle." Louis jumped over a chair.

"Sofia. Please call me Sofia," she said. "But did your ankles hurt when you fell?"

"Oh, yes. Broken bones hurt quite a bit. You'd think I'd get used to the feeling, having broken them both five times now in the past week, but nope. Every night it hurts as much as the first night."

Sofia cringed and shook her head. "Why do you keep going back?"

"I have to. They're helping me." He nodded toward the door. "Rick's a little tough. But I like the other guys. And anyway, by morning I'm good as new."

"But you said you're afraid of heights and that's why you won't jump," Sofia said.

"Right. It's really high." Louis turned the chair to face him and sat down, straddling the back, tapping his thumbs on the table in front of him. "I can't even look out a second story window without getting nervous. I know it seems strange, seeing that I'm more than six feet tall and all. But it is what it is. I'm afraid of heights. I'm not ashamed of that or anything. Although, I am getting a little embarrassed at being tossed off the roof each night. Doesn't help when even the girls jump without effort." His shoulders slumped.

"Are you and Charlie friends?" she asked. She couldn't help herself. They seemed so alike. They even looked alike. Both blonds with bluish-green eyes, though Louis was quite a bit taller than Charlie.

"Oh yeah. We went to school together from first through fifth grades. Then my parents sent me to private school. I only graduated a year ago. I was going to the university when I was attacked on the quad one night."

Sofia nodded. "What were you studying?"

"Engineering. I'm hoping to go back next year. It takes about a year to acclimate to everything. Of course, in my case, it may take longer. If I don't master the jump, they won't teach me to fight. I have to learn to fight." He stared down at his folded hands on the table in front of him. "I don't want to be useless in the war."

"You won't be, even if you don't master the jump," Sofia said.

There was no way she was letting them toss him off another roof. There needed to be some sort of exception so he didn't have to do it. They couldn't keep terrorizing him with the jump.

"Can I go? I have to meet them in fifteen minutes and I need to get changed." Louis tugged at his johnny.

Sofia nodded. "Yeah, but don't go to the roof. There must be something else Osgar can find for you to learn."

"I gotta go. I gotta master the jump. If I don't go they'll just find me and drag me back," he said. "Don't worry. I'll get the jump somehow. Then I'll learn to fight. I don't want to die." Louis left, jogging out the door.

She shook her head and watched him leave. How in the world was she going to fix this? They had this poor kid believing he had to master the jump in order to live. She paged Osgar to tell him to send Rick down and wrote her notes on her pad.

Ten minutes later Rick entered the room. If knowing how he trained the new recruits wasn't enough, his stature was a clear indicator of his status in the pack.

At more than six feet, six inches tall, he loomed over her. A few flecks of silver speckled his cropped brown hair. His face was shaved smooth and a jagged scar ran from his left temple to his ear. Steel gray eyes stared unblinking at her.

"Please have a seat, Rick." She motioned to the chair on the opposite side of the table.

"I'll stand." His gruff voice was a perfect match for his rugged presentation.

Sofia swallowed and nodded. "Very well." She stood, too. "Please explain what happened with Louis last night."

He didn't flinch, just stared down at her, his gaze piercing into her like a steak knife into a cupcake. She could just about feel the jagged edges of a blade ripping into her, but she held her own, never once looking away.

She'd learned a few things about werewolves in the past few weeks. First, they were just like vampires with the dominance issues. There was a hierarchy and the higher up you were, the more capable you were of controlling everyone else. Second, everything was a test of dominance—so never, ever let them see you sweat.

Even if you weren't a werewolf, they tried to dominate you and though they usually existed side by side with humans in a very cordial manner, they believed themselves to be superior.

Sofia didn't look away in spite of the overwhelming desire to rip her gaze from his and duck into the nearby closet. "Your explanation?" If she was going to succeed in this job, she'd have to hold her own with Rick and every other nonhuman working here.

"A training exercise."

Sofia scribbled the words on her note pad then circled them. "That's it? That's how you explain shoving a young man off a roof?"

"Pushing. Yes."

"The difference between pushing and shoving is what?" She stood up straight, gripping her pen so tightly she thought it would snap.

Why in the world they continued to differentiate between the two she could not fathom. Either one explained exactly what had been done.

Rick stared straight ahead as though he was studying a spot on the wall. "Sometimes recruits need encouragement. A little push."

She nodded and noted his response, turned away, and wrote a few more lines on her pad, glanced at Rick, and then continued with her notes. Defining encouragement would become a priority. She'd add it to the Workplace Violence Policy. Encouragement vs. Abuse. She sighed.

"Are we done?" He stood with hands behind his back, legs parted, shoulders squared. He had to be a good three feet wide.

"When you shoved Louis off the roof last night, was it the first time?"

"It was the first and only time I pushed him."

"Are you stating you did not shove Louis off the roof every other night for the last week?" Her pen stopped moving, and she looked up at Rick, studying his face. He blinked once.

"No."

"What are you saying?"

"Last night I gave him the necessary encouragement one time. He was incapable of attempting the jump more than once."

"But you have pushed him off the roof before, correct?" Sofia's hand tightened even further around her pen.

"You know that to be the case."

"So, yes?"

The edge of a tattoo showed on Rick's left bicep below his sleeve. A claw. He nodded.

"And you've felt the need to push Louis off the roof every night for the past week for what reason?" She flipped the page of her notepad.

"Your game grows tiresome." He snickered.

"This would be a lot easier if you'd simply explain the circumstances of what has occurred rather than require me to drag every detail from you." Sofia sighed. "Is there no other way for him to learn this task?"

"He must learn to jump and land in order to be able to fight. The skill is required." His cheek twitched. "If he cannot master this, he is useless."

Sofia's jaw tensed. "Louis is not useless whether he can jump off a roof or not. He, like every other employee, brings something valuable to this organization. You just need to figure out what that is. And requiring him to master something he cannot is insane and cruel. Your training techniques are barbaric, torturous."

"You do not understand our world."

"You do not understand employment law, hostile work environments, or workers' compensation, not to mention the plain and simple fact that assaulting employees, or anyone for that matter, is wrong and just downright mean." She slammed her notebook and pen on the table.

"Your foolish idea that we should apply human resources practices to non-humans is outrageous." He leaned on the table, hands curled, knuckles down. "You are putting this entire organization at risk by attempting to force us to comply with this nonsense. War is a costly endeavor."

"And you are putting this organization at risk by purposefully injuring employees. The cost of every hospitalization alone should be enough to make you stop, if cost is all you're concerned with." She folded her arms over her chest and glared at him. He wasn't the first manager who'd been on the wrong side of the Employment Law. She wasn't backing down. "You are not to force Louis off the roof again."

"You are not to tell me how to run my training exercises." The table groaned under his fists. "We need trained soldiers *now*. War looms around us."

"Are you planning to push him again?"

"I'll do what needs to be done to make him worthy as a member of The Alliance. Whatever it takes." The scar at his temple throbbed, reminding Sofia of the red warning light signaling her car engine was overheating. "I will not risk having wolves who are not prepared to fight to the death. Bas Dubh will not play patty-cake to decide who wins."

There was no way she was allowing anymore workplace violence to occur. Not on her watch. "I'm suspending you. You've left me no choice. I can't risk the safety of even one employee because you insist on continuing these barbaric training tactics. You'll leave the building and stay home until a decision is made on how to handle this situation." She shook her head, picked up her pen, and scribbled her decision on the notepad. She knew she'd have a lot of explaining to do to Dr. MacDuff and Fergus, but Osgar could simply take over the training, and they wouldn't lose any ground.

A loud crack sounded and the table crashed to the floor. Her notepad slipped out of her hand, and she tumbled downward, landing in a heap, still gripping her pen.

"I do not take orders from you!" Rick's voice bellowed above her.

She pulled herself up to her knees and managed to get to her feet, though she'd somehow lost a shoe, torn her skirt, and her stockings had holes in both knees. "Oh, yes you do!" she shouted. "Now get out!" She pointed toward the door. Blue ink stained her hand. The damn pen had snapped in half when she fell.

She glanced up and was shocked by what she saw. Rick, the man, no longer stood in front of her. Instead, some sort of combination human-wolf towered over her. He stood on two clawed feet, was covered in fur, and the only thing about his face that resembled the man she'd just been speaking to was the giant scar that parted his fur and rippled when he opened his mouth to growl. He stalked forward, saliva dripping from his mouth.

She dropped the broken pen and stumbled backward, tripping over her shoe and landing on her ass.

# CHAPTER SEVEN

Dragomir may not have been able to sense her aura, but he could hear her scream. He smashed open the conference room door and leapt between Sofia and Rick. His body tingled, the anticipation of a battle fueling his already burning need for action.

Color faded from his vision. Only hues of black and white appeared before him. How easy it was for him to slide into warrior-mode. Not just easy, but comfortable and welcome. He'd been itching for something to do, some excitement since leaving Rome. Finally, a fight.

He scanned the room, taking in the state of the situation. Smashed table, ink splatters, one angry werewolf holding a notepad. And Sofia, his charge, sprawled on the floor.

Rick growled.

Sofia gasped.

Dragomir's hands flexed around his daggers.

Rick shifted his weight and inched closer.

Dragomir took a measured step toward the werewolf.

Rick lifted the notepad into the air and ripped it down the center, then hurled the halves in opposite directions. Shreds of paper flew about the air. A chair flew at Dragomir, and he batted it away without blinking.

Sofia whimpered. The soft, breathy sound drew Dragomir's attention from the impending fight. He glanced over his shoulder to be sure she wasn't hurt.

She'd fallen on her backside into a disheveled mess, quite the opposite of what she'd looked like not an hour ago. She was missing a shoe. Bruises had formed on both her knees, and a deep red stream of blood ran down her left shin. Blue ink covered her hands and smudged her cheek and the tip of her nose. Long strands of hair had come loose from her bun and floated around her face while the actual bun hung like a ball on the side of her head. Her wide, green eyes stared at the werewolf across the room and her mouth hung open, lips forming a perfect circle.

Something within Dragomir twisted. For a split second conflict rose within him. He must decide. Kill the wolf. Help Sofia.

What was wrong with him? She was fine. She could get herself up and find her shoe and fix her hair and wash her hands. And face. Her nose. And lips. Of course she could. She didn't need a warrior to do those things for her. He wasn't her lady-in-waiting. He was her bodyguard. Her comfort was not his concern. Her safety was his only responsibility.

The fact that she was frightened by the big bad wolf was not an issue he needed to contend with. His issue was the angry werewolf standing in front of him. His job was to thwart all attempts by anyone to harm even a single hair on her silly little head.

Dragomir forced his mind back to the fight and struggled to regain his focus. Not until the blue ink blotch on the tip of her nose appeared black was he sure he was focused enough for battle. And though it only took seconds, it felt like hours that he was trapped in some sort of spell. Trapped by her beguiling eyes.

He snarled and turned back to Rick in plenty of time to see the razor sharp claw take a swipe at him. He darted to the side and came up behind Rick. Dragomir pulled the wolf backward and wrenched his left arm up behind his back while pressing a knife to his throat.

"What is the meaning of this attack on Ms. Engle?" Dragomir demanded.

Rick growled and foolishly attempted to break free of Dragomir's hold. Dragomir slid the knife along Rick's neck to the spot two inches from his spine causing a thin line of blood to seep from beneath the fur. Then he drove the knife into Rick's neck, pinching the scruff into a bunched clump of skin and fur and bringing the wolf down to his knees.

Sofia screamed. "No! No! Help!"

Osgar was the first to reach them. "What the hell is going on in here?" He tossed aside half the broken table clearing a path to where Dragomir stood.

"Stop it! Stop him!" Sofia yelled, scrambling to her feet. She ran at Dragomir. "Animal!" She slapped him.

Stunned, Dragomir released his knife and stepped back. He stood beside Osgar gaping at Sofia.

"Help him!" Sofia pointed at Rick's neck, though she backed away from the werewolf.

Rick yanked the knife from his neck and roared, rising to his feet to tower over Sofia, dwarfing her size so that she appeared tiny and utterly fragile beside the wolf.

Sofia squeaked. Her mouth dropped open but not another sound escaped.

Dragomir snapped out of the daze she knocked him into and scooped her up, carrying her out of the room and down the hall to the security office. She needed to be removed from the Lower Level. Jankin's assertion that she'd be safest down here was completely incorrect. The simple fact remained the Lower Level was probably the most dangerous place for her. In less than two hours' time she'd been attacked twice.

"Put me down!" Sofia's feet thrashed about. She punched Dragomir in the chest and shoulder and wiggled out of his grip, landing on her knees on the floor. "You *are* an animal!" Her voice echoed. "A Neanderthal. Don't ever, ever pick me up again." She pulled herself to her feet, clinging to Dragomir's coat and wincing with each movement. When he reached to help her, she barked, "Don't touch me." Then she sidestepped him and marched out the door, hobbling on bruised knees and one shoe.

Meg and the other four wolves sitting at the first bank of security screens stared up at him. Meg's lips twitched, and Dragomir glared. The smile beginning to form on her mouth returned to a perfectly straight line.

He spun on his heel and followed the sound of Sofia's voice back down the hall.

"Dr. MacDuff!" Sofia yelled. Her high heel clicked, then her stocking foot thudded. "Dr. MacDuff!"

Dragomir measured the tenor in her voice and knew she was fighting with fear and anger. Her pitch was higher than usual, consistent with any woman on the brink of hysterics, but the hard huff that ended each shout told him wild anger bubbled just below her surface.

"In here," Jankin called from the conference room.

"It's unacceptable. Completely unacceptable!" Her voice cracked a few times. And even though she cleared her throat, she could barely contain herself. "Every issue that occurs does not require a physical response."

Dragomir laughed to himself. She could use some self-reflection. Apparently, she had no idea how she was reacting, no concept of her own physical response. She'd hit him three times this evening and ripped his shirt off and her scent didn't simply waft behind her. It was as though the fragrance of raspberry and that damn flower were being piped into the Lower Level with the intent to suffocate everyone.

*What is that flower? Peony? No.*

"He is an animal!" Sofia stood in front of Jankin, pointing at the doorway where Dragomir stood. He wished she'd calm down. She was turning into a highly potent olfactory weapon. He glanced at the wolves, inspecting for drool, but though they were both focused on her, neither showed any signs of hunger.

"Sofia, Dragomir is a warrior and he is tasked with ensuring your safety—" Jankin began only to be cut off by Sofia.

"I do not need him to ensure my safety. I'm perfectly capable—"

Rick growled.

Dragomir edged closer.

Sofia spun to face Rick and Osgar, who had also shifted to his wolf form, a security measure, Dragomir was certain. But it was clear Sofia didn't understand. She backed straight into Jankin, her mouth hanging open.

Dragomir smiled.

"Stop laughing at me!" she snarled at Dragomir, and her display of anger made it nearly impossible for him to remove the smile from his face. She had no idea what she was dealing with. She stepped beside Jankin, keeping the wolves and both vampires in her line of vision. "I just haven't seen them in this state before. It's slightly unnerving. That's all." Her neck flushed and another burst of florally tangy-sweet berry puffed.

"Lass, you are not working with humans anymore." Jankin placed his hand on her shoulder. "You must alter your perspectives on employee relations. Otherwise, I fear you will be continually frustrated and require a guard to even meet with the staff."

Her eyebrows furrowed, her jaw jutted forward, and she shook her head. Dragomir wasn't sure if she was more put out by having to change her philosophy, or the threat of having a guard with her more often.

"Even if I change my perspective, there is still way too much violence in this workplace. He…" She jabbed her finger in Dragomir's direction. "…stabbed a… man for no reason."

"He attacked you." Dragomir stood beneath the air vent, hoping to smell something other than her damn scent.

She glared at him. "Convenient excuse for you to act out with violence. I don't want you with me. You're too quick to resort to physical assaults."

He nodded. She might not have been wrong about that. He knew full and well he did not worry about silly human concerns. He was a warrior. Warriors could be frightening. He understood her feelings. He'd have much rather been on the front lines, leading troops into battle than in Wooddale, protecting one woman from werewolves who were supposed to be on the same side as her. And he would love for her to convince Jankin to let her have a different guard. Though he knew no one could guard her better than he. He also knew Jankin felt the same.

"Sofia, even on the Lower Level with a skilled security team available, myself, Osgar, Fergus, Meg, and half the council, still it was Dragomir who sensed your fear before anyone else."

"With all due respect, Jankin. The woman screamed. The only sense required was the ability to hear." Dragomir may have been highly skilled, but he was not a liar, and in this matter, one so important to Jankin, he would not mislead or allow anyone to think he was better than he truly was.

"I did not scream," Sofia argued. "Dr. MacDuff, he's delusional. I'll admit I was nervous, but I did not scream."

Dragomir shook his head. Typical. How many women had he encountered who pretended to be tough? More than he cared to remember. These were always the most dangerous, always getting themselves into trouble and never admitting their own fault in the matter.

Jankin raised an eyebrow. "Nevertheless, it was Dragomir who responded to your need. He is the best guard for you." Jankin's voice remained calm, not even a hint of emotion.

Dragomir had heard this tone before, knew it well, and was surprised to hear Jankin use it now. It was the one he employed when dealing with other masters, other vampires he could not control, in situations requiring extreme diplomacy.

"But... I..." she glared at Dragomir, then turned to Jankin. "Why can't Osgar train me like he does the wolves? Why can't I learn to defend myself? Then I wouldn't need a guard at all."

"Sofia, you could never be a match for any werewolf or vampire." Jankin glanced down at her. "Even with a bodyguard you've managed to be attacked in the building. There is no training in the world that could make you able to compete with the likes of one of us."

Dragomir had to agree. In fact, he was fairly certain that any amount of knowledge in this area would make her dangerous. She already possessed more confidence than she should. If she had any sense, she'd ask Jankin to send her away to a remote, well-guarded safe haven. She'd go on a lifelong vacation.

"I didn't say I'd be a match, but I'd at the very least know what to expect and have some ability to defend myself, deter an attacker. It can only help, especially if you all insist on becoming violent with every conversation. If I'd known what

Jefferson could do, I'd have been better prepared and never been caught in that situation. If I'd known this…" She waved toward the wolves. "…could happen, I'd have…well, I'd have done something." She rubbed her nose and smudged the ink over her clean cheek.

Jankin nodded. "I think you're correct, lass. You do need some skill to help you. What kind of employer would I be if I didn't teach you what you need to know?" He turned her to face the wolves. "Osgar, here's your new recruit." He nudged her forward.

Osgar grinned, but judging from Sofia's response, she didn't read it as a welcoming smile.

"Not like that!" She spun out of Jankin's grasp and stood behind him. "As a human."

"Oh, no. The wolves train in wolf form first. The human training for this group won't begin for several weeks," Jankin explained. His tone was much lighter than seconds earlier. "I don't want to wait. I should have thought of this weeks ago. You need to be conditioned for battle and not because you'll ever go onto the field. That you will never do. But, it appears I've given you a job in which you'll need battlefield strategy as well as the ability to physically endure each round with the staff." He pursed his lips and inhaled. "Aye, you'll need this type of training after all." He rubbed his chin.

"Well…" She glanced at the wolves.

Rick growled, making it very clear she'd be in for a rough go if he were forced to take her. In Sofia's short tenure at Cader she hadn't endeared herself to the wolf. In fact, Dragomir was certain she'd made an enemy for life. His line of vision narrowed on the wolf.

Rick snapped at Dragomir, baring his teeth.

"Maybe training with the wolves isn't the best idea," Jankin said. He paced a few feet, scratching his beard. "Maybe I can find someone else." He smiled. It was a smile that made his typically pleasant face appear entirely vampire.

Rick growled.

Dragomir snarled, his fangs cutting into his lip.

Jankin nodded. "Dragomir will train you."

The room suddenly smelled like a funeral parlor that had just received a fresh delivery of floral arrangements.

# CHAPTER EIGHT

"Perfect. Just perfect." Sofia scrubbed the ink off her face with more gusto than required. "You are something else, girl." She stared into the mirror, no longer focusing on the ink smudged over her nose or the rosy cheek she'd nearly rubbed down to bone. "Train me. I don't want to be helpless. Blah. Blah. Blah." She did her best damsel in distress imitation. "Sometimes you amaze even me." She bandaged both her knees, using those flexi-bandages that promised to withstand hours of movement. "Well, we'll just see how flexible you are," she taunted the bandage box. "Can you stay on while I spend my night being trained by Vlad? I'll bet he really is The Impaler. The real Dracula." She jerked her jeans up, tied her sneakers, and with an angry huff, slammed her fist on the bathroom countertop as she glared at herself in the mirror one more time before walking into the bedroom.

She left the lights off and snuck up to the window to peek out at Dragomir. He stood leaning against Osgar's giant truck, staring up at the window. "Oooh! Just how many people have you killed, Vlad?"

He mouthed something.

"Can you hear me?" she whispered.

He nodded.

"It is completely inappropriate for you to eavesdrop on my conversations! You're a miscreant." She stomped toward the door, yelling, "Have you no manners?

No respect?" She clomped down the stairs, half shouting and half mumbling. "*Disrespectful.* Inhuman. Dead. *What next?*" She threw open the door.

He hadn't moved from his spot behind the truck.

She pulled on her sweatshirt and descended the steps down to her walkway. "And furthermore—" She found herself on her ass in the mulch bed.

Dragomir glanced at her from the same place she'd last seen him.

"You did that on purpose! What was the point? Obviously, you can knock me down. Just about any one of you can knock me down. Did that make you happy?" She stood up and dusted off her backside. "How is that supposed to help me? What? Is there a certain technique to landing on one's ass that will save me from a werewolf attack? Frankly—"

She was on her ass again, and he was back at the truck when she looked up.

This time when she got up, she didn't bother to say a word. Instead, she marched over to the truck and punched him straight in the gut, sending him doubling over.

"My hand. My God that hurt!" She shook her hand and hopped up and down. "What the hell do you have on under your coat?"

Dragomir stood up, clutching his abdomen. "Nothing." He coughed and gasped. "You've got a good power punch. Let's see what else you can do." He stepped back and circled her.

"I think my hand is broken. I must have hit your belt buckle." Sofia opened her hand and stretched her fingers, then tried curling them back, but stopped midway due to the pain throbbing in her knuckles.

"I am not wearing a belt and stop whining." He removed his coat and tossed it into the open truck window. "Do you think a thirsty vampire will wait for you to ice your hand? What else can you do?" He disappeared into a shadow.

"Where the hell are you? What else can I do? Nothing. I didn't even know I could do that. Had I known, I'd have punched you in the head and knocked you out, then called the police to have you removed from the property. No. Maybe I'd have called Rick to come get you. Yes, that's what I'd have—" She fell on her ass again.

"You know, bruises do form on butt cheeks. And I did not hear Dr. MacDuff say anything about knocking me down every chance you got." She climbed to her feet but didn't bother to dust herself off.

"Where are you?" She couldn't see him at all. Oh, but she could feel him. She knew he was watching her from not too far away, trying to stare *into* her. "Cut the crap. I can feel that and I don't like it. Have you ever heard of sexual harassment?"

He laughed and not just a single chuckle. It was a full belly laugh that echoed in the night.

He was standing not three feet from her.

"Sexual harassment is not a laughing matter." Sofia turned to her right to slap him.

But before her hand made contact with his face his fingers curled around her wrist. His laughing stopped. "I was not sexually harassing you. I have never mistreated a woman in all my years. And I have no intent to begin now." His breath was warm on her face.

He pulled her closer to him, pressing her body to his and slowly twisting her arm behind her back. It didn't hurt at all as long as she didn't fight him.

She stared up into his face. From this proximity she saw the crescent-shaped moon reflecting in his dark pupils. His eyes weren't black. They were the darkest blue she'd ever seen, easily as dark as the midnight sky. Long black eyelashes made his eyes appear gentler than she'd ever noticed, almost human.

She assumed from the bump on the bridge of his thin nose that it had been broken at one time. His face was shaved smooth, and she was tempted to press her finger to the deep dimple centered in his chin.

A mild breeze blew and his hair danced across her face.

She closed her eyes and inhaled. The woodsy scent of autumn, crisp evergreens, and mossy forest mixed with dewy grass flooded her mind. It was a pleasant aroma, one that made her think of home, of all the years she'd spent in the woods hiking and photographing animals, bird watching.

But that other scent was there, too. Clean, but artificial. *Soap.*

She sniffed. *What is that? Lever? No.*

Dragomir released her arm. "I think you've had enough of a break. Back to work. What else can you do?" He stepped away from her, once again vanishing into a shadow.

Sofia stumbled back from him, legs wobbly, arms rubbery. *Damn it! Why does this keep happening?* She landed on her ass once again. "Thanks a lot. Next time why don't you just throw me down?"

"It was not my intent that you would fall." His voice came from behind the truck.

She glared over her shoulder. "Right. Just like the first two times were accidents."

"No. The first two times were meant to help you focus."

"So, let me understand this. You think by knocking a woman on her ass you're helping her focus? Also, you do know that knocking a woman down is typically considered mistreating her, don't you?" She shook her head but managed to get to her feet and remain standing in spite of the fact that she was pretty sure both kneecaps had melted into gelatin.

"I do not claim to know what helps every woman focus. I simply know that you seem to focus best when on your ass. And, it's not mistreating you when—"

"What?" Sofia's voice was caught between a shriek and a growl and she didn't know which part was more upsetting—that she was acting like a silly girl or turning into an animal.

"In every situation that has occurred, I've found you on your ass. It seems this is the best position from which you should learn to defend yourself."

She couldn't tell if he was serious or if this was some sort of joke.

"Isn't the whole idea of this training to help me avoid landing on my ass in the first place?" Was she the only one with any logical thought process?

"That would make sense if I thought you could avoid it." His voice came from right beside her and down she went.

She bounced back up and spun toward where she heard his voice, then promptly landed on her ass again. She clenched her teeth, and for a split second, considered going back into the house to call Dr. MacDuff. Training was turning into a night of fun torment for Dragomir with her ass well on its way to becoming so sore she was certain she wouldn't be able to sit at her desk in the morning.

"I'm calling—"

Down again.

"Your other option is the wolves. I am fairly certain you will not survive a trip off the roof," his voice called from the distance.

"Where are you?" She stood up then went down again.

"That is for you to discover," he whispered in her ear and then vanished.

"How the hell am I supposed to discover where you are if I can't see you? Damn vampires." She stood up again, knowing she was going down, but also aware Dragomir was correct. She wouldn't survive a trip off the roof, and she knew Rick would ensure she'd take one.

"I believe you have other senses. Use them."

She bounced back up, faster than before and turned toward his voice only to be spun around and land on her ass again without so much as a thud.

"Close your eyes. Let your body decide." His breath in her ear made her shiver, and any attempt she made at controlling her body was useless.

Her eyes closed and something else took over, something she'd never experienced. This time when she landed, she noticed Dragomir wasn't simply knocking her down. He was picking her up and placing her on the ground. Because he moved so quickly, she'd thought he was kicking her feet out from under her.

But really he seemed rather thoughtful about placement. He scooped her up, cradling her legs on one arm, the other arm catching her back, then he placed her on the ground. No dropping. No pushing. No pain.

She bolted back up to her feet, but before her new awareness told her where he'd gone, she was down again. This time he didn't leave her side so quickly.

He lingered and she felt it, him, his presence all around her. He silently called to her like a long lost friend welcoming her. She waited, focusing, listening as if some secret was about to pass between them. But before she could think to ask what was happening, he was gone.

His scent wrapped around her and she clung to it, inhaling as deeply as she could and following it thirty feet to her right and up into the maple tree in the corner of the yard. Her head tilted back, and she opened her eyes to find him bathed in moonlight, standing on a sturdy branch.

Dragomir nodded. "Up."

She stood and before she'd even gained her footing she went down again.

This exercise repeated itself several more times until Sofia followed his every move around the yard, behind the house, into the woods, and down the drive. There was nowhere he could go she could not detect him.

"Good. You can track. You must practice." Dragomir appeared at her side. "The wolves will be easiest for you to recognize. Like trying to find an army tank hidden among jeeps. Practice during the day." He pulled her to her feet. "It's late. You must rest. We continue tomorrow at sunset. I will wait for you in the lobby."

And with those words he turned to the woods, leaving Sofia to stare after him, but hard as she tried, she couldn't find him. She glanced up at the moon, then closed her eyes, and *it* happened. She sensed him. He wasn't more than fifty yards away. When she opened her eyes she caught a glimpse of him, barely lit by rays of moonlight filtering through the naked branches.

He turned his head, glancing over his shoulder and their eyes locked. Something mischievous showed in his gaze, daring and dangerous, and his lips tugged up exposing sharp pointed fangs. He stopped walking and turned to face her, his head in a slight downward tilt, hair falling in his face. But nothing, not darkness, nor his hair could hide his eyes. He stared at her like a hunter planning his attack. If she didn't know better, she'd have sworn he was coming back, coming for her.

She gasped and raced for the house.

Once inside, she ran through the steps of her security system, locking everything and hanging crucifixes in windows. She didn't bother to turn on a light on the first floor. There was no need. Between the moonlight and her newly awakened night vision she could see perfectly clearly.

This intrigued her. Everything appeared in crisp detail from the laundry basket full of undergarments and light-colored clothes to the items written on the grocery list stuck on the fridge to the half-naked vampire standing in the woods watching her house. How could this be? And did he know what she could see?

She stood in front of the sliding glass door leading out to the deck and watched him. He paced the woods occasionally glancing toward the house.

At one point her gaze locked on his and his right eyebrow shot up. He didn't look away. Neither did she. Instead, Sofia's vision zoomed in closer, studying him. She noted the slight squint to his left eye, the even pulsing of his left cheek, and the pinpoint fangs resting above his full bottom lip. His tongue slid between them, leaving his lips moist, glistening in the moonlight.

All at once her little training session caught up with her. She was short of breath and flush. Beads of sweat trickled down her chest, pooling in her bra between her breasts.

She yanked off her sweatshirt. When she glanced back at the woods, he was gone. She didn't bother to try to find him, well aware he hadn't gone far. He couldn't. He was on duty.

She headed upstairs to shower. Her unleashed senses worried her. She'd never felt so strong, so alive. But how? She wasn't a vampire. Why should she be able to see at night or register their movements so easily? These damn vampires were causing her more worries than she'd even considered possible.

She swallowed hard. What was wrong with her? And why had Dragomir been able to bring whatever it was out?

# CHAPTER NINE

*Damn Jankin.* He must have known for years, probably from the moment she was born. He'd probably been aware of this little secret from her very first breath.

Dragomir gritted his teeth. He'd suspected Jankin of withholding information, the truth. He'd seen it in Jankin's eyes all those years ago. But he hadn't pushed, hadn't challenged the man he trusted. Instead, he'd nodded and pledged his allegiance to The Alliance, to Jankin.

Now centuries later, the truth was rearing her lovely head. Jankin, the vampire, had conceived a child.

Dragomir and most everyone close to Jankin knew of his love for his descendants, though everyone believed the bloodline to have died out a couple hundred years ago. And no one had thought they were anything but the family he conceived when he was human, when most men were capable of conceiving a child.

Dragomir checked the back door. Locked. *Good.* Then he checked each window and found all but two were locked. The one in her bedroom where the rosary beads still hung and the bathroom window out of which steam from the running shower poured.

Dragomir smirked. "Bruises do form on butt cheeks," she'd said. He'd have liked to check, though he was absolutely certain any bruises she had were formed from her falls back at Cader as he had been very careful about lowering her onto her backside tonight.

He dropped to the ground and moved back into the woods.

Jankin was right. Sofia was very valuable. She possessed qualities far surpassing any other woman, traits that rivaled a vampire's, abilities she had no idea how to control.

Dragomir stalked the woods, rounding the property as he did a sweep to ensure no one breached the perimeter. Easily enough he sent out his presence and sensed that not another being, human or otherwise, moved anywhere near the house, but he made the walk around just to be sure. He wouldn't have bothered with the extra steps if he hadn't been startled by Osgar last night. He grunted at the foolish fact.

If the Alliance gossip machine was correct, Sofia was born twenty-eight years ago at Cader, prematurely, an untimely birth that brought her terrified parents to the nearest hospital instead of making the trek fifty-five minutes north to the state's primary obstetrical hospital.

Rumor had it Sofia arrived a full six weeks earlier than expected. She spent those first six weeks under the watchful eye of Jankin, whose love of humans was well known.

Dragomir always believed this admiration came from Jankin's continual monitoring of the MacDuff bloodline. He had seen the master through many losses of descendants and knew each one affected Jankin more than the previous one.

For nine centuries Jankin watched his children and grandchildren grow up, have children, and die. As far as Dragomir knew Jankin never intervened, never once changed any of them, didn't offer a drop of vampire blood to save one. He'd managed to resist what had to be a nearly all-consuming urge. But if any vampire could, it was Jankin. He, above all others, would not violate vampire law for his own selfish pursuits.

At least not until Sofia arrived. How else could a premature baby survive in a hospital ill equipped to care for her? If she was part vampire, she might have survived.

Dragomir leaned back against a tree watching lights flick on and off as Sofia moved through her house.

Vampire offspring had long been a desire of many a master. Even weaker vampires had dreamt of the feat. Dragomir never had. He'd lost three children as a human and had no desire to worry for another child, whether human or vampire, ever again.

Even though vampires weren't supposed to conceive children, there had always been talk of one vampire who'd been able to conceive. There'd been the question of why it had happened, of who had been able to do it. Was it a gift from God? A curse?

The indelible pain of his losses flared. His mouth went dry. Eight centuries had passed since his babies fell sick. Eight hundred years and still the cracks in his heart had not healed.

*A curse, most definitely.*

A curse that had not only put Sofia's life on the line, but would force Jankin to admit what he'd done in order to keep much more than his own offspring safe from the claws of Bas Dubh.

Dragomir believed Kiernan's desire to conceive a vampire child was more the reason for this dreaded war than anything else. Bas Dubh could easily live a worthwhile existence without the ability to conceive. Their production team effortlessly created fledglings whenever they were needed. But Kiernan believed a "natural" vampire would be more powerful, nearly God-like. And, certainly, the master of such a vampire would be able to rule all.

Somehow Kiernan must have figured out Jankin's secret. He must have known about Sofia. The idea of this perplexed Dragomir. How could Jankin have kept this secret guarded from him for so many centuries and yet their sworn enemy was able to uncover the truth?

Dragomir circled the house, considering this fact and coming back to the same conclusion. He'd been blinded by his friendship with Jankin, too blind to see the dangerous truth.

When Dragomir stopped to think about Jankin's actions over the years, he knew full and well it had been a curse. Jankin had given up so much to keep guard over his lineage. He watched as his male offspring died young, leaving the women to try to manage alone.

The men never lived beyond their mid-thirties, and the ones who lasted that long were rare. Though, Sofia's father lived into his fifties. Dragomir paced along the forest, mulling the idea. Or rather, the fact. It wasn't an idea. It was a fact. The MacDuff males all died early. Natural deaths, though young. However, Brian Engle lived twice as long as most.

What had Jankin been up to? Had he sired Sofia? Or had he crossed a more treacherous line? Had Jankin allowed Brian Engle to drink vampire blood?

The very idea of Jankin breaking such a sacred code was beyond comprehension. Why after centuries of restraining himself would he go against this decree?

Dragomir picked up an acorn and rolled it between his fingers, up and down as he paced. He glanced toward the house at the sound of metal rings sliding along the curtain rod. Steam poured from the bathroom window, and Sofia mumbled something about landing on her ass so many times.

He grinned in spite of himself. She had a nice ass, and he'd have liked to put her on it for reasons that had nothing to do with training.

She was a smart one. That he had to admit. In five hours' time she'd learned to scent and track him. His experience with training was quite extensive, and he could recall only one other who'd mastered the skill as quickly. But Daria had been a vampire, not a human.

He sighed, then threw the acorn deeper into the forest, aiming it at a giant oak. It hit the tree with such force it sounded as though a firecracker exploded in the distance.

"What was that?" Sofia's startled voice came from her window. The light blinked off, and Dragomir saw her silhouetted in the distance, holding a towel to her chest and dripping from the shower. Her wet hair draped over her shoulders and she craned her neck toward the sound. Water droplets rolled down her skin and soaked into the towel she pressed tight against her breasts. Her sweet scent swirled in the steam pouring from the window.

Dragomir stood motionless. If only she'd drop that towel. He swallowed.

Her tongue darted across her lips then she bit the bottom one between her teeth and leaned to the right. She squinted as though she were staring hard into the trees, searching for the cause of the noise. Even beneath those thick lashes he could see the sparkling green of her narrowly focused eyes. She shook her head and huffed before turning back to the running water of the shower.

Her long dark hair dripped water down her backside. The droplets rolled down the curve of her back onto her nice, bare, unbruised ass.

He licked his lips and felt something in his gut clench. His own heart picked up a beat. He curled his hands into fists, digging his fingers into his palm.

He'd risen too late this evening. He would head to town and feed as soon as Osgar arrived. Then he'd rise early tomorrow evening and feed again before training her.

It was hunger, no thirst, just thirst that made him hunger. It wasn't desire. He simply needed nourishment. He turned from the house and tried to recall his previous thoughts, the ones he was thinking before she came to the window, naked, save for a towel covering her front side, a towel he'd have liked to tug from her hands.

His mind wouldn't focus on whatever it was he'd been thinking. Instead, he imagined his hands cupping her bare ass as he held her naked body against his and she wrapped her long legs around him. He thought about the way her soft breasts would feel pressed to his chest, the way her lips would taste, the sting of her nails on his back as he made love to her.

"What am I doing?" He growled at himself. "How can I even consider coveting Jankin's friend or granddaughter or whatever the hell she is?"

He raked his fingers through his hair, then tied the wild mess back from his face. He rolled his shoulders and neck, working to shrug off his indecent thoughts. When that didn't work, he pulled out his bowie knife and lopped a branch from a nearby tree.

A little woodworking could keep him busy. He whittled aimlessly at the wood. Every time his thoughts wandered back to Sofia, he growled and forced himself to think of Bas Dubh and the many battles he'd fought to defeat them. He focused on the ravages of war instead of lovemaking, the bloody fights and death. By 0500 he'd carved an entire tree down to form dozens of stakes.

He held his most recent work in his hand, studying its weight and length. He even took a couple practice stabs at the air.

"Nice stake. Planning to use it on anyone in particular?" Osgar's voice carried from the distance.

But this time he didn't startle Dragomir. It would have been impossible for anyone to sneak up on the vampire. He'd spent the last seven hours forcing himself to be alert, to ignore the soft breathing and sleepy moans coming from the house, to believe petunias could be in bloom in late October in Rhode Island after three frosts had covered the ground.

He was ready for battle. He bolted through the trees, newly carved stake in hand, and pinned Osgar to the ground, stake positioned above his heart. "She sleeps. Trained well. Leave her to rest."

Dragomir focused on Osgar, searching his thoughts for intentions, demanding to know what the werewolf wanted of Sofia.

"Okay. No need to come undone, man." Osgar's hand gripped Dragomir's shoulder, and he pressed up slowly, baring his teeth.

Dragomir snickered as he came up against Osgar's mental defenses. But he pushed past, searching for intent.

Finding Osgar's plans for Sofia was not difficult. The thoughts lay right at the forefront of Osgar's mind. *Protect Sofia.* That was all he intended. His more primal interests lay deeper, hidden, and they didn't include Sofia.

"She will come out when she's ready." Dragomir's voice was lower than he'd intended. The stake pierced through Osgar's jacket.

"Man, I don't know what's gotten into you, but I'm not a vampire. Cut the crap." Osgar's grip tightened and he snarled. His eyes shifted, pupils widening. His muscles vibrated. Dragomir felt him focusing his energy, preparing to shift.

Dragomir loosened his grip on Osgar and jerked the werewolf up to stand.

"What the hell is wrong with you?" Osgar shoved Dragomir away. "You've been acting weird since you got back from Rome. And I've been tolerating it. But one more move like this and I'm letting loose." He straightened his jacket and brushed the dirt and leaves off his jeans. "You hear me? Cut the shit, man. You may be the vampire, but I'm no pup." He headed toward the house. "Oh, and I'll come and go as I please from the house." He glared over his shoulder. "She allows *me* inside in spite of what *my master* might want, remember?"

Dragomir returned to his pile of stakes and watched Osgar ascend the front steps, open the door, and go inside. Not more than ten seconds later Osgar appeared on the back deck. "Hey, dummy. Get the hell back to Cader. The sun's coming up." Osgar pointed toward the sky and shook his head. "You'd better talk to Jankin. There's something wrong with your brain. I may be bound to protect you, but there's no protecting you when you lose all common sense." He went back inside.

The lock clicked shut.

What was Dragomir doing? He'd always respected Osgar, trusted him, cared for him even, in spite of the wolf's very relaxed presentation. The sun was nearly up and here he stood outside and dumbstruck. He scooped up his weapons and ran for Cader.

Osgar was right. Dragomir would speak with Jankin. He had every intention of getting the answers he needed.

# CHAPTER TEN

"Conversion Code W. Conversion Code W. Conversion Code W." The overhead page blared.

"We'll continue this later." Rick crumbled the draft of the Workplace Violence Policy in his hand and threw it on the table, then shoved his chair back and followed Fergus from the conference room. The entire third floor cleared for the third time that day. This time Sofia did not stay behind as Dr. MacDuff had advised her to do during orientation. She ran to the Emergency Room with everyone else. Something strange was happening and she wasn't sitting by the sidelines.

She'd been practicing tracking the wolves all day, which was probably the reason she hadn't made any headway in her actual work. To her surprise, the closer she got to the ER, the less she had to try to notice anyone. Energy moved in fits and bursts all across the ground floor.

Jamieson had left his post. Now sitting at the front desk was one of the volunteers. Mrs. Sheehan looked up from her magazine. "It's a madhouse in there." She hitched a thumb toward the ER and turned back to the article.

The ER no longer looked like a hospital. It now resembled a news scene after a prison riot. Furniture was tossed about. Loose papers floated in the air. Light fixtures dangled back and forth by thin cords. Growls erupted behind curtains. Doctors barked orders at nurses. The pharmacist ran back and forth handing out medication and trying to help where she could.

The curtain for room one jerked open and the charge nurse, Janet, marched out. "Just hold him like that Jamieson. I'll get the chain."

"Yes, ma'am."

Sofia's jaw dropped. Old Mr. Jamieson, whom she was certain had to be in his eighties, sat on the floor with a burly young man at least twice as wide as he trapped between his legs in a scissors hold. He wrenched the man's arm behind his back and held his head cradled against his chest in a chokehold.

The young man panted and moaned, rocking as if in some sort of trance.

Sofia stood at the nurse's station, watching the nurses and doctors deal with what appeared to be complete chaos. Screaming patients threw equipment and the staff dodged, ducked, and restrained. It was absolute pandemonium.

Fergus removed a pair of thick winter gloves hanging on hooks above the nurse's station. "Janet, what's the report?" He reached beneath the nurse's desk and slid a box forward.

"Six victims. Two in tachycardia, two in shock, one subdued with Dilodid, but the effects are wearing off, one still holed up in the ambulance." The nurse put on a pair of gloves and reached into the box to pull out a long silver chain. "You and Rick take room three. Room one is almost done, though we'll need someone to sit with him. Then I'll get room two. Room four should be fine for a few more minutes. But once her body processes the meds, forget it. She ripped the door off the hinges coming in."

Screaming, Charlie sailed through the emergency room entrance, where the doors no longer hung. He landed on his back beside Sofia. "Hey! What are you doing down here?" He scrambled to his feet and ran toward the door before she could answer.

Janet shook her head.

"He's doing fine." Fergus pulled on the gloves and wrapped a length of chain around his hand. "Osgar with him?"

Janet nodded.

Fergus handed one end of the chain to Rick. "Let's get these done. They need to be moved to the Lower Level right away. This department wasn't built to handle this magnitude of traumas."

The three shot off in opposite directions. The ER had gone from a medical unit to a wrestling ring.

From the nurses station Sofia watched as Janet knelt beside the man in room one. "What's your name?" Her tone was matter-of-fact and her movements firm, yet gentle. She wrapped the chain around his neck, appearing unfazed by his groans.

He glared and panted through gritted teeth. His eyes bulged and darted from left to right and back again, never settling on anything.

Sofia hadn't ever seen anything like this. She wasn't accustomed to being with screaming, frightened patients. The ones she'd seen on the units upstairs were calmer, quiet. Someone cried out, a piercing, terrified cry. Sofia's heart sped. She had to focus on remaining calm, pushing back her fear of what might happen.

Janet's fingers went to the man's wrist, and she remained silent for several seconds. "His pulse is two-twenty. He may not even make it to sunset." She draped the chains down his back and around his wrists then hogtied him, winding the chain in and around itself in a figure eight.

"Sofia, come here." Janet waved her over. "I need your help."

Sofia stumbled forward, wanting to help and praying she didn't lose courage and run. "Is this how you typically care for psych patients?" Sofia knelt down beside the man. "I'm pretty sure this isn't legal." She motioned to the chain restraint.

A metal pan clanged on the floor across the department and skittered past room one as if it had been launched from a cannon. Instruments pelted the nurse's desk and a feral scream pierced the air. Sofia ducked in time to avoid being hit by an IV pole that had been thrown like a javelin straight into the room.

"Call Osgar," Dr. O'Rourke yelled. "Stat." He ran past them into room two, drawing the curtain behind him and barking orders. "Let's get him on the table. Get the straps. We'll secure him and move him down."

"Osgar! Osgar!" The secretary yelled toward the open door.

"This guy's not a psych patient. None of them are. They just think they're going crazy. Stay with him. Yell if anything weird happens," Janet said. Then she and Jamieson ran from the room, Janet giving orders and Jamieson running toward the open doors of the ambulance.

"Osgar! Osgar!" The secretary leaned over the desk toward the door, yelling even louder than before.

"Betty! He's outside and busy. Stop yelling." Janet swatted at the secretary before darting into room two.

A woman cried in room five. "What's happening to my son?" She tried to lean past the technician in the doorway.

"We're taking care of him, ma'am. Let me help you. What's your name?" He guided her back to a chair.

"Melanie. Melanie Andrews. That's Michael, my youngest boy. He's sixteen." Her voice cracked.

Michael screamed, a sound the likes of which Sofia had never heard. It was a cry of pain, of agony. She looked down at the man she'd been told to stay with. His breathing quickened, every breath a shorter, faster pant than the one before. She rubbed his arm. "It's going to be fine. They'll take good care of you here." Though she wasn't entirely sure she believed herself. She'd never heard of a hospital where they restrained the patients quite like this.

Sofia forced herself to focus on room two, to try to sense what was happening behind the curtain.

Dragomir hadn't been kidding. Wolves were obvious. There was no doubt about it. They were entirely different from him. Tracking him was like monitoring a phantom, difficult at best. His energy seemed to fade and disappear, then reappear elsewhere. Sofia had stumbled several times trying to keep track of him.

But the wolves were another story. Their energy never faded. Instead a constant stream of busy life flowed from one wolf to the other literally connecting each of them with one another. And if emotions or excitement were involved, the energy raged.

As easily as she could see the secretary standing at the desk, she felt four different werewolf energies in room two. Each individual current coursed into the next, merging together and focusing in one direction, for one cause.

"Get his shirt off and find the bite. The least we can do is ease the pain," Dr. O'Rourke said.

"Aye, doctor." The sound of shredding clothes followed.

"It's here, on his waist. Let's get the jeans off," another voice said, and the shredding continued.

A tortured scream ripped through the air.

"Michael, look at me," Dr. O'Rourke ordered. "Look at me, son. We're going to help you. Pay attention to my voice."

The four energies flowed together, and the young man's screaming quieted to whimpers. Soft murmurs escaped from behind the curtain. Sofia strained to understand the words, but it was useless. She couldn't comprehend the low chanting.

Coming through the doors from the ambulance, Osgar wrestled with another panting and grunting man. "Get the straps. We'll bring him down after we secure him." He tumbled to the floor with the man, rolled over, and grabbed the man's arm to keep him from pulling a nearby stretcher down on top of them.

"We need more help in here," a nurse yelled from room five. "Call the floors. They need to send someone down."

Melanie Andrews stood on a gurney screeching. Her blond hair was a wild mess above her contorted face. She breathed with an open mouth, groaning with each exhale. Her body hunched forward as though she was about to launch herself off the table.

"Sure thing," Betty called.

Sofia scooted further into the room dragging her panting patient with her, but keeping her attention focused on the open doorway. She did a double take when she found Betty, her desktop computer, and phone all under the desk.

The secretary smiled at her. "Oh, this job gets a little hairy sometimes. I'm better able to get my work done down here." She held the phone on her shoulder, fixed the headband holding her hair back, and smiled. "It's been crazy around here lately. But that just makes the time pass quickly." She held up a finger to her lips. "Ruth? Yeah, it's Betty…"

The man on the floor with Osgar growled. "Get off me!" His deep voice held an almost demonic tone.

Osgar wrapped a length of chain around the man's neck, across his chest, and around his knees. "Damn that burns." He stood up and blew on the palm of his hand. Blisters oozed and the skin peeled.

A pair of gloves flew over the desk. "Use these," Betty yelled from her cubby.

"Thanks, Betty." Osgar grimaced and slid the gloves on.

"What's your name?" Sofia asked the patient on the floor beside her.

"Ollie." He managed to answer. His teeth chattered and his body shook. "What's wrong with me?" Sweat poured down his face and neck. His short salt-and-pepper hair matted to his head.

"I don't know." Sofia wiped her sleeve across his face. "I'll get a nurse."

"No. Don't leave me." He glanced back at Sofia. The pupils of his wide brown eyes constricted to pinpricks. The fear in his voice frightened Sofia. He was a big, rugged man, yet his voice cracked and his jaw quivered.

"I won't." She reached up for a towel and settled back behind him, dabbing his face and neck. "What happened to all of you?"

"We were taking a break out behind the barn. Two wolves came—" His teeth chattered, and he groaned when his body jerked into a giant cramp.

Sofia rubbed his arm. He tensed with such force she couldn't comfort him.

The spasm lasted about half a minute, though it seemed like an hour. When it ended Ollie gasped and choked. Sofia worked her fingers under the chain around his neck, trying to wiggle a little breathing room for him.

"I ain't seen a pack of wolves around in twenty years." He coughed. "Water. Can you give me a drink?"

"Yes, of course." Sofia grabbed a cup from the counter around the tiny sink behind them. She cradled Ollie's head as she held the cup for him. Just a few sips were all he took. "Were you bitten?"

"Yeah. All of us." He closed his eyes. "I didn't think rabies took hold so fast." He panted.

Poor guy. Even Sofia knew they didn't have rabies. This was something far worse and with no known cure or vaccination.

She wet the towel in her hand with the remaining water and pressed it to his forehead.

Convulsions gripped him again, only this time, they didn't let up. He remained cramped for several minutes at a time, getting only a few seconds of relief between each attack. His eyes remained wide. His breathing stopped and started in short fits. Sofia rested her hand on his chest. His heart pounded so fast she thought he might have a heart attack.

"Janet! Janet!" Sofia yelled, not willing to leave Ollie alone to suffer.

Ollie screamed a low guttural roar. His body contorted, head twisting back to stare at her, a look of raw terror. He curled back his lips and his face changed. His body thrashed against the chains that bound him. Right in front of her Sofia watched him begin to morph into a wolf.

Trapped in the damn little room, she scooted as far away as possible.

Ollie's body stiffened, veins bulging in his neck, muscles constricting over bone. He howled. The chains around his feet came loose, and he jerked into a seated position, spinning toward Sofia, eyes fixed on her. He twisted his body, wriggling his shoulders and banging his hands back and forth against the chains until the metal slid down his chest.

His head jerked back and he howled at the ceiling. When he lowered his chin and his gaze returned to Sofia's, his face was anything but human. His jaw had elongated to a snout. Fur covered his face. And drool dripped from his snapping jaws. He lurched forward.

# CHAPTER ELEVEN

"Again, on your ass." Dragomir yanked Ollie from the room, securing the silver chain around him and clamping a padlock into place. The noises Ollie made alternated between grunts and bloodcurdling screams. "Osgar, take this one."

Osgar and Jamieson gathered the new werewolf onto a stretcher and wheeled him into the elevator.

Dragomir helped Sofia to her feet.

"For your information, I put myself on the floor to help *him*." She pointed toward the elevator. "Ollie." Her eyes filled and she turned away. "He was afraid," she whispered.

"Naturally." Dragomir tossed his gloves onto the stretcher and retrieved her shoe from underneath, holding it for her to slip into. "The idea is to stay off your ass and keep your shoes on your feet. You never know when you're going to need them." He stepped aside to allow Sofia to pass. "Did you practice?"

She swiped at her cheeks then squared her shoulders and stepped from the room, looking both ways like she was preparing to cross a street. "Yes. All day on the wolves." She straightened her blouse and dusted off her pants. Half her hair fell around her shoulders with the rest still trapped in a very loose bunch at her neck. She tugged the fastener free and let the rest fall in black waves sending that floral scent wafting.

Dragomir quietly inhaled. *Lilacs? No. Berries—yes. But what is that damn flower?*

"Though it didn't require much effort today." She looked around, eyes wide, head shaking.

The Emergency Room was quiet, and though it didn't appear to be able to handle more patients any time soon, Dragomir was certain they'd see another round like this one before dawn.

"I imagine not. Jankin has asked that you attend the debriefing on this afternoon's events." Dragomir motioned toward the open elevator where Ollie lay on a stretcher flanked by Osgar and Jamieson.

Sofia sighed. Dragomir knew she'd only been asked to attend one other meeting. That was her first introduction to The Board. And she'd been very clear about never wanting to be invited again. Dragomir understood how meeting with them wasn't the most relaxing or welcoming experience.

They didn't trust anyone until you'd proven your loyalty and even then they reserved judgment for a few hundred years. Then there was the little issue of the power contained in the room when they were all assembled.

It didn't bother Dragomir and never had. By the time he'd attended his first meeting with The Board, he'd been a master for several hundred years and was closely aligned with Jankin, thus they accepted him fairly quickly. He'd heard newer, weaker vampires describe it like being forced to sit in a high voltage room with live wires sparking.

Dragomir nudged her forward.

"I thought we had other things to practice tonight." She stepped into the elevator.

"We do." Dragomir pressed the button marked "LL" and down they went.

"Hmm. So you'd rather spend a night alone with the dead guy than go to a board meeting. Interesting," Osgar commented, staring straight ahead.

Sofia tucked a lock of hair behind her ear. "Be quiet." She glanced at the wolf strapped to the gurney. He twisted and howled. Sofia flinched and her breath caught.

"Don't worry, Sofia. He can't get loose." Jamieson yanked a strap.

She nodded. "I know." Her words were merely a breathy acknowledgement, barely concealing her emotions.

Still in the throes of changing, Ollie's face was partially morphed and his hands and feet had turned to claws. In a few hours he'd be a fully developed werewolf with little to no self-control and more than slightly terrifying.

Sofia reached over and rubbed his arm. "I'm so sorry this happened to you, Ollie." Then she swiped her sleeve across his sweaty brow.

"Sofia, once he gets through tonight it will get easier," Osgar explained, handing her a handkerchief.

She nodded and dabbed Ollie's forehead.

"I gave that to you for these." Osgar brushed his fingers over her cheek and wiped away the tears running from her eyes.

Dragomir clenched his jaw. He shoved his hands into his pockets to keep from removing Osgar's hand and not just from Sofia's face. The sudden desire to rip Osgar's arm from his shoulder was almost too much to bear.

Sofia wiped the back of her hand over her cheeks. "It's awful, isn't it?"

"The first change is always the worst. They fight it. It's instinct and fear, but once he's done it and found he'll live through it, he'll be able to do it faster and with less pain." Osgar patted Ollie's back.

Dragomir had seen hundreds of humans change, knew it hurt, but never thought much of it. It was part of the process, like becoming a vampire, which hurt like hell and lasted longer than the wolf transformation. This guy would be physically fine in a few hours. Vampires took a full twenty-four hours to change, and if you'd been bitten just before dawn it could take another eight to twelve hours depending on the time of year. New vampires always rose in the dark.

Would Sofia have shown this much concern for a "dead guy?"

Before the elevator doors opened to reveal an awaiting medical crew, Osgar and Jamieson began chanting. The low hum was meant to calm and guide a wolf through the transformation. Janet, Meg, and Dr. O'Rourke's voices filtered into the elevator, and the five wolves escorted Ollie down the hall to the room where he'd spend the rest of the night and most of the next couple weeks.

"This way." Dragomir motioned for Sofia to take a right out of the elevator. He knew the moment she felt The Board. Her back stiffened and her pace slowed like a prisoner walking those last steps to the guillotine. He placed his hand on the small of her back. "It shouldn't be a long meeting."

At least it wouldn't be, if they didn't get sidetracked again. Lately, board meetings seemed to run amuck with members bickering over foolish points and aligning based on history and old wounds being reopened. Jankin had long tried to run this branch as a democracy, but the truth about vampires and werewolves was they required a dictator to tell them what would be done. Someone had to be the supreme master, super alpha, or everyone fought for control.

Jankin hadn't risen to this position by playing childish games. He'd come into power driven by an almost consuming need to destroy Bas Dubh. But Dragomir no longer knew if Jankin wanted to destroy the rebels because he believed in a higher, more important cause, or if he sought only to protect the woman he believed to be his heir.

Sofia turned her head toward Dragomir. Her green eyes were wider than before and a crease formed above her nose. She took a deep breath as though to steady herself and nodded before stepping into the room.

The entire Board had assembled, all thirteen members. This was a change from the typical sixty to seventy percent attendance rate. A debate was in full swing. Commodus stood at one end of the giant table banging his fist on the mahogany as he yelled, "We can wait no longer! We must advance."

Seamus argued, "We are not prepared. We need more time. Our allies have not sent enough support. Our brethren from the British Isles have pledged warriors. We need them." He sat back in his chair and crossed his arms over his chest. Behind him his second in command snickered. The other wolves around the table knocked on the wood and a few echoed his sentiments.

"Bah! Our newest recruits are nearly ready. They can go to battle now. Let them learn in real war." Commodus pointed at a woman seated at the far end of the table. "Josette, too long silent on this issue. What say you?"

The ravishing blond very slowly blinked heavily mascaraed eyelids and turned her head in equally as slow a manner until she'd locked gazes with Commodus. Her crystal blue eyes nearly glowed. "I see no point in rushing. Again Commodus, you'd have our fledglings and pups die unnecessarily." Her voice coated the room like soft, plush velvet.

Knowing Josette's approach better than most, Dragomir prepared for what was next. He'd always admired her way of handling Commodus. She was forever one of a select few to convince him of rational thought. Though she looked the part of the lady, her technique was all warrior. Dragomir tensed his own energy, wrapping it around Sofia and himself, then he watched.

Josette's slight smile never wavered, but her power shot toward Commodus like a whip being cracked at the back of a slave.

Commodus bristled. He stood straight, head tilted toward the ceiling, but gray eyes focused on Josette, a sly grin on his lips. "Ever the voice of reason, sister." He bowed his head. "I acquiesce to your perspective." With as much grace as any master could display after having tasted another's power, Commodus backed to his seat, quiet until his next opportunity for an argument.

Tonight's display was more effective than usual, and obviously designed to influence the rest of the room. Have finished with Commodus, Josette turned her power on the other masters, testing each one. Though most were prepared for her approach, one by one the leaders not focused on her discussion with Commodus flinched or glanced at Josette with an irritated expression.

Josette waved a gloved hand at Commodus and inclined her head. Smooth honey-colored hair tumbled over her shoulder. When she glanced up, her smoky gaze landed on Sofia, and then quickly darted to Dragomir.

He nodded.

Josette's eyebrow shot up and her attention turned to Sofia. "You've decided to join us. A welcome surprise." A smile teased the corners of her mouth, further enhancing her uncanny likeness to a 1930s film star.

"Yes. I've asked that Sofia attend tonight's meeting." Jankin sat at the head of the table and offered the chair at his left to Sofia.

She glanced around the room, raised her chin, and took a step forward out of Dragomir's reach. The sound that escaped her lips forced Dragomir to her side. If he didn't know better, he'd have thought someone punched her in the gut. But he knew what had happened. Josette had tested Sofia.

"That's enough," Jankin commanded, his voice a rapid boom in the conference room.

Josette's attention moved back to Commodus, whose grin was nothing short of wicked.

Dragomir placed his hand on the small of Sofia's back and directed her to the seat beside Jankin, who rested his hand on hers. Jankin's power blanketed Sofia and Dragomir.

It was a strange sensation, like a warm current flowing around him. Dragomir stopped touching Sofia and stepped back, breaking the connection, leaving Jankin to protect her. He still hadn't had an opportunity to question Jankin, but he would, when they were alone and Jankin could take the risk of answering honestly.

Dragomir stood behind Sofia, studying the group assembled. Seven masters and six alphas, all leaders within The Alliance, gathered around the giant table, most with an entourage acting as protection. The last time this group had been assembled, at least one of them managed to scare Sofia. Because he'd been in Rome, he hadn't attended that meeting so he wasn't entirely sure who'd been responsible. However, he wasn't about to let that happen again.

When he'd heard about the last meeting, he hadn't thought anything of the incident. Hadn't believed there to be any problem with a human being shooed out of a board meeting and made to feel that she didn't belong.

But now he knew differently. If she was Jankin's descendant, she did belong. She, above all others, needed to be in these meetings. She needed to come up to speed on the war, The Alliance, and what Bas Dubh could do to her.

# CHAPTER TWELVE

Sofia edged closer to Dr. MacDuff, wanting nothing more than to run from the room, up to the first floor, and straight out of the building to her car where she'd gun it the whole way home. In a meeting with a group of volatile vampires and werewolves was the last place on earth she ever wanted to be.

She had yet again been zapped. It was like walking into an invisible electric field. A painful burning that sizzled along her body with lingering aftereffects. Her toes curled in her shoes as her muscles twitched. She reached down to rub her left calf, willing away the cramp knotted in her muscle.

The warmth flowing around her from Jankin brought some relief, though not quite the same as when Dragomir had touched her. Dragomir's protection seemed impenetrable. With Dr. MacDuff, she continued to feel crackling as though sparks bounced off his shield.

She cast a sideways glance at Dragomir. He stood behind her, still as a statue. She wished he'd touch her again, place his hand on her back, fingers splayed to cover the entire lower half. When he first touched her, she hadn't realized what he was doing, not until she'd stepped away in a rush to prove she could hold her own in this meeting. *Wasn't I sadly mistaken?* She straightened her leg under the table, making sure not to point her toes, lest her cramp get worse.

"Seamus, when will Rowan's brigade be here?" A tall blond man took a seat half way down the table. He leaned his forearms on the wood, hands raised to form a triangle. On his right hand was giant gold ring, containing the Cader House Crest of black onyx dragons on an ivory background.

"In one week's time. No more than that," a burly black-haired man answered. He reached back and handed an empty glass to the man behind him. The glass was whisked away and a second man stepped into the first's place. A third man slipped into the second's empty spot. The two men stood at attention, wearing dark suit jackets, tartan kilts, and expressions that said they'd kill without a second thought.

Sofia glanced around the room. Most every seated member had at least two guards in attendance. *If you're on the same team, why so much security?*

Fergus sat to Jankin's right with Osgar, Rick, and Dragomir to their backs. After sizing up the rest of the group, Sofia was thoroughly pleased to have her own bodyguard. For once she had to agree with Dr. MacDuff on this issue.

"One week? Too long. We cannot risk more death." A robust female vampire said. *Margot.* Sofia struggled to keep a neutral face. Margot shifted her weight like a Botticelli woman preparing to sit for a portrait, only she wore clothes, though barely. The neckline of her black dress dipped so low Sofia half expected to see nipples peeking out.

Sofia had met Margot just over a week ago while working after sunset one evening. The vampire had sauntered into her office under the premise she was looking for Dr. MacDuff. She'd made herself perfectly comfortable propped on Sofia's desk. So comfortable, in fact, she began quizzing Sofia on several rather personal issues—marital status, dating status, sexual preference. That evening a nipple did make an appearance. Sofia was so uncomfortable she left her own office to find Dr. MacDuff. When she recalled the incident to Osgar, he was tickled to inform her that Margot "liked" her.

Sofia glanced at Osgar, who stood directly behind Fergus. The left corner of his lips twitched and he winked. She knew perfectly well Osgar's mind had wandered back to that conversation or some image surrounding the topic. She also knew to expect some ridiculous comment from him in the not too distant future.

"There is nothing to be done. We wait one more week," Dr. MacDuff said. He sat back and sighed, never breaking the connection with Sofia's hand.

"Bas Dubh moves now!" Margot argued. She scooted to the edge of her chair until her breasts rested on the table. "Fourteen more vampire attacks, twelve werewolf attacks in my region alone. I can barely keep the incidents hidden. And we haven't recovered even one of the victims. His army grows, Jankin, too fast. We are not keeping pace." She slapped her hand on the table.

"We will be outnumbered before long," Commodus added.

Dr. MacDuff's solemn expression did not fade. He listened as board members argued over what to do and why.

"Jankin, too many innocents have already been sacrificed," Margot said.

"Reports from Rome indicate a rise in missing tourists every day. It is becoming more dangerous. Since Dragomir left the region we've struggled to keep control," a werewolf with wavy silver hair said. He stared at Dragomir. "Your choice to leave has had catastrophic impact for many."

"I go where The Alliance needs me." Dragomir's voice was low.

"The Alliance needs you in the field, brother. Trent has not seen enough battle to handle that command." The werewolf stared over Sofia's head.

"Richard, Dragomir is needed here," Dr. MacDuff said.

"The ones you care for are safe, hidden in the stronghold of this organization. What about ours?" Commodus stood. "What about my bloodline? I will not sit back and watch it bled dry. I will send my troops into battle with or without you," he roared. His fangs descended and his face contorted into an expression that made a horror movie vampire look peaceful. He turned toward the door, motioning for his guards to follow.

Before Sofia could register what was happening, Dr. MacDuff was across the room. The door slammed shut and both Commodus's guards lay on the floor, cowering at Dr. MacDuff's feet. He caught Commodus by the throat and held the vampire face to face. Josette's men moved in, but Noelle, Osgar, and Fergus beat them to Dr. MacDuff and Commodus, blocking their paths, weapons drawn.

"Last I recall your bloodline died out in the 1400s." Dr. MacDuff's voice remained even, and though it held no emotion, his power pulsed in the air. He stared at Commodus until the vampire averted his eyes. "You will hold your men until I give the order."

Silence hung in the room. Even the deep breathing of nervous wolves ceased. Finally, Commodus spoke. "As you wish, Master."

"If your progeny are too weak to remain alive, then they should curse their master." Dr. MacDuff's gaze fell on Sofia as he released Commodus to slump into his chair. "Of this Board only the wolves have cause to worry for the protection of their bloodlines, and we've not seen any movement by Bas Dubh against them."

Dr. MacDuff paced the length of the table, walking behind each board member, forcing every personal guard to step back to allow him to pass close to the seated leaders. His face was anything but gentle. Fangs had descended beneath his curled lip. His eyes glowed, and as he passed each person, standing or seated, his attention lingered for a second as though he focused his powers at them.

"We will wait for Rowan's men. In one week we meet again to define our strategy. I will not jeopardize what The Alliance has spent nearly a millennium trying to accomplish. I will not rush into battle ill prepared." Dr. MacDuff returned to his seat beside Sofia, though this time he did not touch her. "If anyone is not satisfied with this plan, tell me now."

Sofia watched her boss. His hard features did not at all resemble the kind man who'd been patient and tolerant of her refusals to comply with his requests that she attend these meetings or take up residence at Cader. His narrowed eyes stared ahead and every muscle in his face hardened as if made of stone. She found it difficult to believe the vampire sitting beside her was the same man who'd negotiated with her about a personal guard and respected her wishes only to enter her house when she allowed him. Now she thought she might not press her luck with him in the future.

"I agree with Jankin and the wolves. Waiting is our wisest move. We should not attempt a weak attack. Let us fortify our army then move against Kiernan."

The tall blond silently tapped his fingers on the table. "Kiernan has built an army bigger than before, but his lunacy grows and he becomes sloppy in his work. He's leaving victims in his path instead of taking them into his ranks. We may be able to ascertain information about his plan from those he's left behind. Let the vampires work with the new wolves. Let our interrogators uncover any clues locked within their memories." He looked to Fergus.

Wolves all around the room grumbled and growled. Seamus shushed his men. "Laurent, you know this idea does not sit well with wolves. We do not appreciate having vampires playing mind games with our own."

"It is forbidden in our charter!" A short, very muscular dark-skinned man jumped up from his seat. "How dare you suggest such a treasonous tactic?"

Around the room wolves standing guard began shouting. "It's a Bas Dubh plan. An attempt to control wolves!"

The alpha who'd started the tirade pointed at the blond. "I've never trusted you. You've always wanted to hold more power on this council. I will not allow my wolves to submit to this."

Fergus rose to his feet. "Enough. Hold your tongue, Joachim. Your temper is getting the better of you. Again." He paused for moment. "It is true. The wolves will not like it."

Grumbling continued from the ranks. Joachim dropped into his chair, snickering.

"I cannot approve of the mind search for any wolves who've completed their training, but any new wolves, those still within the first month, shall be searched." Fergus turned to Meg. "We will need a formal order to cover this."

She nodded. "It will be ready for your signature before daybreak."

"Absolutely not! No wolf should be mind raped!" Joachim again jumped up from his chair. "Traitor!" He pointed at Fergus.

Around the room gasps erupted and wolves and vampires alike were shoved against the wall as Osgar and Rick barreled up the sides of the conference room to descend on Joachim. Meg and Noelle flanked the men, setting upon Joachim's guards and dispatching them without any trouble.

Sofia gasped. In the rush of movement she hadn't been able to distinguish all that happened, but when the melee stopped, the only wolf of Joachim's entourage left alive was Joachim and he was face down on the table with two snarling wolves holding him in place.

Meg no longer looked like her pretty, well-kept self. She was tall and covered with fur. Blood splattered Noelle's face and chest. She held a sword up by her head and slowly turned, keeping her back to the table and her sword toward the wolves lining the wall.

Fergus remained where he stood, watching, unblinking. "This is not a decision I make lightly, but we must have the information. Laurent, you will personally supervise the interrogations."

"Of course, Fergus. It will be handled with complete consideration and respect for the wolves." The tall, blond vampire bowed his head.

Fergus stepped around the table, and though he spoke to Laurent, his focus was on Joachim. "I'll expect nothing less. No wolf should come from the experience violated. And any information ascertained not related to Bas Dubh will be guarded with the highest levels of care." Fergus's hands flexed and curled.

Sofia swallowed and choked. She hadn't breathed since before Osgar moved, and now the air seemed too heavy for her lungs. She'd just seen her first killings and already she couldn't remember what had transpired.

Fergus stalked to the other end of the room. Anger poured from him.

Sofia's heart pounded in anticipation of what horrible thing would happen next. With each step Fergus took, her heart sped a furious beat.

"You have my word. No harm will come to these wolves." Laurent rose, and his guards gathered behind him. "We begin tonight with the victims who arrived today."

"I offer my team as well, and I request Sheila and Cristof participate. They and their wolves will be able to calm the victims while we work," a petite female vampire with a vicious scar running from below her right eye to her jaw said.

"Very well, Rosemarie. But remember, any missteps will cost the ultimate price." Fergus's eyes darted toward Rosemarie.

She nodded and followed Laurent. Three women, equally as short as Rosemarie, followed the interrogators from the room.

"This meeting is adjourned until the interrogation team has a report." Dr. MacDuff brought his hands together, motioning for everyone to exit the room.

Sofia stood.

"Sit," Dr. MacDuff said. Sofia froze at the harsh order. Dr. MacDuff closed his eyes for a moment. "Please stay, Sofia."

She sat and watched as only the vampires left. All but Dragomir and Noelle. The wolves remained.

"Joachim, you have yet again disagreed with the decision of this Board," Dr. MacDuff said.

Joachim strained under the hands of Osgar and Rick. He twisted his head to peer down the table at where Sofia and Dr. MacDuff sat. "You have what you want." His cold stare centered on Sofia. "All that matters is pleasing The Master." His gaze locked with Sofia's. "Remember, your life is his."

A cold hollow pit opened in Sofia's stomach and fear rippled through her. She bit back a scream. Her life was her own. It had to be. From the corner of her eye she watched Dr. MacDuff. He sat unmoving, watching the action across the room.

Taking his attention from the scene unfolding in front of them for one brief moment, he glanced at Sofia. His cold, harsh stare didn't linger, nor did it tell her anything about what he thought. As quick as he looked at her, his attention snapped back to the men at the opposite end of the table.

Sofia waited for what would happen next, terrified of how this would end.

Joachim fought to break free of his captors, growling and clawing at the table. Osgar and Rick jerked him to his feet, holding him to face Fergus.

"We know you spend time with a known Bas Dubh sympathizer. That you've attended meetings."

Joachim's eyes widened for a second, then his lips curled back and an angry growl ripped from his chest. "Kiernan is right. We are supreme. We should not hide in the darkness while weaker beings control our fate." His jaws snapped and he attempted to lunge for Fergus. "Bas Dubh will take control. Kiernan's plans have already begun. Soon The Alliance will be no more."

"Take him down to the cells. Chain him in silver and leave him to wait for Laurent. We'll learn what we can then dispatch him." Fergus turned his back to Joachim.

Joachim's eyes bulged in his fur-covered face. "I will not be mind fucked!" He thrashed against Osgar and Rick, who yanked him off the ground. "Fools! He'll only use you for his own benefit. We've been pawns for Jankin's desires." His screams were cut short when Dr. MacDuff's intense stare caught his eye.

Their gazes stayed locked together for several minutes until finally Dr. MacDuff broke the connection. The somber, intense expression could not mask the fury ravaging within him.

The dazed look left Joachim's face, replaced by terrified recognition. His focus left Dr. MacDuff and he gaped at Sofia.

Through all the energy levels pulsing in the room she felt horror emanating from Joachim. At the same time a savage rage rolled over his energy, swallowing him. Sofia followed the flow to its source. Her gaze met Dr. MacDuff's blazing green eyes.

As if from thin air, Dr. MacDuff drew a sword and thrust it into Joachim's heart. "Fool. No one takes what is mine."

Sofia swallowed the scream rising within her. Dr. MacDuff was no different than the others. He might even be worse.

# CHAPTER THIRTEEN

Tea sloshed from Sofia's cup. She couldn't stop her hands from trembling. They more than trembled. They shook like a can of paint being mixed at the hardware store. She tried to put the cup on the countertop but ended up breaking it against the Formica.

Tonight she had watched four killings…murders…executions. Whatever they were, she didn't care. The fact was she'd been forced to watch four people die.

"I want my old life back." She used a dishtowel to push the glass and spilled tea into the sink. It might not have been the greatest life, but at least no one got hurt and she was able to fit in.

This worrying about big secrets like vampires and werewolves only made life much more difficult.

"There's no going back," Dragomir said.

She glared at the kitchen window. He stood outside the house, leaning against the wall, occasionally glancing in at her.

She still hadn't acquiesced to letting any vampires into her house, and she'd revoked Dr. MacDuff's invitation as she was leaving Cader. Actually, she'd done something she'd never, ever done. Too shocked and afraid to tell him face to face, she'd called him from her cell phone as she drove. Neither the talking nor driving had been a good idea, but she refused to allow anyone not human to get into a small space with her so she drove herself, followed again by Dragomir driving Osgar's monster truck.

"Stop eavesdropping."

"You opened the window and asked me a question. I thought we were still conversing."

She had done that. Of course, his response was what made the shaking worse. Apparently the occasional death at board meetings was not unusual. If this was the case, why in God's name had Dr. MacDuff asked her to attend? He knew she was not a fan of violence. He had to know death involving swords, werewolves, and vampires fell into the violence category.

It was going to be virtually impossible to change the culture of this organization regarding workplace violence if board members killed each other at meetings, especially if the head of the organization was leading the pack.

She was completely out of her league. She did not belong with them. She belonged in a nice company where everyone respected each other, and nobody got killed as part of the disciplinary process. There was no point in talking to Dr. MacDuff. He couldn't understand her perspective at all. She'd simply look for other employment, find another suitable job and then if Dr. MacDuff wanted to send someone to stand guard outside her new job, so be it.

"That's what I'll do." She reached for the bottle of coconut rum in the cabinet and had to use two hands to steady it enough to get it to her mouth. She didn't often drink and never straight liquor, but this was a different situation that called for drastic measures. *Liquid courage.* She gulped a couple mouthfuls and ended up coughing and wheezing and trying desperately to swallow away the burning sensation running from the back of her throat straight to her belly.

Dragomir watched. "Do you think that will sharpen your skills tonight?"

"Shut up. I'm taking the night off. Go sit in the woods or in the truck. Just leave me alone." She swiped her sleeve over her mouth.

He nodded. "If you think that's the best use of our time, fine. However, I suggest we practice. You need to learn to disengage yourself from situations."

"I'd like to disengage myself from this situation. Got any suggestions?" She took another swig, then breathed out, expecting to see fire shoot from her mouth.

"Your best bet is learning to sense trouble and how to get the hell out of the way before it finds you." He stood square in front of the window. He'd tied his dark hair back at the nape of his neck and moonlight lit the left side of his face.

He had the darkest eyes, well, eye. Sofia squinted at him. She couldn't exactly see both, though she knew plain and well they were the same. Two of the darkest eyes she'd ever seen. He was clean-shaven tonight and the cleft in his chin looked very inviting. Her hand twitched, ready to touch it, to just graze her finger around his chin and along that line, then down his neck to his chest.

She bit her lip.

Dragomir cleared his throat.

Her eyes snapped up from the middle of his chest, where the first buttoned button lay below a dark swirl of hair.

His eyebrows crept upward. "If I didn't know better, I'd say you were just undressing me with your eyes, Ms. Engle."

She glowered at him. "I most certainly was not." The next swig of rum went down fast. It didn't taste that bad anymore and barely burned.

"I'm fairly certain that sort of behavior would be in direct violation of your Sexual Harassment Policy."

"I was not harassing you, not undressing you. Not at all." She turned away from him, fumbling for the cap.

"Not that I'd mind you doing that sort of thing, though truthfully, I'd much rather you did it in person, not in your imagination." His voice held a clear note of amusement.

"For your information, I was not undressing you and second, it is not harassment if the recipient is not offended by the behavior." She took one last sip before capping the bottle and smacking her lips.

"Well, then I'm not harassed, but I am intrigued. Did you stop at my shirt or did you have my pants off, too?" He smiled.

"I was not undressing you." Sofia stomped to the door. "Let's just get this over with."

Of course, now that he thought she had some sort of interest in him, which she most certainly did not, she'd need to be on her guard. Everything she'd ever read about vampires, the ones in horror novels and romance novels, indicated they were all sneaky, doing everything they could to get their prey. She was nobody's snack. She pulled on her sweatshirt, licked her rum-flavored lips, and marched out to learn how to disengage.

*Disengage. I'll disengage him. Damn vampire.*

Dragomir was, after all, dead, and since accepting the actual, real existence of vampires and werewolves, Sofia had added them to the list of men she did not date or do anything else with either.

Unable to see him, she stood in the driveway staring into the darkness. *Shadow man.* She shook her head. *Show off.* She closed her eyes and inhaled. His scent wafted on the breeze all around her. The woodsy scent of clean, crisp air and soap. His bold presence emanated from the side of the house near the kitchen window.

Sofia opened her eyes and saw him. He still leaned against the wall, a luminescent outline surrounding him. He wasn't wearing his duster tonight, just a white shirt, sleeves rolled to his elbows, and jeans with combat boots. Even as a shadow he looked delicious.

The longer she watched him, the sharper her vision became. The top three buttons on his shirt were open. His arms folded over his chest, and for whatever reason, it made his shoulders look broader than she recalled.

Her gaze wandered lower. His shirt was tucked into his jeans, which appeared to strain against the muscles of his thighs. She wished he'd turn around so she could see if they were having the same trouble on the backside.

She hated to admit it, but he was the type of man she liked. Muscular, tall, broad. She guessed he'd have a nice ass. She sighed. And his eyes—they were like none she'd ever encountered. Thoughtful and deep, like they hid the answers to every question she could ever think to ask.

The first time she'd met him in Fergus's office, she nearly fell into the depth of those eyes. She'd felt him size her up and would have, should have reported the incident to Dr. MacDuff. But she hadn't. Because she liked it. The way his gaze lingered on her face as if he was seeing a woman for the first time felt so good. She'd noticed him focus on her lips and the way his tongue slid across his own, like he was thinking of tasting her, made her nearly melt. When his attention wandered lower, she hadn't felt at all violated. In fact, he was so tender, so interested, she couldn't help but turn a circle for him.

She'd been sized up many times over, but no one ever made her feel like he did, like she was special and beautiful. Not even human men had done that.

She bit the inside of her cheek hard, drawing blood and pulling herself back to reality. She would not fall prey to some dead guy with vampire magic. She wouldn't no matter how damn handsome he was.

"Well, what are you waiting for? Attack me." She widened her stance in anticipation of the assault. She'd show him about disengaging.

When he didn't move, she stood up straight, jammed one hand onto her hip, and used the other to wave him over. "Some time tonight."

He remained at the window.

Sofia tapped her foot impatiently.

He watched her. He was doing it again. That annoying thing he did when he simply waited for something to happen. He did it all the time. Stood there, melting into the landscape like the invisible man, waiting, sizing up his surroundings.

It was irritating. Sofia was not the stand-around-and-wait type. She liked to get to it and be done with it so she could move on to the next event.

"Fine." She marched up to him intent on provoking him. However, her newly acquired night vision was not honed enough or maybe it was simply to narrow. She didn't notice the leftover logs from her fire pit as she barreled at him. Her foot caught on one and down she went.

This time she didn't land on her ass. Instead Dragomir moved. He caught her before she hit the ground, arms around her, cradling her against his chest.

"Whoa." The first thing to register about her situation was not that he'd moved or that she'd tripped, again in front of him, or that her arms and legs had begun their transformation into gelatin. Instead, she noticed how quickly his heart beat beneath her hand, the one that had managed to land flat against his chest, inside his shirt.

She pressed her palm to his skin, and the beating sped. Her fingers caressed the hair tickling her skin, and his grip on her backside tightened.

She glanced up at him. His gaze was focused on her and once again warm. His chest rose and fell with more rapid breaths than she'd previously noticed. He licked his lips. She bit hers as the desire to kiss him swelled.

Would it be so bad to kiss him just once? Then she could say she'd done it, kissed a vampire and that she hadn't enjoyed it and she wouldn't recommend it and she could swear them off for good, having just cause to make such a finite decision.

His head dipped toward hers. She swallowed. Her legs had given out. She couldn't decide to avoid this even if her life depended on it. She was staying in his arms unless he dropped her down on the ground, and if he did, she'd stay there, unable to drag herself to the house and wishing he'd kissed her.

She tilted her head back and his lips brushed hers. *Soft. Warm.* She parted her lips. His tongue slid between them, and she welcomed him. She removed her hand from his chest, sending it up and around his neck.

Her other hand stayed put, holding onto his bulging bicep. *Hard. So big.* Sofia's mind went blank save for one thought. *Dragomir.* He was the only thing she could consider. Wanting him. To hold him. Touch him. Kiss him. To…

Not one other thought came to mind. She couldn't remember what she'd been doing before this kiss or why she'd ever wanted to do anything else. All she knew was she had to have more of him.

She managed to will her legs out of their goo state and with a little lift from him she wrapped them around his waist. His hands cupped her ass, squeezing and kneading and pulling her closer to him.

She delved deeper into the kiss, crushing her mouth against his and exploring every inch. She finally broke the kiss when her back hit the side of the house and he pressed his hips into her.

"Oh," she moaned. Her breaths were so heavy she could barely catch them.

He kissed her lips, her cheek, her ear, then her neck. The feel of his warm, wet mouth tugging on her skin drove her nuts. She writhed against him, knowing she was about to lose it. "I…I…oh…"

"Let go, Sofia. Come for me." His low voice, softer, sexier than anything she'd ever heard drove her over the edge.

She dropped her head against the wall and cried out, "Oh God" as the wave of ecstasy washed over her. She squeezed her legs around his hips and pumped against him, moaning for more.

His mouth came to her neck once more, his tongue working the skin. Soft suckling sounds alternated with her moans, and the feel of his mouth tugging on her skin brought tears to her eyes.

The low rumbles vibrating from his chest sent zings of excitement through her breasts. His muffled groans of pleasure pleased her. He enjoyed her, wanted more. She held his head to her neck and ground her hips into him.

"More. More," she begged.

His mouth came to hers and she felt his fangs. His tongue delved deeper. Sofia thrust her tongue into his mouth, wanting him to taste her, to have her. His fangs pricked her tongue and tiny pangs of pleasure shot through her. She cried out.

He broke the kiss, threw back his head, and growled. The sound echoed around them.

When finally their moment of pleasure ended, her head drooped to his shoulder. Dragomir propped his head against the house. His slowing breath puffed against her neck. His hands held her firm against his body. They stayed like this until her senses returned, until she was able to realize she had not only kissed a vampire, she'd dry humped him, against her house, begging for more until she came. And worse than all of that? She'd loved every second of it.

She scrambled out of his arms, awkwardly tumbling out of his grip in spite of how he tried to keep her from falling.

*On my ass again.* Leaves crunched beneath her.

This time she got to her feet on her own, completely embarrassed by her behavior. She didn't bother to look at him, just spun on her heel and ran back toward the house.

"Good night."

She slammed the door shut behind her, locked it, and raced up the stairs to the shower.

# CHAPTER FOURTEEN

"What the fuck?"

Dragomir paced back and forth behind the house for three hours. The lights had gone out twenty-two minutes after she'd run into the house. Twenty-two minutes and fourteen seconds to be exact. Not that he purposely monitored her so closely, but that was the exact time the lights went out.

*Did I just…? I did.* "What the fuck?" He marched back toward the woods.

How was he going to explain this? How was he going to tell Jankin what he'd done? He raked his fingers through his hair for the hundredth time, then down over his face.

"Damn it." His hands smelled like her. His hair smelled like her. His entire body smelled like her. "Damn it!" He glanced toward the house to be sure he hadn't wakened her with his shout.

Her respirations continued in the slow rise and fall of a sleeping woman, one who'd been pleasured by a vampire. A vampire who'd been contracted to ensure her safety, but who apparently thought taking advantage of her was part of the job.

"I didn't take advantage of her." He snapped a branch from a nearby pine tree. "She attacked me. She told me to attack her, but then she attacked me."

He spun around and beat an oak tree to his left, pounding the pine bough against the trunk of the tree until all that was left was a two-foot stick.

"She was falling. I caught her. That's all I did. She…" He tossed the stick to the ground. Sap covered his hands, and when he tried to push his hair back from his face, he ended up with sap on his cheeks and forehead and hair stuck to his fingers. "Damn it!"

He froze and listened. Still the quiet breathing of a pleased woman was all he heard.

He sniffed his hands, aggravated by the persistent desire to smell her. Now he smelled like pine and flowers and fruit. He still couldn't figure out which flower, but this was not the time for deciphering what she smelled like. This was the time to practice an explanation. *Still, what was that? Hyacinth?*

He shook his head and continued pacing. He hadn't bitten her. He'd managed to keep his fangs to himself. But he'd wanted to bite her, wanted to sink his fangs into the soft, supple skin of her neck. And she'd wanted it. She'd offered her neck, held his face to her skin, begged for more.

"Fuck!"

He had wanted to bite. Wanted to mark her as his own. The pull to mate her was overwhelming. But he'd resisted. He hadn't crossed *that* line.

"I'll just tell Jankin she'd had too much to drink and she came on to…" He sighed. "I should have known better." He fell back against a tree and banged his head repeatedly. "Jackass."

He licked his lips, still able to taste her. The heady flavor of lust combined with coconut rum. Her lips had been sticky, sticky and sweet. As if she needed to add a little something more to her already unbearably intoxicating scent. And, the flavor of her…

He hardened just thinking of her. The idea of undressing her, kissing every inch of her, touching her in places no other man should ever touch her, being inside her. His cock throbbed.

"Fuck!"

He glanced toward the house. This fucking woman was killing him. His pants were stained and sticky. His hands and hair and face were sticky. His lips were sticky. And he had the most horrible desire to pleasure himself right here in the woods outside her house just because thoughts of her plagued his mind.

He wanted to sink his fangs into her flesh in so many different spots. Her neck, her breasts, her thighs. His cock strained against his jeans, rubbing on the zipper.

"What the fuck?"

He adjusted himself, glaring at his cock as if that could quell his desires. He'd never in more than eight hundred years felt this way for a vampire or a werewolf and certainly not a human, though he'd happily enjoyed all three plenty of times.

"Fucking Jankin. This is all his doing." He kicked at a pile of leaves. "Come to Wooddale. I need the most skilled warrior for this assignment." He did his best Scottish accent. "Bastard. A setup. She's like the devil. Dressed in her business suits with her hair up and pretty green eyes batting at me. Why not just offer me the damn apple?" He rubbed his temples.

Dragomir spent the next hour practicing what he'd say, deciding how he'd explain pinning Sofia, possibly his boss's descendant, against the back of her house, bringing her a level of ecstasy he was sure she'd never experienced with any other man, and then having his own orgasm when he was supposed to be teaching her to disengage herself from compromising situations.

He groaned and cursed the day he turned vampire. "If I can't disengage myself, how can I teach her? Fuck. Fuck. Fuck!" His voice echoed in the woods and his gaze darted toward the house.

*****

Six hours later, Osgar arrived to relieve him. "Ever the disheveled mess," Dragomir said as he rose from the porch steps.

"Look who's talking." Osgar sipped coffee from a Styrofoam cup. "What happened to you?"

"She sleeps. All night." Dragomir turned toward the woods and trudged back to Cader, both dreading and needing to speak with Jankin.

"I like what you've done with your hair." Osgar laughed after him.

He'd get answers. What woman could upturn a vampire? Only one with special power. Dragomir had managed to convince himself of this during the long night. It was the only possibility.

After this last event he was absolutely certain she was a descendant of Jankin MacDuff, the vampire. How else could she be so damn beguiling?

Dragomir couldn't afford to waste time when he needed answers, but there was no way he'd face Jankin stinking of clumsy, immature sex with Sofia. There'd be no getting a single question out, never mind an answer, if Jankin thought he'd defiled Sofia. In his quarters Dragomir showered and dressed in clean clothes before finding the master.

Jankin sat at a black oak desk, focused on the computer screen. His main office, the one deep within the Lower Level, was larger than the conference room, holding a giant table that matched the desk at one end, a more comfortable sitting area with sofas and chairs at the other end, and another door, hidden by an oil painting of Scotland. The hidden door led to Jankin's private chamber.

The only movement Jankin made came from his right hand as his fingers worked the mouse. He was a man Dragomir admired, strove to be like. Reserved, usually, and naturally pensive and understanding, Jankin was one of the most powerful vampires Dragomir had ever met. A leader among leaders. A friend.

Dragomir swallowed the lump in his throat. His chest tightened. *What have I done?*

Many others sought council from Jankin. Dragomir had witnessed Jankin pardon, even accept men and women he himself would not have thought twice of killing. Could Jankin pardon him for touching Sofia? If he could, would he?

A low hum of power emanated from Jankin. He was relaxed, not at all bothered by the events of the previous evening. In a state of rest he still gave off a vibe no one could miss. Even humans, dense to any metaphysical energy, felt it. They revered him, were drawn to him, trusted him. And they should. Above all else, Jankin loved humans. He had sworn his life to protect them from Bas Dubh.

*Bas Dubh.* The black death.

It was the reason for all their troubles. The attacks. The threats. The wars breaking out across the globe. It was the excuse Jankin had used to lure Dragomir to Wooddale. Memories of Jankin fighting side by side with him flooded Dragomir's mind. Swords in hand, covered in blood, dead enemies fallen at their feet. Together they'd fought many a long, miserable battle.

Jankin stormed many a compound, slaughtering followers of Kiernan. Vampires, wolves, and mind-washed humans alike. He had no tolerance for Bas Dubh. No ability to believe humans should be slaves. As long as he lived, he would never consider wolves second class to vampires or humans to be walking, talking meals. He would not allow any members of The Alliance to simply turn a human for fun or lust or one-sided love.

Respect was to be given to them or else plan to meet your death.

Dragomir stood silently in the doorway. Somehow all those hours of practice didn't seem like enough. He clenched his fists. He was no coward. He would own his actions, tell Jankin everything, or at least an overview of everything. No need to bend his ear with details. Then, if Jankin didn't kill him, he'd request a transfer back to Rome or out into the field in New England. Hand-to-hand combat was what he needed. It would clear his mind. Help him forget that damn woman.

Jankin's green eyes narrowed. "You might as well ask."

Dragomir stepped into the room. Jankin had always been a sentimental man. Portraits of his descendants hung about the room, one after another, so many of them with a likeness to Jankin. *Strong genes.*

Pictures of Sofia and her mother and father adorned the wall to the left of Jankin's desk.

On the bookshelves behind the desk albums of old photos, scrap books of clippings from newspapers hundreds of years old, written works from descendants long dead, trinkets belonging to others and locks of hair from babies filled the shelves.

One shelf held framed report cards belonging to Sofia, an original birth certificate, a picture painted for Jankin, marked grade three, prom pictures, announcements regarding her academic and athletic achievements.

Dragomir groaned.

"What it is?" Jankin finally looked at him. "Something's been on your mind for several nights. Now's the time." Jankin motioned Dragomir toward a chair.

Dragomir couldn't bring himself to look the man in the eye. He'd betrayed his friend. He'd broken his confidence. He'd molested the apple of Jankin's eye.

"I…she—"

Jankin raised his hand. "Before you begin, tell me how the night went. Sofia was rather upset when she left. Called and banned me from the house. Och." He shook his head. "She needs to understand the dangers we face."

Dragomir nodded. "Agreed." In all honesty he couldn't have agreed more. She had no idea how dangerous her life had become. Even her guard couldn't be trusted.

"I hadn't anticipated Joachim's loss of allegiance to The Alliance or to Fergus. We should have known it was coming. The wolf had been sneaking around for months. Commodus's behavior was no surprise. His boldness knows no bounds, but he is a coward in the end." Jankin leaned back in his chair. "How did the night go? Did she relax any? I hate for her to be so tense all the time. It's unhealthy for a human not to find some release."

Dragomir's eyes widened for a flash. "Yes, she did seem to release…" He cleared his throat. "…relax."

"She's wound quite tightly, having to be as restrained as she is. She's frustrated at not getting what she's wanted."

"I think her frustration might have diminished after last night," Dragomir mumbled to his feet.

"Less violence? We're at war. She doesn't understand." Jankin glanced toward the Sofia shelf. "War is violent." He picked up a framed document. "But you wanted to ask me something."

Dragomir finally looked at his boss. As Jankin admired the birth certificate a slight smile tweaked his lips.

"The Legend. It is true. Isn't it?" Dragomir studied Jankin's face, measuring every muscle and the millimeters of movement or lack thereof.

Jankin replaced the birth certificate on the shelf and turned back to Dragomir. "I wish I knew." That same smile remained on his face. His eyes were gentle, amused. "I've nearly driven myself to madness trying to figure it out."

"How could you not know? You were there." Dragomir's voice was gruffer than intended, but Jankin's lack of commitment and foggy answer were unacceptable. Jankin must know the truth.

Jankin laughed. "I have been a bachelor all these long years including those twenty-eight I lived before the change. I held several women at that time, enjoyed my share, plus, but I never called one my wife, never tied myself to one to protect and cherish 'til death or vampirism do us part." His eyebrow ticked upward.

"Since I was turned, I've held hundreds." His voice lowered. "Ah, more than that. This you know, old friend." He sighed.

Dragomir shifted in the chair. He did know. In their younger days they'd caroused together. They knew each other's histories. For the first time he wished he didn't know Jankin so well. And God help him, he knew Jankin had far more knowledge about him than a grandfather should have about a man who touched his granddaughter.

"I left Scotland for a time." Jankin's gaze seemed to focus on some far away memory. "Nearly two hundred years later I returned to my lands and found the family living there, clearly mine. Eara was the name of the one woman I bedded before *and* after the change." He reached for the whiskey on the corner of his desk, pouring some for himself and some for Dragomir.

"I could never know for sure if the conception happened before or after." Jankin sipped his whiskey then stared down at the glass, watching the amber liquid roll around in his hand. "I'd be lying if I said I haven't wished it to be true." He looked at Dragomir. Gone was the laughter from his eyes. Worry now plagued him.

"She can scent, Jankin." Dragomir reached for the glass in front of him. "Me and the wolves. She spent yesterday practicing. Can even track me." He shrugged. "And the wolves as well."

"Many who spend time with wolves can scent them. This is nothing out of the ordinary."

"Bull. We both know it's odd for her to scent or track them. But let's give her the ability to scent." Dragomir drained his glass. "That still does not explain her ability to track me, my energy or the wolves."

"I don't believe her to be anything more than human, Dragomir. As much as I'd like to believe something different she is not my child." Jankin sat back and sighed. "I've traced her bloodline. She is not mine."

Dragomir bolted from his chair to pace behind it. "Let's say she possesses a superior sense of smell than most humans. That does not explain her ability to track. If she was not conceived by a vampire, what explains this phenomena?"

Jankin poured himself another measure of whiskey. "I should have known you'd come to question me."

"You dragged me here from the front. How could I not notice?" Dragomir slid his glass to Jankin and waited for another pour.

"She'd have died." Jankin refilled Dragomir's glass, eyes fixed on the smooth flow of liquid. "I couldn't bear it."

Dragomir listened. Something told him what he was about to hear might be worse than the idea of Sofia being part vampire.

"Helpless little creature, not even able to cry. It was a few weeks before her lungs were stable enough that she could howl out that first scream, a call to battle, to fight for her own life." Jankin's eyes misted. "A warrior from the first. Her father had been one of my best friends. How could I not save her?"

And there was the truth. Jankin had bound Sofia to him. His blood was probably the first thing she'd ever consumed. Vampire blood. So potent it could bring a dying man back from the brink. Vampires rarely shared. It was one of the laws of their society. Do not play with a human's fate.

Only two occasions were considered acceptable for allowing a human to drink from a vampire. The first was simple. The creation of another vampire. Humans couldn't be transformed without consuming the blood of a vampire.

The second was the marriage ritual. Vampires bound themselves to their mates. The sharing of blood was considered an intimate exchange, one done only when lovers made the highest commitment to each other—to live *for* each other and to die *with* each other.

"Who else knows?" Dragomir growled. A secret this dark had to be buried, hidden forever. Death was the penalty for such a crime.

Death for the vampire and the human.

"Noelle." Jankin sighed like a burden had been lifted. "Not another soul. Not even Fergus."

"Did you bind Noelle?" He knew it was foolish to question Jankin, but he couldn't stop himself. Something forced him to demand answers, to know who he needed to monitor, who, if the need arose, he'd execute.

Jankin shifted in his chair, regarding Dragomir through narrowed eyes.

Dragomir leaned forward. "They would take her. They'll use her." He whipped away from Jankin unable to look at his mentor. "If the wolves ever realize she can track them…" He ran his hands through his hair and stared up at the ceiling. "…*our* wolves would not accept it." And if that wasn't bad enough, the idea of Kiernan taking Sofia, torturing and enslaving her entered Dragomir's mind. "No one else must ever know." He slammed his fist on the table. "Ever."

"As I suspected you've come to realize her value. You now understand your importance in maintaining her safety."

Value? He'd realized more than her value. For the first time in centuries a woman piqued his interest in ways only his beloved wife had. Sofia intrigued, surprised, beguiled, and befuddled him. She aroused feelings in Dragomir he'd forgotten ever existed.

She made him excited to rise in the evening.

Dragomir looked deep into Jankin's eyes. The fleck of hazel slicing through the deep green of his irises glowed.

"I fully understand. Your life as well as hers would be ended. All our work against Bas Dubh would be for naught. Without you, The Alliance will not survive."

"The Alliance would continue, just not as it has." Jankin inhaled. "You smell of her."

Dragomir held Jankin's gaze. He'd come to confess. "Yes."

Jankin's presence swelled. His power prickled along Dragomir's skin. His eyes flashed with an angry light and all his attention drilled into Dragomir. He was almost as good an interrogator as Dragomir. Almost, but not quite. Dragomir locked away many of the details of the evening's events too personal to share with anyone. Many things a man did with a woman were meant to be kept private.

Jankin searched and Dragomir did not stop him, rather he allowed the master to know his thoughts and feelings for Sofia. It was necessary to ensure Jankin knew Dragomir would defend Sofia to his own death.

"I've seen the way you look at her." Jankin stood and faced the bookshelf. He picked up a picture of Sofia as a young girl with pigtails. She was dressed like a pumpkin. "Like a man admires his woman." His fingers traced the smiling face. "And I've seen the way she watches you. She would deny it, of course, but I've seen. I know she is drawn to you."

Jankin replaced the frame, spun to face Dragomir and lunged across the desk, knocking him to the floor, his fist meeting Dragomir's chin. "I am not ready to give her up." Jankin's words ripped through Dragomir's mind. "She is like my own child."

"But are you ready to die for her?" Dragomir withstood the blow and dodged a second, ending up across the room. "Would you give up your work to save her life?" Dragomir swiped away the blood running from the wound on his face. "I would."

Jankin glared at Dragomir. His fangs lengthened as he spoke. "Would you?"

"We both know there is only one way for her to be truly safe." Dragomir raised his head to look down his nose at Jankin. "There's only one way to ensure you both remain safe."

# CHAPTER FIFTEEN

Sofia folded the turtleneck collar down and took one last look at the giant hickey she hoped she'd only imagined. But nope. There it was. Dark blue and black with purple-y spots nearest her throat.

"Oh my God." She pushed the words through gritted teeth.

She straightened the collar up over the bruise, tied a scarf around her neck, and pulled her hair down over her shoulders to lie on her chest.

"I look like crap." She tugged the collar, loosened the scarf, and fussed with her hair.

The turtleneck wasn't even hers. It didn't fit well and wasn't comfortable. She'd found it in a box in her mom's room. "How could the woman have been that much smaller than me?" Sofia yanked at the underarms, futilely trying to stretch the fabric so it didn't constrict the blood flow to her arms. The sleeves ended a good three inches above her wrists, and the waist kept slipping up and out of her skirt.

"I'll have to keep my damn jacket on all day." She buttoned her suit jacket. "This is a fine mess."

How could she have possibly done that last night? How did she let him do this? She…he touched her. He did this with his vampire magic. "That sneaky son of a bitch. I'll bet he'd planned this the whole time."

Vampires couldn't be trusted. She'd known this. She'd felt them testing her, probing her with their vampire abilities. "Pigs." Every one of them was not to be trusted.

Now she could get rid of Dragomir. She'd tell Dr. MacDuff he'd attacked her, show him the proof and be done with that vampire. She swung open the bedroom door and marched down the stairs.

"Get your feet off my coffee table," she barked at Osgar.

"Geesh!" He jumped up. "I didn't even hear you." He did a double take. "What are you wearing?"

"Shut up." She was well aware she looked ridiculous. Beyond the shirt being too small it was bright orange. She couldn't even remember seeing her mother wear it. She couldn't imagine why the woman had owned such a foolish thing. But she was thankful to have it and reached into her jacket to tug at the armpits again.

She poured black coffee into her travel mug and snapped the lid shut. As she rinsed the pot she noticed the bottle of coconut rum. *Liquid courage, my ass. More like the devil's brew.* She opened the bottle and poured the last little bit down the drain.

"Rough night?" Osgar leaned against the counter.

"Why do you always look like you just rolled out of bed? Don't you ever comb your hair?" She threw the bottle in the recycling bin, grabbed her lunch and coffee then slung her handbag over her shoulder.

"Okay, maybe today I look a little worn, but is there any need for both of you to point it out? Did it ever occur to you I might have feelings and having you and Drag mocking my look might hurt those feelings?" He pouted and shuffled his feet, only briefly glancing at Sofia.

"You're kidding. Since when have you given a crap about what anyone else thinks of your looks?" Sofia opened the kitchen door. "Get out." She hitched her thumb toward the porch.

"Fine. I don't care. But you oughta know you're in no position to complain about me. Your shoes don't even match." He walked past her, pointing to her feet.

They didn't. She wore one brown and one blue. "Shit!" She shoved her bags and drink into Osgar's hands and ran up the stairs.

*****

The drive to work was more treacherous than Sofia could have possibly anticipated. "I'll just walk in to Dr. MacDuff's…" She ran a red light. "No. I'll call
him and ask him to come to my office. No sense in getting trapped on the Lower
Level." A horn blared, but she kept going.

"I'll tell him Dragomir provoked me, baited me. He convinced me to go behind
the house with him." She swerved over the yellow line. Another horn blasted and
she jerked the wheel to the right. "He *lured* me back there."

She wiped her face with her sleeve as she remembered the feel of his mouth
on hers, his hands on her ass, her legs clamped around him. She squirmed in her
seat and breezed through a stop sign. This time when a horn sounded lights shined
in her mirror. Osgar was flashing his high beams and waving his hands at her.

She yanked the mirror sideways and stopped at the next red light.

While she waited she thought about that first kiss and how gentle he'd been.
His soft lips pressed to hers, parting so smoothly, then his tongue slid into her
mouth. And his taste. Ooh, he tasted like, like man, like heaven, like wine and
chocolate and *man.*

And his…his…it was hard and big and so hard. She bit her lip. Her hips wiggled
as she thought about how she'd rubbed herself against him with such force, such
desire, like nothing she'd ever experienced. God, he was good.

Someone banged on the window. "What are you doing?" Osgar shouted.

Sofia's eyes snapped open and she gunned the gas. A pedestrian dove out of her
way, rolling into the gutter. She slammed on the brakes before rear-ending an Audi.

She gripped the wheel with two hands and kept her eyes open, focusing on
the road and not on Dragomir or his body parts and how he seemed quite adept
at using them. All of them.

Still the memory of his mouth pressed to her neck, his lips sealing over her
flesh, and the way his tongue worked her skin made her moan aloud. The sound
startled her. "What is wrong with me?" She glanced at herself in the rearview

mirror. Beads of sweat had formed on her flush face. She dabbed her lip and cheeks and turned on the air conditioner.

The turtleneck, scarf, and her hair were too much. She was so warm she thought she'd overheat. She tugged at her collar and caught a glimpse of the love bite marring her neck.

"But he didn't bite me." Sofia fingered her skin. "Why not?" She nibbled her lip.

Why wouldn't a vampire bite a woman? Why wouldn't *he* bite *her?* Why, when he lured her back to him, wouldn't he take advantage of the opportunity? Why not feed?

"Am I not good enough?" She clenched her jaw. "Why not?" Didn't he want her?

She turned into the parking lot and pulled into the first empty spot. "Did he think I'd taste sour?" When her bumper smacked the light pole, she put the car in park.

"What the hell was that all about?" Osgar asked, jumping from his truck. He parked immediately behind the Camry, so close there was hardly enough room for Sofia to wedge a finger between her rear windshield and his bumper.

"Is that necessary? And do you have to drive such a mammoth truck?"

"Yes. Absolutely necessary. You are not driving again today. You practically demolished the town. I think they called an ambulance for the poor guy you chased off the crosswalk. What has gotten into you?" Osgar carried Sofia's handbag and lunch box as she tried to hobble toward the door.

"I'm tired. That's all." No way was she telling Osgar what had happened with Dragomir. In fact, she'd decided not to mention it to anyone, least of all Dr. MacDuff. The thought of it, him, the incident made her wet in places she'd prefer stayed dry during work.

There was no way she could honestly report such an incident as harassment or assault or inappropriate behavior when her body had this reaction. Traitorous flesh. Her mind screamed "tell, tell." But her body begged, "more, more." She sighed and hobbled along.

"Nice shoes," Mrs. Sheehan said. "You setting a new trend?"

Sofia glanced down. Her shoes were the same color, both blue, which in and of itself looked ridiculous with the purple tights, brown skirt, and green jacket. But the kicker was the three-inch heel on the strappy sandal. It dwarfed the flat loafer.

"Well, at least they're the same color." Osgar looked up toward the ceiling and over toward the Emergency Room entrance. "Where's Jamieson?"

"We had another group arrive. He's in the ER helping Rick."

Osgar stepped toward the Emergency Room.

"No need to go, Osgar. They've got it. Only three this time and two are down already." Mrs. Sheehan waved him back.

He nodded but stared toward the door.

"That's a nice scarf, honey. But you might want to wear it with something a little less orange." Mrs. Sheehan leaned over the counter, her finger pointing toward Sofia's neck, and then circling the air as though to draw a bull's-eye where Sofia stood. "You know fuchsia is a pretty color and the lime green with the yellow really brings it out. But it's not the best choice for an orange turtleneck or that hunter green blazer."

Sofia's fingers gripped her coffee cup so firmly it cracked. It was going to be a long, long day. She held out her hands for her bags.

"Oh, no. Let me carry them to your office. We'll take the elevator. It's safer." Osgar led the way down the corridor.

Sofia followed, her head hanging, one foot bumping along while the other clomped beside it. How was it Dragomir didn't want her? She had practically thrown herself at him. Actually, she did throw herself at him. It was more of a fall at him, but the fact remained she went to him. And he didn't want her. But why?

She'd seen and felt him watching her these past few days. She was no love expert but those were not the looks of a man with no interest in a woman.

*Fine. If all he wanted was a dry hump behind the house, that's all he's getting. See if he ever has the opportunity to…to…to do that or any other thing to me again.*

"Easy there." Osgar pulled the nearest trashcan under Sofia's hand. "You're dripping coffee everywhere. Housekeeping's gonna love you today."

Sofia looked back at the trail of coffee starting at the elevator and following her up the hall. She dropped the broken cup in the trash. Huffing, she turned to the ladies' room to retrieve a towel.

"Don't worry about it. I'll get it. Is there something you want to talk about? Something happen?" Osgar urged Sofia toward her office.

"No." She grabbed her bags from him and kicked her office door shut. It closed with a slam. "Sorry," she mumbled and trudged to her desk.

She hardly left her office all day. Too ashamed to be seen dressed like the company clown and physically incapable of walking the halls with her shoe situation, she'd managed to get everyone to agree to meet in her office or at the farthest, the conference room on the third floor.

Whenever her mind wandered to Dragomir she forced herself to remember Mrs. Sheehan's disapproving gaze. Every time her mind wandered to the incident or any reminder of it, like Dragomir's breath on her skin or the way his tongue slid from her mouth down her chin to her neck or the sound he made when he finished, she looked at her feet.

*Setting a new fashion trend. Yeah.*

The day was not an entire loss. She did manage to get some work done, though she was certain her appearance did not help move her agenda along. After the events of last night's board meeting and the current investigation into the training process for new wolves, she'd decided the most important order of business was completing the Workplace Violence Policy in spite of Dr. MacDuff's recruitment initiative. She figured she had plenty of ammunition for reorganizing priorities.

However, between the persistent urges to relive every vivid detail of the encounter with Dragomir and her inability not to sense the werewolves in the building, remaining on task was a near impossibility. Progress was slow.

Sofia closed her eyes and focused on the energy bubbling up the stairwell. The air charged and wisps of loose hair floated around her head. Only one person had literally changed the atmospheric pressure all day. Constantly. She was beginning to get a headache from the highs and lows.

*Rick.* Sofia inwardly groaned.

Whenever he came to the third floor, the pressure dropped. Since he was suspended from commanding any training exercises while she was still investigating the concerns with Louis and she'd drafted a policy that prohibited physical assaults during training, Rick felt the need to be on the third floor campaigning for werewolf laws.

She'd suggested a policy to limit the amount of physical contact that occurred during werewolf training or at the very least limit the number of times a werewolf could be assaulted. But nothing seemed to stick. Rick consistently presented a rationale for attacking his charges. They hadn't even begun to tackle the concept of verbal assaults.

It was a quarter past three and she was preparing for her fourth meeting of the day with Osgar, Fergus, and Rick. Judging by the fact that Rick was plowing toward her office like a stampede of angry buffalo, Sofia knew he wasn't pleased with her latest revisions.

"Don't even bother coming in. I'll meet you in the conference room with everyone else," she called down the hall before the stairwell door opened. "I refuse to have another pre-meeting argument." Having given up on trying to appear professional, she picked up her notepad and padded out of her office barefoot.

The last three meetings had begun with Rick yelling, Sofia debating, usually in a professional manner with a low volume and appropriate tone, though she did lose her cool once. Osgar and Fergus played referees, attempting to keep Rick in human form and Sofia from causing him to explode into a rabid fur ball, which was a term she only used in her own thoughts of him, never aloud in spite of the term dangling on the tip of her tongue all day.

In the hallway she met Meg, Osgar, and Fergus.

"Who are you talking to?" Meg asked. She wore a red suit with red shoes and a black blouse. Her lipstick matched the suit and her blond shoulder-length hair fell in waves around her round face. She was an attractive woman with a lot of spunk. Anyone who could pull off that outfit had to be.

Sofia sighed. "Rick. He's coming up the stairs." She turned into the conference room and tossed her notepad and four copies of her latest policy on the table. "His tactics are getting pretty old."

The trio followed her into the room. A surge of power pressed against her back, and she could have sworn the three wolves were right behind her. Collectively they were a force nearly as agitated as Rick. She glanced over her shoulder to see them still standing in the hall. The energy surrounding them sparked and pulsed as though it might burst into an inferno.

Meg stepped closer, breaking away from Fergus and Osgar, blocking the path out of the conference room. "Dragomir was correct. You do have a gift of some sort."

Sofia hesitated. Did they know? What had Dragomir told them? "I wouldn't call it a gift." Sofia rubbed her temples. "He's just a loud walker." *Lame-O.* She got the very distinct impression Meg was annoyed. "He's been pissed all day. It's hard to miss."

Meg nodded and a slight smile tugged her lips. But behind her pretty violet eyes, Sofia saw something wild stalking.

As Rick moved down the hall, an invisible wall of hot, angry energy came with him making Sofia's head pound. If they didn't get this policy resolved there was a good chance her brain would ignite.

She did her best to ignore Rick's energy and find Mr. Jamieson's. The old guard was probably the gentlest soul in the building. His entire being was calm and relaxed. She'd spent a good part of the day focusing on him. Tracking him was better than taking an aspirin.

"This policy is still too restrictive." Rick stormed into the room, yanked a chair back, and dropped into it. He slid a paper across the table to Sofia. "I've edited your policy. This is much more acceptable."

Osgar and Fergus filed into the room, and although Meg returned to her own office Sofia had the very distinct feeling she was keeping an ear tuned to the conversation in the conference room.

Rick had vehemently disagreed with every single draft Sofia submitted, which did not surprise her and was the reason he no longer got to vote on the policy's approval. He only had campaigning power. The current process required Sofia, Osgar, and Fergus to come to an agreement, then the policy would be presented to Dr. MacDuff for final approval. Thankfully, Dr. MacDuff had managed to get The Board to agree that he and Fergus needed to be the only ones involved, otherwise this policy would never get finished.

Sofia read the policy. "One line. You think one line covers what we need?" She stared at him.

"Yeah. All your words get in the way." He handed out copies of the policy to everyone else. "As you can see this allows for progress in the training arena and manages to set expectations in the *Employee Relations zone*." He said the words "employee relations" as though he was trying to pronounce some Greek term he'd never before heard.

Sofia read the one-liner out loud. "Violence will be used on an as needed basis during training exercises and only with the intent to weed out the weak."

Unblinking, she pursed her lips and stared at Rick. Hours of arguing her perspective that violence should be a last resort to control someone who has displayed the potential for violence toward others or has already become violent, and this is what he gets out of that?

She tapped her foot. "No."

Osgar shifted his chair to face Rick.

Fergus removed his glasses. "I think this policy is definitely a step closer to where Sofia is heading. Certainly it's better than your last suggestion of 'Violence will be used whenever I see fit' but it still needs some work." He cleared his throat and turned toward Sofia. "Generally speaking we don't have policies."

"I know. It's a major problem. I'd venture to say it's the reason people end up dead for misbehaving or tossed off roofs and considered useless for being afraid of heights. It's not right." Sofia shook her head. "Not at all." She continued scribbling notes all over Rick's draft of the policy, adding lines and commas, drawing arrows so the lines she added would get typed in the correct order.

"Oh, there she goes. Look at what she's doing!" Rick pointed at the policy in Sofia's hands. "She's ruining it. How am I supposed to train these soldiers with her around?"

"In a more *humane* way," Sofia answered without looking up.

"Humane? Humane? Is it humane to have your throat ripped out? Or to be attacked while you pump gas? Is it humane to end up becoming a vampire or werewolf just because some psycho felt like having a good laugh?" Rick's voice echoed in the conference room.

"Of course not. But that doesn't mean you terrorize employees," she snapped.

"Oh, okay. I'll just sprinkle fairy dust on them and wave a magic wand so they don't have to feel sad about Bas Dubh killing their families, raping their women, or eating their babies!" He slammed his fist onto the table and the wood cracked. "Why don't you go write policies for Bas Dubh? Maybe one of your policies can end the war."

Sofia stood up. "You are the most unprofessional, extremist, coercing...ruthless...mean man I know. We are not having a policy that allows you any opportunity to stretch the intent of the policy to meet your own sick and twisted desires!" she shouted, pointing her finger in his face.

Rick rose to his feet, towering over her. "We are not having a policy that limits my ability to develop a team of highly skilled wolves to combat one of the most evil vampires to ever exist," his voice boomed.

Sofia watched his jaw muscles pulse. His nose twitched, and deep within his eyes, something savage moved.

Fergus and Osgar jumped to their feet.

"So this is probably a good time for another break." Osgar nodded toward Fergus.

"Sofia, come with me. Let's go review the changes you'd like to see." Fergus attempted to lead Sofia from the room, but she didn't move.

Instead, stunned by what was happening to Rick, she stared. Fur began to flow over his face. His bone structure changed, growing into the wolf she'd seen earlier in the week. His teeth enlarged, jaws snapping. Ears pricked above his head. He stood to his full height, nearly eight feet tall, swung his head back and howled, an angry growling sort of call.

"Sofia, let us leave Rick and Osgar." Fergus pulled her from the room, but not before her gaze locked with Rick's. A cold shiver spiked down her back and her heart hammered in her chest. For the first time since she came to Cader, she realized the wolves might be deadlier than the vampires. She knew Rick would kill her given the chance.

# CHAPTER SIXTEEN

The howl of an enraged werewolf has the power to wake the dead.

But could it pull a man from a dream of ecstasy?

Dragomir rolled to his side, trying to hold on to the illusion of Sofia's soft lips pressed to his.

Was the warning of danger within the stronghold powerful enough to disrupt a vampire's fantasy?

He squeezed his pillow, clutching it against his chest, holding her safely in his embrace.

Again the wolf howled. This time a second wolf joined.

The scent of wild berries and flowers swirled. It mixed with the spicy scent of desire. Lust. Need. She wanted him. He must have her.

The howls changed. The tone lowered. Growling ensued. Banging began. Louder and louder. Harder and harder. The sound of someone hitting metal over and over.

The illusion of Sofia vanished.

"Dragomir! Wake up!"

Dragomir bolted from his bed and ran toward the door. "What it is?" He flung the door open and grabbed the throat of whoever disturbed him. He spun quickly, slamming the body to the floor, his hand still gripping the neck.

"You're needed upstairs," Noelle hissed. "Your charge is, yet again, irritating the wolves." She didn't fight him, instead she glared and curled back her lips to flash fangs at him.

Dragomir knelt on her right side with his right knee pressed into her abdomen, resting between her ribs just below her diaphragm. One sharp thrust and he'd crush her chest, then he would remove her heart with his bare hands.

"You know." His words were so harsh Noelle flinched. His vision faded to black and white.

The sound of her sharp intake of breath was her only response.

Dragomir felt her try to throw her mental defenses into place. An invisible cold wall erected between them. His eyebrow twitched and he watched her squirm, her fingers digging into his hand.

Noelle's attempt to block his intrusion was no match for Dragomir. He'd interrogated many over the years and his skill for finding weak points and unlocking hidden secrets buried deep within the psyche far surpassed her abilities to stop him.

He wandered in her mind, looking for the secret, the one little bit of knowledge she held that could destroy everyone. He moved past current worries, memories of lives long past, and minutiae.

Nothing. Not a hint of what she knew or how or why laid exposed anywhere. Not in the open or hidden away.

Dragomir probed, pushing ideas and thoughts aside as if rifling through boxes of old clothes. Finally, tucked away deep under layer after layer of mental shield, he found it locked up tight where few would have ever looked.

He moved around it, testing it, prodding her, working to loosen her hold on that one bit of information. But she held tight, sending wave after wave of defenses at him, shoving him back, ramming him as though she could remove him from her mind.

*He told me, you know.*

*I do.* Her voice sounded tired, pained. *I have known since her birth and have never told. I will not betray him.* She struggled to keep control of the blaze of information. It lit like a hot poker as Dragomir prodded.

She believed herself, a genuine statement. She would not mean to betray Jankin.

*But will you betray Sofia?* Dragomir attacked. His hands tightened around her neck. His knee came up high and hard. His presence in her mind grew to consume every single molecule of space, crowding her out of her own mind and forcing her to drop her guard.

Noelle screamed. She clawed at his chest and her legs thrashed about.

Dragomir did not yield. Instead, he bore down harder than before, focused on the one bit of information that could destroy so much.

The secret vanished.

Pulling back from Noelle's mind, Dragomir loosened his hold on her body. She lay silently, having forced herself into a death-sleep, shutting down her mind, making it impossible for Dragomir to remain within. Impossible for anyone to take the secret from her.

Dragomir released her. He stood, showered, and dressed.

Noelle was loyal. Always had been. He could trust her with Jankin's life. She'd protect him to the death. But Dragomir would trust no one with Sofia's. She was his concern.

Dragomir found Noelle's key in her hip pocket then carried her back to her chamber and placed her on the bed. Left on her own she would sleep for days. Dragomir would find Jankin. He sired Noelle. He'd be able to wake her.

As he drew closer to the exit from the Lower Level, the racket coming from the upper levels neared the riot stage. Between the howling wolves and yelling vampires there might have been a mutiny occurring.

Dragomir raced up the stairs from the Lower Level onto the ground floor and into the ER. Raised voices and chanting came from behind the doors. Metal clanged. He pushed open the doors and found the nurses and Dr. Schwartz gathered around the nurse's station arguing over takeout menus and who would go pick up dinner. Clipboards clattered as nurses argued over Chan's or Asian Dynasty while two technicians and Jamieson chanted for Italian and banged metal charts against a filing cabinet. The three men pounded out a beat and demanded Gino's Rustic Kitchen.

Dr. Schwartz glanced over, grinned, and pointed up, then loudly made the argument for Italian because they'd ordered Chinese last time.

Dragomir gritted his teeth. He marched out the door and bolted toward the stairwell. Not being able to track Sofia was becoming a nuisance. Every wasted stop he made meant she continued to dangle in peril's way. The woman was going to be the death of him.

He took the stairs three at a time, finally getting so frustrated he launched himself up the last flight to hit the landing with a hard thud. The voices coming through the open doorway indicated chaos had broken out.

Rick and Osgar were shifted, but the tone of their gravelly growls was different than usual. The pitch was higher. Dragomir registered shock instead of anger. The wolves were surprised by something.

*She has to be up here.* He pushed open the door and heard Fergus say, "Sofia, please come into the office." He was pleading, not demanding or suggesting.

"How the hell are you doing that?" Meg asked.

"And I don't see why you constantly resort to this response whenever you don't get your way!" Sofia shouted.

Dragomir entered the third floor hallway.

Osgar stood in front of Rick. Meg and Fergus stood behind Sofia, Meg tugging on Sofia's waist. Sofia faced the shifted wolves, using one hand to push Osgar aside and the other to jab at Rick's chest.

Rick snarled.

Dragomir took one step forward, prepared to block any attempt Rick made to harm Sofia, but he didn't move another inch. The woman seemed to have complete control over Rick.

Sofia's green eyes held all the angst she'd been carrying for days. They narrowed and her gaze centered on the stunned werewolf standing in front of her. Dragomir was glad Rick was on the receiving end of that look. That was an expression he never wanted aimed at him.

"Oh, don't give me that. I don't want to hear it. You're not even willing to see my side." This time Sofia lunged at Osgar. Meg's hold on her waist slipped and Sofia slammed into him. He stumbled back and fell through the doorway into the conference room. Sofia scrambled to her feet and closed the door between them.

She flipped back the waves of black tresses tumbling over her face and sent that florally scent wafting into the air. Dragomir silently inhaled.

*Not jasmine. Definitely not.*

"And furthermore..." Sofia turned to Rick, finger poised to jab into his chest. "...I have been nothing but reasonable with you. I've been shocked, but reasonable. It is not out of the realm of rational thought to ask you to develop and share a training plan." Rick stepped back until he was pressed against the wall. She followed, poking the entire way. "It is not an outrageous leap to believe tossing a man off a building and breaking his ankles every night is cruel. Especially, when you know he's terrified of heights." Her finger drilled into Rick.

He growled something.

"Unacceptable. No." She shook her head.

The conference room door opened and Osgar came out rubbing his head, no longer in wolf form. "Sofia! Dude! Come on. How do you know what he's saying?"

"Not now, Osgar." It was the only acknowledgement Sofia gave him. "Well? What's it going to be?" She jammed her hands on her hips. "Are you giving me the training plan or are we going with zero tolerance on the Workplace Violence Policy?"

Dragomir's eyebrows rose and he bit back a smirk. He had no doubt she'd try it, but no faith it would pass. Training wolves or vampires without some violence was an absolute impossibility.

Rick grumbled something.

"That's what I thought. I'll expect it on my desk tomorrow morning."

Meg's mouth dropped.

Fergus stuttered. "So...So..." He scratched his head and rubbed his beard, then gaped at his wife.

"Where the hell have you been?" Osgar snapped at Dragomir.

Sofia turned from Rick and her eyes widened just a touch when she faced Dragomir. Her mouth dropped open for a split second and then clamped shut into a tight line. She straightened her skirt, yanked her shirt hem down, fixed her jacket sleeves, and adjusted her collar. Her fingers fussed with a brightly colored scarf then she pulled her hair around her neck.

Desire bolted through Dragomir. He forced himself to remain where he stood, not to go to her, take her in his arms, and kiss her like no man had ever kissed her. His mouth watered and he clamped his jaw shut.

Sofia's left eye narrowed while her right eyebrow inched up. "We don't need you. I have Osgar." She glanced toward Osgar and her mouth dropped open again. She spun around, turning her back to him. "Maybe you could put on some clothes."

Dragomir nodded toward Osgar. "And I see he did an admirable job of keeping you safe by falling into the conference room."

The tone of his voice was deeper than Dragomir had intended, surprising not only himself, but catching Sofia's attention as well. She glanced in his direction, and he had to remind himself not to go to her. He was fairly certain she'd do worse than give him that glare if he groped her again. Not to mention what Jankin would do.

"She caught me off guard." Osgar rubbed his head again. "You'd have been knocked over, too, if she suddenly started reading vampire minds or something. She understands us when we're in our wolf form."

"It's shocking," Meg said. "Sofia, how long have been able to do this?" Meg's tone was less than encouraging. An angry alpha female was, generally speaking, more dangerous than a male. As Dragomir remembered they were more unpredictable.

He stepped closer to the group, shooting a sharp look at Meg.

She nodded. "How long?"

"I don't know. I didn't know I really could until just this conversation." She waved toward Rick and peeked over her shoulder. "It's because of him. If he didn't constantly become *that* whenever we meet, I wouldn't have to learn to understand him." She looked down at the floor and sidestepped toward her office.

Rick growled.

Dragomir positioned himself between Rick and Fergus, keeping one eye on Rick and trying not to watch every move Sofia made.

"It's not like I understand every wolf," she snapped, caught another glimpse of Osgar, and shuffled a few steps closer to her door.

*Shoeless. Interesting.* Dragomir took in the entire package. She was not quite as fashionable as she'd been every other day. Today her clothes didn't fit right, she had on a silly scarf knotted like one of those cowboy bandanas, and he was pretty sure the colors of everything didn't go together.

Her silky black hair fell past her shoulders, framing her face. The dark locks made her eyes appear brighter than usual. He had the desire to run his hands through her hair, down her shoulders, and over her entire body.

She bit her lip.

Was he making her nervous or was she finally realizing she'd tried to go hand-to-hand with a werewolf more than three times her size?

"But the only non-wolf who can understand a wolf in this form is the master vampire bound to him." Meg stared from Rick to Sofia to Dragomir and finally at Fergus. "Do you know why this is happening?"

"No. I've never seen this before. Not once have I ever encountered a human who could speak to wolves." Fergus pulled out his cell phone and scrolled for a number.

Sofia walked toward her office. "Great. Now I'm the werewolf whisperer."

Less than a full ring completed before Jankin answered Fergus's call. "Jankin, Sofia seems to be able to speak to the wolves."

Dragomir heard Jankin's response. "She *speaks* to them?"

"In English. But she understands them as though they were speaking English to her. Do you know the explanation for this?"

Jankin remained silent for several seconds. "I'll be up."

"Get dressed. Both of you," Fergus said. "And do not mention this to anyone." He walked back to his office. Meg followed, the pained look in her eyes said she knew this was a problem.

Dragomir followed Sofia to her office. He leaned in the doorway. "Have you ever seen a werewolf in wolf form before the incident with Rick in the conference room the other day?"

"No. And don't come in." She faced her computer screen, but every few seconds her eyes darted to the left, then back to the computer.

"So just two days ago you had your first encounter. At that meeting did you understand what Rick was saying to you?" Dragomir crossed the threshold.

She glanced in his direction and huffed. "I told you not to—"

"Answer the question."

"He wasn't talking to me. He was talking about me." She turned back to the computer. "And it wasn't very nice."

"You didn't mention it."

"No one asked."

Dragomir nodded and walked to the window. In the distance a very small glow faded into the horizon. Night had fallen. He watched Sofia's reflection in the window. She shuffled papers and straightened little piles on her desk. Every five or six seconds she glanced at him. When she bent over to reach for something below the desk her hair fell forward, covering her face. He hid a smile as he watched her watching him through the dark curtain.

"You are full of surprises, Ms. Engle."

"Look who's talking." She ducked beneath the desk to reach for something and her chair shot backward dumping her on the floor. "Damn it."

"Are you all right?"

"Fine. Just stay over there. And you're not supposed to be in here." She sounded as though she was in a cave.

A blue high-heel shoe appeared on the desk. Beside it she tossed a flat loafer, similar to ones he'd owned, only blue and much smaller. She crawled up into the chair and slipped the loafer on then unbuckled the strap of the sandal and placed it on her other foot. "You have a lot of explaining to do," she whispered in a harsh tone and glanced from Dragomir to the door and back.

"Yes. You must learn to disengage." Dragomir remained calm, unaffected. "Why are you wearing two different shoes?" She certainly had a way of keeping him perplexed.

"Never mind. It's not your business," she huffed and bent over to secure the strap to her ankle. Her nimble fingers worked the tiny clasp.

His gaze ran the length of her leg up to her knee. A well-defined calf muscle drew his attention. The way her leg looked in that heel made his mouth water. Even her reflection excited him. He maintained a slow pulse and tried only to breathe when he spoke. But he struggled. Being this close to her made him want to pin her against the wall, rip her clothes off, and grind himself into her until she screamed in ecstasy.

He couldn't even consider turning around at this point. She'd see her effect on him. *Why the hell is this happening?* He'd encountered plenty of other beautiful women in his existence. Most of whom did not argue about the meaning of his world. Why was this happening now?

Could Jankin have been correct?

Dragomir quickly ran through a series of ideas that should have quelled his desire: fish guts, target practice, werewolf breath. When none of it worked he called up the vivid images of headless men in battle. The gruesome pictures did the trick.

"Tonight we practice disengaging." He turned to face her.

"We are not practicing anything tonight or any other night." She stood up. "You are not to come onto my property or into my house or my office or near me ever again. You animal." Again her hands flew to her hips. Little fists resting on those lovely curves.

Dragomir smiled. He rather enjoyed her antics. Dramatic. Over-the-top. Silly. Her face reddened. She was just getting started. He sat on the windowsill and waited.

"If you think you're ever putting your hands on me again, you've—" She took one clumsy step forward and dropped down three inches.

"Got another think coming?" He finished her sentence.

She stepped onto her left foot and went back up. "What? Yes. That's right. Don't think I can't put an end to you. I'll just share this with Dr. MacDuff." She yanked her collar down.

Dragomir's eyes bulged. He moved across the room, reaching her before she had time to tell him to stay away or put her collar back in place. He surveyed her neck. He'd bruised her badly. A giant round of black and blue covered the entire left side of her throat. If he hadn't known better, he'd have thought someone punched her. No wonder she wore the ridiculous scarf.

He brushed his fingers across her neck, inspecting. No fang marks. He sighed in relief. At least he hadn't claimed her. How would he explain that to her or Jankin?

Somehow he'd managed to avoid the entire "I-defiled-your-Employee Relations Manager" conversation. It hadn't been easy but he'd managed, though he had been forced to admit his feelings for Sofia. He never thought he'd have been thankful to hear Jankin admit to breaking the law. It was the one thing that saved him from an all out battle over Sofia.

She closed her eyes and tilted her head back. With one hand he caressed her head while the other touched her neck. She whimpered the faintest sound he'd ever heard a woman make.

Dragomir licked his lips. The desire to kiss her mouth and then her neck surged. He wanted to kiss away her worries and the bruise he'd left on her. His heart throbbed when he looked at it. How could he have hurt her?

"Sofia," he whispered. "Open your eyes."

Her long dark lashes fluttered open and she looked down, not meeting his gaze.

His fingers caught her chin, drawing her closer. "I never meant to hurt you." His thumb rubbed over her chin. "Forgive me."

Sofia nodded and pulled away. She rushed past him in an off-kilter sort of bounce and exited her office.

"Sofia? Is everything all right?" Jankin asked.

Dragomir didn't bother to turn and watch her go. He'd heard Jankin enter the hallway seconds earlier, and he needed the moment to mask what he felt before facing what might come next.

"I just need a minute." Her voice cracked. A door opened down the hall and clicked shut.

"What have you done to her?"

# CHAPTER SEVENTEEN

After jiggling the little slide lock on the ladies' room door into place and managing not to burst into a fit of hysterics, Sofia leaned on the countertop, rocking and staring at her reflection. What was happening? And why? Was he trying to control her? Was this some sort of vampire game, some cruel and unusual ritual or something? What was he doing to her?

She splashed water on her face. Her makeup had all but worn off hours earlier. She was fairly certain she'd sweated it off. Between the turtleneck, scarf, and suit jacket she'd had to keep on all day, three debates on the Workplace Violence Policy, and the fight with Rick she'd stood no chance of looking presentable at the end of the day.

She untied the scarf and yanked the turtleneck away from her skin. That damn hickey was still there and it hadn't faded even a shade. She didn't have another turtleneck. What the hell was she going to do tomorrow?

Calling in was not an option. What would she say? "Can't come in. I have a hickey to beat all hickeys." She pressed her hands to her cheeks. She'd be tempted to flat out fire herself for that stupid excuse.

The more she stared at the bruise, the less offensive it seemed. It sort of grew on her. She'd never had a hickey like this before. She leaned closer to the mirror, swaying left to right to allow the light to hit it from different angles. Certainly little love marks had appeared on her neck from time to time, and she'd had arguments with her mother over how they got there. But nothing like this ever formed.

She brushed her fingers over it, pressing to make the skin turn white. *He* made this happen. The memory of his mouth on her skin, his tongue lapping at her, his lips sealing over her flesh made her breath hitch. She'd thrown her head back and pulled him to her, thrusting her neck to him, holding his head against her. All the while riding him. Outside. In the backyard. Like a teenager sneaking around.

And she wanted to do it again. She'd like a matching hickey on the other side and maybe a couple on her breasts and two or three on her thighs. She moaned.

Her hands flew to her mouth. In the mirror she watched the door. Was she making a lot of noise in here? What the hell was she doing? Why did she want him to touch her like this? More importantly, why did she want to rip his clothes off and ride him hard like she hadn't had sex in a century? Was he trying to turn her into a nympho?

*He is!* She gasped. "That's it."

That was why he didn't bite her. He was some sort of sexual vampire. Was it succubus or incubus or something? That had to be it. She wasn't a sex fiend. He was making her this way. Normally she would never want to fool around with the likes of him. She liked refined men, upstanding men, the kind you could take out in daylight.

She rinsed her face again, fixed her collar, knotted her scarf around her neck, and prepared to meet with Dr. MacDuff. He'd explain the werewolf whispering, and then she'd tell him she no longer wanted Dragomir. She cringed.

Not that she ever wanted Dragomir. Dr. MacDuff would understand she meant she no longer wanted him as a guard. He wouldn't assume she meant physically or sexually. At least she didn't think he would.

She hobbled back to her office and found Fergus with Dr. MacDuff and Dragomir.

"We're closing the door for this conversation, Sofia." Fergus held the knob and motioned for her to enter.

*Great. The cone of silence.* Every room on the third floor was soundproof as long as the doors and windows were shut. It was the reason she always kept the door open when she met with Rick. Someone had to be able to hear her scream.

"Sofia, I hear you understand werewolves." Dr. MacDuff sat in one of the chairs opposite her desk. Fergus leaned against a file cabinet at the far end of the room and Dragomir remained seated on the windowsill.

"It seems so. Any idea why?" Sofia walked to her desk, trying to keep her focus on Dr. MacDuff, which proved more challenging than walking in one high-heel and one flat.

Her attention kept falling on Dragomir and the way he followed her every move. She was suddenly conscious of her purple tights. How in God's name had she ever left the house like this?

"No. Can't say I do." Dr. MacDuff rested his ankle on his knee.

"Must just be a gift." Sofia sat in her chair leaning on her desk. "First vampires exist, then werewolves and…" She waved her hand in the air. "…there's a war brewing and now I'm a werewolf whisperer. What more could a girl ask for?"

*Sex with Dragomir?*

"Yes, well that sounds amusing but I'm not sure it's appropriate," Fergus said.

She bit her tongue. She hadn't answered her own question out loud, had she? "What? I…I…he…you…" She pointed at Dragomir.

"What is it Sofia?" Dr. MacDuff frowned. He glared up at Dragomir then leaned closer to Sofia.

"It sounds as though she is as confused by this werewolf whispering as the rest of us." Dragomir's jaw muscle ticked. He shot Sofia a look that caused her to drop her hand.

She nodded at Dr. MacDuff. "Yeah." She covered her neck with both hands and lowered her chin onto them. "The whispering."

Dr. MacDuff watched her. His steady gaze made her feel as though he might be able to read her mind. She looked to Fergus.

"You're sure you've never heard of this?" she asked.

"Positive. The only existing reference is from three thousand years ago when Folki drank from the vampire Brynhilder." Fergus paused as though he'd heard something at the door, shook his head and continued. "The blood gave him the power to speak with the wolves."

Sofia wondered if he could truly hear anything beyond the door. To her understanding the entire third floor had been remodeled in 1939 to ensure for soundproof meeting rooms.

This new job was like being inducted into a secret agency. When would she get her weapon? She tried not to giggle when the idea of her as a secret agent crossed her mind.

"Sofia, is there anything you'd like to tell us?" Fergus asked.

She looked at him. "Well, no. I don't think so. I mean outside of the obvious. I'm still a bit weirded out by the vampire-werewolf situation. I'm not entirely in agreement with having guards, and I don't ever want to attend another board meeting." That seemed to cover most of her worries.

The three men stared at her. No one moved. Not one reaction. Did they want more?

"Oh, and there's way too much violence here. I don't like it at all." She shuffled the files on her desk and held up the one containing multiple drafts of her policy. "But I think you know how I feel about that."

"Anything else?" Fergus asked.

She was not admitting to her sexual desires for Dragomir, who smelled so damn good. That forest-y aroma wafted, not at all overpowering the soap scent, and she didn't mind. She'd just ask what soap he used. Or maybe she wouldn't. Maybe she'd continue guessing until she got it right. *Lifeguard?*

Just the very front of his hair was clipped back this evening. The rest hung down to his shoulders. And those shoulders bulged under his t-shirt. The black cotton stretched over his muscles, leaving nothing to her imagination. His hands rested on the wood beside his legs, biceps screaming to be squeezed. His pecs flexed once or twice. Strapped to the waist of his blue jeans was a huge knife.

Sofia shifted in her chair. She'd forgotten about the question. All she could think about was running her hands across Dragomir's chest, then giving him a nice hickey to match hers.

"Sofia?" Dragomir's voice made her nipples form peaks.

"Yes?" Her reply was so breathy even she was caught by surprise.

"Sofia?" She jerked her gaze from Dragomir to face Dr. MacDuff. His sharp tone frightened her. "Is there anything else you want to tell us?" His stare bore into her.

She shook her head. "No. Nothing. Not at all. Nothing. Unn-unnn."

"Dragomir." Fergus glared at the vampire. His eyes were different, like an animal's, and his personal energy roiled around him. Sofia's mind registered a volcanic explosion with boiling hot magma shooting from its core. "Have you allowed her to feed from you?" Fergus's voice was nearly feral. Sofia wondered if everyone else understood him.

"No." Dragomir rose from the windowsill. His hands hung at his sides, fingers open and ready. He faced Fergus.

Sofia rose. "No. No he hasn't. Why would I do that? Why would..." She couldn't even finish the sentence. The idea of it made her stomach turn. She swallowed. "Why would I ever do that?"

"When a vampire mates, he feeds his love to bind her." Fergus glared at Dragomir.

"Mate?" Sofia asked. "Mate? What? We're not—"

"It's quite clear something has happened here," Fergus spit the words through clenched teeth. Sofia wasn't entirely sure, but she thought his face might have changed. He appeared thinner beneath his beard and his mouth seemed larger.

She wondered if her mind was playing tricks. Was she beginning to associate any angry man with a giant mutant wolf?

"Nothing has happened," Sofia lied sort of. They hadn't even done *it*, really.

All three men turned to her.

"You're a terrible liar, my dear." Dr. MacDuff watched her. His demeanor remained neutral, though Sofia felt something different about him.

"I'm not lying." She didn't make eye contact with anyone.

"You cling to each other." Fergus breathed loudly, the same way a bull does as it stalks a matador.

"Dr. MacDuff, we're not even touching each other. And you know how I feel about this whole guard situation. This is ridiculous, and I don't see how it has anything to do with anything." She leaned on the edge of her desk, hands gripping the wood to keep them from shaking.

The truth was she'd felt it. She couldn't explain it and she really didn't want to understand. But the moment Dragomir had appeared on the floor she felt him come to her, surrounding her, and she dove for him, holding on to his invisible presence like he was the very air she needed to survive. She felt herself reaching for him even now.

"Dragomir, tell me what has happened." Dr. MacDuff's voice never rose, nor did the tone change to be anything other than calm.

But Dragomir flinched. His fangs descended. Hands fisted. His body shook.

"Have you tasted Sofia? Have you claimed this woman?" Dr. MacDuff continued to watch Sofia, never once looking at Dragomir.

Dragomir dropped to his knees and fell forward onto all fours. "No." His breathing came labored. His back rose and fell as the sounds of his struggled breathing shocked Sofia.

"Stop it! Stop it!" Sofia rushed to Dragomir. She knelt beside him, wrapping her arm over his back. His muscles pulsed, contracting to rock hard bulges, then releasing and repeating. He groaned. Sofia looked up at Dr. MacDuff. "Leave him alone! You're hurting him."

"Has he fed her? That's the more important question," Fergus said. "Has he broken the supreme law?"

Dr. MacDuff stood. "Have you fed her?"

Dragomir's body shook, muscles vibrating. Sweat poured down his face and arms.

Fergus grabbed a handful of Dragomir's hair and jerked his head back. "Answer the question."

Dragomir's eyes focused on Dr. MacDuff and after an unbearable silence he answered, "Yes."

"What?" Sofia pried Fergus's fingers free from Dragomir's hair. "What are you talking about? No. No. You have not."

Dragomir slumped back on his butt. His head lolled back on his shoulders.

"He said that under duress. Again with the violence. He lies because you torture him," Sofia yelled at Dr. MacDuff. "You're worse than the wolves." She turned to Dragomir and brushed his hair from his face. "You didn't do that. I wouldn't have done it. We didn't break any laws." She held his cheeks between her hands. "We didn't."

"I did." He closed his eyes.

"The Supreme Law? You're not the man everyone thinks you are," Fergus spat the words. "You have no honor."

"No. No, it's not true." Sofia didn't understand. She didn't remember ever doing anything like that. She could hardly tolerate the thought of it now. Her stomach lurched. "It never happened."

"You don't remember." Dragomir opened his eyes. Something deep within his midnight blue gaze told her not to argue, not to fight.

She nodded.

Did she really drink vampire blood? She couldn't remember.

"Jankin, you know the law." Fergus appeared behind Dragomir and from under his suit jacket pulled a stake.

# CHAPTER EIGHTEEN

Fergus stood over Dragomir, gripping a pale wooden stake in one hand and holding Dragomir by the hair with the other. "Dragomir, you have admitted to breaking the most supreme vampire law. This is a crime punishable by death." The stake rose high above Dragomir and Sofia.

She did the only thing she could think of. She lunged onto Dragomir, draping her body across his chest and locking her hand over her wrist behind him. "No!"

Dr. MacDuff squatted beside them. "Sofia, you must remove yourself."

"I can't let you kill him." She blinked and tears trickled down her cheeks. She couldn't let him die. Her heart ached at the thought of his death.

There was far too much violence in this world. This couldn't be where she belonged. But while she was here she would do her best to stop as much as she could.

"You must. This is not an issue for you. This is a much higher rule than a simple policy." Dr. MacDuff's voice was not steady. It wavered and broke.

"There are always exceptions. Why can't this be an exception?" She straddled Dragomir, her thighs gripping his hips.

Dragomir's hands moved along her legs, sliding from the back of her ankles along her calves over her bent knees and up her thighs. Her skirt hiked up to her hips.

Something began tingling inside Sofia. She caught her breath. "An exception," she repeated. He was an exception. She knew it. An exception to several rules. She crushed her chest against Dragomir's.

His hands came to rest on her backside.

"Too much risk. She exhibits signs that reveal the truth." Fergus shifted. "She tracks and scents. She speaks to werewolves." Fergus raised the stake once again. "Remove her, Jankin."

"Please. You said you'd work with me. You said you wanted Cader to be a better place. Prove it." Sofia peered at Dr. MacDuff through the mess of hair hanging in front of her eyes.

Dr. MacDuff closed his eyes and shook his head. "It is as it must be." His voice was so low she barely heard him.

Something inside her knew she had to help Dragomir. She had to prove her willingness to belong, to understand their ways in order to win them over. But she didn't know how.

Dragomir wasn't a bad man. Sofia knew there was an explanation. Something wasn't right, but she wouldn't let him die. She'd save him now and get answers later.

"There's no other way? Nothing? Not one thing could save him?" She felt Dragomir's heart beat against her breast. The fast pounding told her he was frightened. She squeezed herself closer, rubbing her cheek against his.

"If she's so inclined to save him, she will have to mate him," Fergus said. "Are you willing to bless a union with him?" The disgust in Fergus's voice stabbed at Sofia's heart.

Dr. MacDuff blinked at her once. Something lit beneath his sparkling green irises. He brushed the hair from her face and nodded. "A union would save him. Save you both."

"Wait. What? Union?" She blinked rapidly, unsure of whether the tears on her cheeks were for Dragomir or herself. "Save us both. What's wrong with me?"

"They'll hunt you. When word spreads that you drank from him, you won't be safe anywhere. Even the other members of The Alliance will want you dead." Dr. MacDuff dropped his head and sighed. "Mating Dragomir is the only way out of this."

"You mean…is that like marrying him?"

Something in Dragomir's pants moved. Hardened. Sofia couldn't help but bear down on it. Dragomir groaned. She squeaked.

"Yes, Sofia, except the ties of mates are more than just words. It's an eternal, spiritual bond that links your energies. The existence of each mate is intertwined. They need each other to exist." Dr. MacDuff rested his hand on her head and held her hair away from her face.

Sofia wished like all hell he'd stop touching her. She honestly wished he and Fergus would get the hell out and let her have a few minutes alone with Dragomir. She bit her lip hard enough to draw blood.

"Forever? So Dragomir would be dead in about fifty to sixty years or whenever I die?" She tried to think clearly, to ask the right questions. "I'd be condemning him to death in this lifetime."

"Possibly, but unlikely," Dr. MacDuff answered.

Dragomir's fingers dug into her. His chest tightened. His arms locked around her.

Sofia swallowed. "What? Oh, can't you just explain it?" She couldn't stop the moan that escaped her lips and had to turn her face into Dragomir's neck, unable to stand the thought of Dr. MacDuff or any other person seeing her like this.

The smell of Dragomir's flesh filled her nostrils then her lungs and she could barely follow the rest of what Dr. MacDuff said.

"As your mate Dragomir would be free to feed you whenever you desired. It would extend your life."

"Like I said, we'd be dying in about fifty to sixty years," she mumbled into Dragomir's skin. And as she thought about that she couldn't help but feel selfish. She was pretty sure she'd be getting fifty to sixty years of damn good sex and then he'd have to die. But he had to believe that was better than dying here and now without sex.

"You will drink from him tonight, if you mate him," Fergus snarled. "We will know the truth. We will see the union sealed."

Sofia stiffened. Just the thought of someone's blood in her mouth was enough to cool her desire. Her mouth was suddenly dry.

"It would only be a small amount, Sofia. Just enough to form the binds," Dr. MacDuff said.

"It's drink or he dies," Fergus said.

"Oh all right. Let's just get this over with," she said.

Dr. MacDuff sighed. He stood and placed one hand on Sofia's head and one on Dragomir's. "Witness now the joining of two souls."

Dragomir moved with speed Sofia could not have anticipated. He ripped her turtleneck and scarf from her neck and lunged for her skin, biting into her flesh with such drive she thought he'd bitten through her. Instead, a wave of pleasure even more amazing than the one from last night hit her and she slammed her hips onto his, moaning. He held her tight against him and drank. He sucked and swallowed, sounding like a starving man feasting after weeks with no food.

Sofia's mind went completely blank. She couldn't focus on a damn thing. Not until he spoke to her. She heard his voice, felt him inside her, in her mind, in her heart, in her body. He was everywhere. His scent. His essence. His love.

"My mate, I swear to protect, cherish and honor you. I will provide for all your needs. I bind you to me as my mate, my wife, my friend, my lover from this day until the end of all days. Eternally bound, I will love no other."

His lips left her skin and he held her before him, her body slack from his feeding and her own pleasure. She blinked lazily, then licked her lips.

"Do you take me as your mate?" He asked the question out loud for all to hear.

She stared at him. His face was flush, hair a mess, skin slick with sweat. Deep within his dark eyes hunger burned. He wanted her, truly wanted her for his own. It was a desire she'd never seen in a man before, not even in a ravaging animal. He needed her as though *she* was the very air *he* breathed.

Her heart pounded. He would be hers for eternity.

Eternity was a long time.

He didn't blink, just held her and waited.

She hardly knew him. Could she possibly spend eternity with someone she didn't know? He was beautiful. And strong. And he had been kind. Though he was also pigheaded. And difficult. And ruthless.

A devilish grin tugged at his lips.

He loved her. She felt it. The way his energy swirled around her and within. He never pushed or tried to influence her. He waited eagerly, hoping she'd say what he wanted to hear.

"Yes," she whispered.

"I give myself to you, my mate. Everything I am, my very essence is yours." He pulled her to a seated position and removed the knife from his side. He ripped his shirt from his chest and drew the blade over his heart. A thin line of red appeared. "Take from me. Bind me as your mate."

His hand slid up Sofia's back to rest on her neck but he didn't force her.

She swallowed hard and closed her lips, pinning them together between her teeth.

The moment of truth. Could she truly bind herself to him? Could she drink blood? She tried to swallow again, but her mouth was so dry her tongue stuck to the roof. She coughed.

"It's all right, Sofia. Relax. He will not taste like blood to you. He will taste like your mate." Dr. MacDuff knelt beside her.

"It's dripping." She moved to wipe Dragomir's chest.

Dragomir caught her hand and shook his head. "Use your tongue."

In a bedroom alone with him those words might have been very erotic. But with an audience including her father's friend and a pissed-off werewolf the mood was slightly more distressing and much less arousing.

She couldn't catch her breath. She tried to inhale but came up short. Loud gasps and her thundering heart made her more uncomfortable.

"What does he smell like to you?" Dr. MacDuff asked.

"The forest." She huffed. "And soap."

Dragomir smiled and laced his fingers with hers. "Calm, my love."

"Clean. Fresh. Inviting. Wild. Familiar." Dr. MacDuff's voice was suddenly distant.

Dragomir surrounded her, held her close. "Drink, Sofia. I will taste as sweet as nectar for you." His voice, so gentle moved within her.

She rested one hand on Dragomir's hip and clung tight to his other then leaned forward and let her tongue catch the blood trailing down his chest. Her lips sealed over the slash and she tasted him.

He was sweet, yet manly.

She felt him writhe against her. He released her hand and both arms encircled her, holding her to him, squeezing her body to his. His cock throbbed against her so hard it hurt her abdomen. He moaned and then yelled her name.

She suckled the wound, transfixed on the idea that her lips and tongue were bringing him such pleasure. Her hands slid around him, her fingers digging into his back, her mouth working his chest. She held on, never wanting to let go, wishing his pleasure would last forever.

The wound sealed and she rested her forehead on his chest. Dragomir curled forward, cradling Sofia on his lap, his head resting against hers.

Their breathing rasped, uneven breaths announcing their completed bond.

Dr. MacDuff stood behind Dragomir and replaced his hands on their heads. "What bond has formed tonight no entity may destroy. Eternal happiness be yours."

Sofia heard the door open and footsteps exit the room but she was too comfortable in Dragomir's arms to care what was happening.

# CHAPTER NINETEEN

It was several minutes before either Dragomir or Sofia moved. And when finally he shifted, he scooped her against him, stood, and carried her to the desk where he gently placed her on the edge. He stood silently in front of her, his legs brushing the insides of her knees.

Sofia reluctantly let her arms drop from around him. Her skirt had crawled all the way up around her waist and her plum-colored stockings now sported holes in both knees with runs shooting up to her hips and down to her toes. She straightened her skirt, wiggling it down to her thighs and fussed with her shirt, the collar of which hung open to her waist, exposing lots of cleavage and a bright pink bra. She tucked the collar back up and tried to button her jacket, but the buttons were no longer attached. She wrapped the blazer one side over the other and folded her arms across her abdomen.

"Thank you for doing this." Dragomir's hand touched her thigh.

She nodded.

"Sofia, I—"

"Don't." She put her hand up to stop him from saying anything else.

She couldn't look up. She couldn't look him in the eyes. She'd done it again. Only this time with an audience. She stared at a file on her desk. *Personal and Professional Conduct.* The lump in her throat literally hurt to swallow. Was she truly fit to be the Employee Relations Manager? She'd just dry humped Dragomir in her office in front of the Chief Medical Officer and the CEO. Was it even possible to step any further over the line of professionalism?

She sighed and tears pooled in her eyes.

She hardly knew Dragomir. All she really knew was he was handsome. Beyond handsome. Gorgeous. Oh, and dead. Of that she was also absolutely certain. She'd done the deed with the dead guy again. Her mother would be so proud.

A tear ran down her nose and hung on the very tip, dangling like a single raindrop poised to fall into the torrents of a whirlpool, to forever be lost, void of its own being. She wiped the back of her hand over her nose and sucked in a shaky breath.

She'd done more than just fool around with him. She'd vampire-married him, an eternal commitment. She'd tied herself to a stranger for all eternity. And for what reason? Because he'd broken some vampire law?

"Is it true?" she whispered. "Did I drink vampire blood? Before tonight, did I do it before tonight?"

"Yes."

He needed to leave, to just exit the room, turn off the light and get out. Then she could slink to her car, which she'd probably drive off the nearest bridge.

*What have I done?*

"Why?" She tried to inhale, tried to pull some clean, non-Dragomir-smelling air into her lungs. It was a pointless endeavor.

He didn't answer.

She gasped and more tears ran down her cheeks. She tried to cover her sob with a cough. "You should probably go."

He didn't.

Instead, he stepped closer and tilted her head toward his.

Sofia wanted to push him away, slide off the desk and curl into a ball on the floor. Staring up into his dark eyes was not what she needed. Watching him study her face, feeling his thumbs tenderly wipe tears from her cheeks, letting his warm skin touch hers—none of it was what she needed. But it was everything she wanted. None of this made sense.

"I am sorry for all that's happened."

She blinked and tears poured down her cheeks. "I just married you." She pressed her face to his chest and sobbed. She'd always imagined marrying a man she loved, one she'd dated for a while, one who loved her, too. She never in a million years expected to marry a man eight hundred years older than her. A cold-blooded killer. A criminal vampire.

He stepped forward until his legs were flush with the desk. His arms wrapped tight around her and he held her to him. He stood there silently, just holding her.

And she cried.

And cried.

Between sobs she mumbled, "Married." She cried some more. "Vampire." What was left of his t-shirt was soaked to his skin. "Eternal." She wiped her nose on his sleeve. "Blood." She coughed and choked, and he finally reacted.

"Calm down."

The two words did not have the effect of calming her down. She shoved out of his arms. "Don't tell me what to do. You're not the boss of me. I'm the boss of me." She wiped snot on her sleeve. "I'm going home. And you're not welcome in my house."

She jumped off the desk and toppled to her right. Dragomir caught her. "Damn shoes. Let go of me. I don't need your help." She jerked her arm and teetered on her high heel.

He propped her back onto her feet and released her.

She grabbed her handbag and lunch bag. "I don't drink blood. How dare you?" She marched toward the door. "Get out of my office." She held the door open and glared into the hallway.

Dragomir gathered his knife from the floor and stepped past her, keeping one eye on her.

She flicked off the light and slammed the door behind her, then walked to the elevator. "I ride alone." She pushed the button and watched the doors close between them.

When she stepped from the elevator on the ground floor, Dragomir was already waiting at the entrance. Sofia walked past him refusing to make eye contact with him or anyone else. She noted Jamieson at the desk, flanked by Fergus, Osgar, and Meg. No one looked happy.

Fergus cleared his throat and Sofia couldn't help but look at him. His eyes narrowed and she thought his lips curled back. It was hard to tell with the mustache and beard. "She's expected back in the morn. And in the same condition." Fergus looked Sofia up and down. "Human." His attention fell to Dragomir. "Do what you will, but keep her as she is."

*He saw me with him.* She whimpered and rushed to the door trying to make it out of the building before the blubbering started again.

"Nice. Real nice," Osgar said. "The least you could do, Dragomir, is not make her cry." He stepped around the desk. "Sofia, wait."

"Leave me alone." The cool night air hit her cheeks making her skin sting below the tears. She didn't bother to wipe them away. More kept coming, so what was the point? Osgar's truck was no longer parked behind her Camry. She climbed into the car, jammed the gear into reverse, and hit the gas.

A horn blared behind her and she swerved to avoid an oncoming car.

The Camry spun out and landed in a ditch, where it stalled. She put her head on the steering wheel and cried some more while she fumbled in her handbag for her phone.

Before she could call for roadside assistance, Dragomir had pulled the car from the ditch and opened her door. "I will drive."

She'd have argued, but the truth was she didn't want to drive. She just wanted to go home. She climbed out and he walked her to the passenger side, opened the door, and waited for her to get in before closing it.

They rode the remainder of the twenty-minute ride in silence. At least Dragomir was silent. Sofia whimpered and hiccuped and sniffled and then sobbed again. "Forever," she blubbered. "That's a long time." He'd trapped her. He'd done something heinous to capture her. "Vampire tricks."

"It doesn't have to be, if that's what you'd prefer."

"It what?" She rummaged in the glove box for a napkin or paper towel, but came up empty. She leaned into the backseat and found a file full of drafted policies. She grabbed one titled *Personal Appearance* and blew her nose.

"If you would prefer we die sooner, it can be arranged." He didn't take his eyes off the road. "We do not have to live long lives together." It was a statement, not a threat or promise. "We can die." His unemotional comment simply hung in the space between them, sort of like an annoying dog who's supposed to sit in the backseat but keeps sticking his head between the front seats.

She looked out the window and gulped. Then she rolled it down so the wind blew a chilled blast into the cabin. He'd rather die than live with her. He'd rather die now than live forever *with her*. After all this he wanted his freedom.

"Until you decide how long we shall exist together you must train. You must learn to defend yourself." Dragomir parked the car in its spot across from the porch. "With Bas Dubh's open attacks and your refusal to stay at Cader, we can spare only one night. Tomorrow you will train."

The crying started again. "I never wanted you, either." Sofia yanked open the door, jerked off her high heel, and ran for the house. "Stay out. Just stay out." She slammed the door and the deadbolt clicked shut.

# CHAPTER TWENTY

Dragomir stared after Sofia, more confused now than he was when she threw herself between his heart and the stake.

The woman kept him dumbfounded. Even when he thought he understood her motives, she fooled him.

He'd been fairly certain she'd interrupted his execution out of her nonviolent workplace philosophy. She so firmly believed Cader should become a gentler place to work. It only made sense to believe an execution would not align with her goals.

He'd have gone to his death willingly to keep The Alliance strong. No one could ever know about Jankin's deed. That information must be kept hidden. Dragomir's false confession guaranteed Jankin's safety. Even if Noelle ever admitted to knowing the truth, no one would believe her. They would question why Dragomir would have admitted to something so egregious if he hadn't committed the crime.

Dragomir glanced at the passenger seat. Sofia had forgotten her bags, left them in disarray among a dozen tissues and crumpled papers on the floor. Lipstick, a wallet, and some sort of hair clip had fallen out. He tucked them back in and set the bag on the seat.

His new wife didn't understand the danger surrounding her. Each time Sofia let loose a new ability she announced that something unnatural had occurred. Either someone had done something or she wasn't entirely human. She had no idea how to control herself or how much danger she posed to herself or Jankin and in turn, The Alliance.

Dragomir watched the house. Not a light lit anywhere. Sofia moved about in the dark, sobbing. "What have I done?" he heard her ask the question over and over, never once stopping for an answer.

He leaned his head on the headrest.

Squeaky pipes rattled inside the house and water began running, then splashing. She showered. To wash his scent away, he was sure.

He closed his eyes and slouched down in the seat. He'd never planned to marry again. Not after losing his Elena. First their babies, then his wife. He'd never felt such pain. The losses of the children devastated them both, but then to have her taken, too, drove him to near madness.

The shower stopped. The rings holding the shower curtain slid along the metal pole and then slid back.

The taste of Sofia laced his tongue. His mouth held the sweet flavor of her blood. He hadn't tasted another like her, not ever. Sweet, yet smoky as though fire stoked in the depths of her soul.

Sofia had reacted so passionately to him during the mating ritual he believed she'd agreed to marry him because she cared for him. The way her body moved with his, the way her energy flowed to him, the way she looked at him—he believed she wanted him, maybe loved him.

He'd allowed himself to forget what he was and to succumb to her wiles.

He hadn't seen that look in a woman's eyes since...since his first wedding night.

Women looked at him. They always looked. But they never saw. Their libidos responded to someone who could bring them pleasure they'd never experienced. And for them that was enough. Never mind the rest. Ignore the monster who lay in wait. The vampire who'd feed on their flesh, on their blood.

Sofia saw. She knew. She'd known from the moment she laid eyes on him, and he repulsed her.

She hadn't wanted him. Strong beliefs in a nonviolent workplace led her to throw herself on the pyre for him. She foolishly believed she could force his kind and the werewolves to play nice. Now look what her ideas got her.

His world was not nice. It was violent. In his world people died. They were killed. Many had been killed by him.

Jankin was right. Sofia wouldn't understand. And now she hated him. If she knew the truth, she'd hate them both.

Had he done the right thing? Was there any other way?

He stared into the trees. Nothing moved. Not a single night animal crawled among the leaves.

The bed creaked. Sofia was finally lying down to rest. She needed to sleep. It would strengthen their bond, and it would give her mind time to process the evening's events.

The union existed. They'd spoken the words, shared their blood, even performed some sort of consummation of the act. For now this was all there would be. He wouldn't, couldn't even consider forcing her to seal the bond though he wanted her in his bed.

If she ever offered, he'd weigh the option. He knew if they committed the last act she'd never be able to leave him. She would suffer by refusing to consummate the union with him, but she'd have some amount of freedom. Over time she could grow accustomed to the urge simmering inside her. She'd live with the feeling that something was missing, a constant reminder of the promise she'd made tonight. He wasn't sure he could allow her to make the final commitment and condemn herself to him.

When the time was right, he'd offer her the option to leave him. After he had ensured her ability to defend herself like any warrior's mate, he would discuss it with her. If she wanted to go, he wouldn't stop her. He wouldn't let her go unprotected, and he was certain that would keep her enraged for the rest of her natural life, but at least she wouldn't have to see him. In the meantime he'd prepare her for what was to come.

They simply had to keep up a good front for safety sake. Tomorrow he'd explain. One thing was certain, he'd never coerce her into anything she didn't fully comprehend. From now on he'd ensure she went into everything with a full understanding of the impact of her decisions.

Dragomir's job was to guard her, to keep her safe, no matter what the cost. He'd taken a blood oath to Jankin to protect her. Then he married her. Twice in less than a week he'd sworn his life for hers. He'd protect her even if it meant battling with her over foolish human ideals.

In his entire vampire existence he'd managed to avoid this sort of tragedy. But in five night's time he'd lost all common sense. He married a woman he hardly knew. He'd allowed her to wreak havoc in his life. Now his own fate was tied to hers. His existence depended on her. *Fool.* He'd do it again without a moment's hesitation.

How had he come to this point? How was this little woman able to do this to him? If he'd never met her, she'd be much happier, maybe even living her silly little nonviolent fantasy. She'd have never been burdened with him. He'd be happier and have fewer worries. The sudden thought of losing her caught him off guard.

What if something happened to her when he wasn't around? What if she fell down a flight of stairs wearing the wrong shoes or got into an accident?

The car door groaned when he opened it. He checked the hinges. They needed oil. He popped the hood, checked the fluids. She needed windshield wiper fluid. He closed the hood and did a sweep of the perimeter.

As long as everyone thought they were married, Sofia would be safe within his world. No one needed to know he wasn't allowed in her house or that the pleasures of her flesh were only his when fully clothed and she'd somehow forgotten she hated him.

Keeping her safe from herself was another issue altogether.

He rounded the property. Nothing new on site. No tracks, scents, evidence of an intruder. The only thing of note was the heavy floral scent. Dragomir stood below her window, eyes closed, head tilted to the sky. Being bound to each other made it a thousand times easier to scent her.

*Magnolia?* He shook his head and went back to checking the property.

Finally he settled into a tree opposite her bedroom window, the one perpendicular to her bed, the one with the view of his sleeping wife. As long as everyone believed they'd consummated their union, consummated in the true definition, no one would bother Sofia. The Alliance would recognize her as his and give her a wide berth.

Of course, she'd still need to control her ability to understand the wolves. Even though certain true mates of the most powerful vampires possessed this skill, it never settled well with the wolves.

Who knew what other talents she possessed? He'd do his best to figure that out before she accidentally let them slip.

For tonight he'd leave her to her tears. But tomorrow her training would continue. Whether she liked it or not she was his mate. Mating him may have saved her from a modern day witch hunt for possessing vampire powers without turning, but it didn't mean she was safe from battle. And no mate of his would be caught unprepared and unable to defend herself should Bas Dubh come knocking. That included a mate who touted a nonviolent workplace resolution policy.

# CHAPTER TWENTY-ONE

Someone growled.

Sofia rolled over. The bedroom was dark.

"Keep her safe."

"Why don't you stay and guard her today? Oh, that's right, you have to go hide from the sun."

"Do not test me, wolf." Dragomir's gravelly voice nearly matched the wolf's growl.

Even a flight above with a wall between them Sofia could hear Dragomir and Osgar argue. Had she developed supersonic hearing or were they yelling? She sat up and focused on their voices.

"Not quite the man everyone thought. Couldn't keep your hands off her."

She crawled toward the foot of the bed. The sun barely crested the horizon and in the far off distance a yellow glow lit between the darkness of the tree trunks.

"Do not forget. I am your master."

"Well, Your Highness, your fall from grace has left us both feeling the pain."

"Someday I will explain."

"When? How long do I have to carry your burden?" Osgar snarled. Even in his wolf form his indignant tone was clear. His voice was harsh and cutting and he continued a low growl even when he wasn't speaking.

"That I cannot answer."

"Fucking vampires." Footsteps on the porch below interrupted the conversation. Osgar's human voice continued, "The least you could have done was win her over first. Are you so removed from humanity you can't remember how to court a woman? Why? Why'd you do it?"

A long pause hung between them, and Sofia leaned off the bed toward the window, equally as eager to know the answer.

"You can't even tell me that? You can't even admit why you'd do something... You've executed vampires for this. How could you possibly do this to her?"

Heavy boots clomped on the porch. "Another time, Osgar. For now keep my mate safe. In my stead I charge you with her life."

Osgar sighed.

"You understand your duty?"

"Yeah. I get it. Keep her alive so your life stays happy. Got it, Master." Osgar's human voice held all the venom of a man on the edge of rage.

"My life is not my concern. And neither is yours." Dragomir stepped off the porch. "The Alliance must always remain strong. Always be our first priority."

"Right. The Alliance." The porch swing creaked. "No worries about a wife. Just concern for duty, no more honor, of course. Let's just do our duty."

"Safe day."

"Yeah, sure. I'll get her back to Cader as usual which is where you should be since you aren't hiding in her basement. The fucking sun's up."

Sofia leaned to her left and spied Dragomir at the edge of the woods. The sun still sat low, not even lighting the tree line. She couldn't make out his features, but she felt his gaze land on hers. She shot backward, flopping down on a pillow.

"Stay safe." Dragomir's voice brushed along her skin like a feather. She shivered and pulled the blanket up to her chin.

"Whatever. Just get back to the fucking stronghold," Osgar griped. "Be a shame for her to live the rest of her life in mourning because you forgot to take cover."

Sofia curled into a ball, squeezing her eyes shut against the world. For an hour she lay in that same position, willing herself back to sleep. But nothing worked. Her mind replayed the conversation she heard over and over, analyzing each word.

Did he not care for her at all? Was he simply married to her to keep The Alliance safe? And how had marrying her done that? She did not recall drinking from him before last night. She'd have remembered something so heinous, wouldn't she?

Had she really married a man with no honor? Dr. MacDuff thought so highly of Dragomir. Had he been wrong? They'd known each other for centuries.

It must be true. You never really knew a person. Or a vampire.

She blinked into the darkness. Her mind raced. Married. She'd married Dragomir. Eternally. The ceremony took place on the floor of her office. She drank from him. It hadn't been disgusting. When she tasted him, she'd enjoyed him. She'd enjoyed everything about it. The flavor, the feel of him coursing within her, his clear and overwhelming pleasure at her mouth on his skin. She'd wanted it to go on, to never end.

What had she done?

As the sun rose above the treetops sleep finally took her. She didn't drift into it. She plummeted. Her eyelids grew too heavy to hold open. Her mind spun. She fell into slumber the same way a rock tossed from a dock drops to the bottom of a pond.

Sofia didn't dream. She simply slept. At last her mind was silent.

# CHAPTER TWENTY-TWO

At noon Dragomir rose. He'd rested in spite of needing to prepare. He hadn't been tired and did not want to sleep, but the choice was not his. Sofia needed to rest. So he needed to be still for her. He'd keep his energy quiet to try to allow her more sleep. But he knew it would be a challenge. He felt her blood coursing through his veins, teasing him until his desire for her was nearly impossible to control. He wanted her in his arms.

Dragomir stood naked in his sparse quarters. His bedroom held simply a bed and a side table with one lamp. Not even a bureau. The bed held one pillow. He'd need two, if she was ever going to sleep here.

The stark white walls were a definite contrast to Sofia's home. She didn't have a white wall in the place, not one he could see from any window. Color, color, color. Warm sunset shades and greens, yellow in the kitchen, blue in a bathroom, even a red wall in one of the rooms.

He stretched his hands over his head then out to his sides and down to his toes. When he stood tall, he let his head roll back and over to the side onto his shoulder, around to his chest and up to the opposite shoulder. He inhaled, held the breath deep in his lungs. His scent was different.

Florally.

He raised his hands to his face. He smelled of her. *Sofia*. How quickly it happened. She would smell of him now, too. The scent was their mark. The two individual scents joined as one. Vampires and wolves would smell them both and know they were bound. Even humans would sense it.

He groaned. *God I hope I don't smell like petunias.* He sat on the floor to finish his stretching routine. When he was done every muscle group was thoroughly awakened, limber, and ready for action.

A quick shower in his equally barren bathroom. One large shower stall. One sink. One mirror and a john. He did own towels, several. They'd been a gift from Meg. A joke. Something fluffy to add a homey feel to his quarters. She made him promise to keep them and he had.

After pulling on his jeans he moved through the rest of his chamber making mental notes of the tools he needed, his plan for training Sofia, and the alterations needed in his living quarters.

He stood in the common room and surveyed its contents: a sofa, a lamp, one chair, and a bookshelf. On his desk sat a computer, one pen and one notepad. Not one thing hung on his walls. And no rug on the floor.

He wasn't here that often. He traveled a great deal. He didn't require much to exist. She'd get used to it. She'd be traveling more, too. She had a passport. Didn't she want to use it?

The coffee pot beeped. Dragomir poured a cup and added a good measure of cream, one cube of sugar. Then he sat at the small table in his kitchen. He'd need more kitchen stuff. Pots. Pans. More than beverages. He'd have to eat food while she was here.

He'd stopped eating hundreds of years ago. Most vampires only ate to fit in. He didn't even bother with that anymore. Now he'd have no choice. It was very clear he needed to do whatever he could to help her acclimate. Eating food was probably going to be expected.

He rubbed his eyes. How had this happened?

He finished his coffee, scrubbed the pot, coffee grounds basket and mug and replaced everything. Then he swigged a couple mouthfuls of cherry juice from the bottle in the fridge before he finished dressing.

Sofia must train. She must learn to defend herself. Their lives depended on her ability to hold her own. Dragomir unlocked his weapons chamber. He chuckled. Pantry—weapons chamber. Pretty much the same thing in his mind.

After gathering several stakes and knives of different lengths he headed down the hall to see the blacksmith.

"Congratulations, man." Dice laughed. "Who'd have thought you'd take the leap?" The blacksmith greeted Dragomir with genuine happiness. "Welcome to the club."

Dragomir nodded. Apparently, Dice hadn't heard about how he joined the club or the welcome would have been much cooler.

Dragomir nodded. "My blades need honing. As well as these stakes." He laid the weapons on the table.

"Ah, training her already. No time to keep her soft, enjoy her a bit?" Dice grinned.

"No. She's too weak. She must learn to defend herself." Dragomir forced the memory of her writhing in his arms last night from his mind. There was no time for any of that. She'd never acquiesce, never offer, never even consider making love to him. He'd have to enjoy helping her become indestructible. That's the only way he was going to find his pleasure.

"Ah, sometimes they are more fun to wrestle anyway." Dice laughed. "Are you training her on the stake already?" He held one in each hand, gripping them like a warrior, ready to plunge them deep. "It might be a little too early in your bond to teach this technique." A look of concern flashed on the blacksmith's face. "They do tend to question our righteousness while we train them. You are training her hard enough to handle combat, should she be ambushed. Yes?"

Dragomir hadn't thought about the fact that she'd question his motives for existing more than she already had. She didn't trust him at all. How could she possibly trust him less? Maybe teaching her the specifics for dispatching a vampire should be delayed. Maybe they'd stick with self-defense. "Eventually, I will train her on the stake, but first the basics." He inspected one of his swords again before handing it to Dice. "Sharpen it. I haven't used it in many years."

The blacksmith nodded. "Has she mastered hand-to-hand combat?"

"No. We have only begun to train." Dragomir added two more knives and six stakes from under his coat to the pile. "Sharpen them all." Hand-to-hand combat? He stifled a laugh. She could barely remain standing in an argument never mind if anyone touched her.

She was defenseless and foolish. She challenged werewolves, literally argued with them when she'd already angered them to the point of shifting in front of her. How many women did that? Couldn't have been many. She was going to get herself killed. He needed to call upstairs, make sure she hadn't pissed anyone off yet today.

"You worry." Dice turned a dial and the sharpening stone began to spin.

"She's human." And she had no ability to think rationally. He closed his eyes. How could he train rational thought? Impossible.

Dice nodded. "So was Jade." He ran his hand along the sword then held it out in front of him, staring down the blade. "That was sixty something years ago now." He placed the sword on the anvil and grabbed his hammer.

Dragomir remembered. Dice and Jade had been in love. She chose to be turned on their honeymoon. Then Dice trained her—when she was much less fragile.

"She'll turn." Dice banged the hammer against the sword several times then flipped it over and worked the other side.

Dragomir knew better. Sofia wouldn't turn. She could barely stand the thought of being in the same building as vampires. She was not about to become one.

The sound of the metal being held against the sharpening stone drowned away Dragomir's thoughts. He watched sparks shoot from between the sword and the stone.

"Did she sleep well today?" Dice grinned. "Does she still sleep, my friend?" His voice dipped and he gave a hearty laugh.

Dragomir could not say. He still could not sense Sofia. His best guess was that she'd slept well enough for the few hours he'd rested. He knew she needed complete sleep. It was the reason he slept—to give her mind time to relax, to stop racing, to stop thinking about what she'd done.

"I'd say she rested just fine."

"Ah, your bond strengthens. I kept Jade in bed the first full week of our joining. By the time we came home our bond was so tight I couldn't bear to have her out of my arms for more than an hour." He laughed again. "And she wasn't for several months."

With each rest period they shared together the bond between them would strengthen. If they lay together, touching, caring for each other, it would seal to a strength nothing in the world, not time or man or death could destroy. He sighed. It was going to take a lifetime for it to become a true bond, forged by something more than words and a blood exchange, if that ever happened.

She'd married him, but that didn't mean she liked him. She'd even dropped her guard twice and drove his desire to fever pitch, but that didn't mean she wanted him. Would she ever learn to love him? Could she?

"I'll be back in a few hours to get these." Dragomir left Dice to work.

"Two hours, tops," Dice called after him. "Go. Enjoy your mate while I work."

Dragomir prowled the halls for a bit before going to see Jankin. Enjoy his mate? The idea of it was superb. The reality was hell.

The halls were quiet. The sun was still too high in the sky for most vampires to wake. But Dragomir had long ago established his ability to stay awake in these hours. He'd spent many a long day thinking. And it appeared he'd spend many more worrying.

He hadn't seen Jankin since the ritual, and he didn't really want to see him now, but he knew they needed to talk.

He knocked on the office door.

"Come."

The room was dark, lit only by the computer screen. Dragomir closed the door behind him and walked through the outer room to Jankin's office.

"How was she?" Jankin looked older. His more than nine hundred years seemed to be taking a toll. Tired eyes. Sagging cheeks.

"She cried. A great deal." Why should Dragomir pretend she wasn't unhappy? He wouldn't. If he had to watch his mate's misery, Jankin would, too.

It was Jankin's fault they were in this predicament.

Jankin nodded. "No surprise."

Dragomir couldn't disagree. When he thought about it logically, it was no surprise. But it still hurt.

"What's the report from the front?" Dragomir asked. He watched Jankin. The way the vampire moved was slow, deliberate. The burden he carried seemed greater today than in all these long years since Sofia's birth.

"There is movement. Orion and Pax found evidence of a fortress just over the town line at one of the local farms. In Exeter. Vampires and wolves."

"Still active? Or is it abandoned?" Dragomir's hands ached. A battle was coming. He felt it, wanted to be a part of it.

"Active. Wolves come and go from the area in large numbers. They've scented only four or five vamps."

"Sounds like a possible daytime attack. When will our wolves be ready?" Dragomir had seen this in Norway. A small contingent attacked when they thought the vampires slept. Bas Dubh wasn't prepared for the wolves The Alliance had trained or for the master vampires to awaken their progeny. Vampires fought below the ground all day long. It had been a good battle.

"Not soon enough. We have the weaker wolves, left behind by Bas Dubh. The ones he thought would die." Jankin's gaze never left the computer screen. "Laurent believes Joachim had known about the assault for months."

"Has he unlocked any details—the timing?"

Jankin shook his head. "Still working the new wolves. Laurent will get it."

Dragomir stood. "How has her day been? Any arguments with Rick or have the wolves taken her under their wings?" He dreaded having to undo whatever Fergus and Rick did. They weren't the type to happily accept this new development.

Sofia's ability to understand the wolves would likely be a sore issue for quite some time. He had no doubts they'd already begun to make her believe he was some villain for making her drink vampire blood without a bond. Osgar was less of a worry, but he knew even Osgar could not understand the situation.

"She hasn't arrived to work yet. Osgar's been at her house all day."

"Blasted woman!" Hearing that she'd not arrived at the stronghold unleashed the pent-up rage Dragomir had managed to control. "She's not safe outside this building. Doesn't she understand why she must come here?" He slammed his hands on the desk. "You should have told her years ago." His face was only inches from Jankin's. "How did you expect to get away with this?"

"When it happened, I did not think about the consequences. I only knew I could not let her die." Jankin glanced up slowly, fangs already descended, eyes glowing.

"You brought me here for this sole purpose, didn't you? Guarding her was a cover. A lie. You wanted me to take the fall for you." Unable to keep the disgust out of his words, Dragomir faced Jankin.

"She needed a strong guard, someone she could trust." Jankin's eyebrow darted up. "Someone I could trust."

Dragomir dropped his head and glared at the desk. Jankin was a genius. Dragomir would never tell, would have died with the secret last night. All to protect The Alliance. To protect humanity.

His head snapped up. "You will tell her the truth. Then she will decide." Dragomir would not force her to live a lie. She would learn what really happened. Then if she chose not to honor their bond, he would understand. He wouldn't let her go, not alone, not without someone to protect her, but he wouldn't force her to stay.

"What good would it do? You've seen how she reacts. She'll run. Do you want her out there without you, without me?" Jankin stared up at Dragomir. His eyes were no longer glowing, nor were they green. They'd faded to a near black color.

"Guilt? Is that what I see?" Dragomir's mouth ticked to the left. "Who'd have known guilt would overcome you?"

"I know what I've done. I know the burden you both carry. There's no way to undo the past. You must help her live with this." Jankin turned back to the computer.

"You will tell her. When the time is right, you will confess." Dragomir would hold Jankin to this, if it was the last thing he did.

"If that is the price you believe I should pay, so be it, old friend. But I ask you, how can a man be angry with the vampire who gave him his mate?"

"She's only my mate by force. She didn't choose." Dragomir turned from Jankin, unwilling to watch as the man he'd trusted more than any other tried to twist this truth.

"No one mates by choice. They only think they do. True mates are born to each other. There's only one for each. No other will do. Can you sense her?"

Dragomir shook his head. "What are you saying?"

"She is your mate because creation says she is, not because of me or circumstance." Jankin removed his cuff links and rolled up his sleeves. "She was born to be with you. Had I not saved her, you'd have lived your existence alone." Jankin sat back. His stare bore into Dragomir. "You can't sense her because you are not bound to each other. It's a cruel joke of love. And it will drive you mad if you don't mate her."

"How could you have known we were fated? *Did* you know?"

Jankin shook his head. "I cannot lie. I did not know. I only knew I could not lose her. And as the world has changed, I knew she needed the best to keep her safe, but I did not know she was your mate."

"She can hardly stand me. She refuses me access to her house, doesn't even speak to me unless she has to. She is not happy." Dragomir couldn't stand hearing the words come out of his own mouth. His mate hated him.

"Not every mating is easy. Not every mate is consciously willing. Some are stubborn, refuse to see what their soul knows is right. Mating is like marriage. It takes work."

# CHAPTER TWENTY-THREE

Bright sunlight streamed through Sofia's bedroom window. She grumbled and pulled her blanket up over her head.

Tick.

Tick.

Tick.

She buried her head under a pillow but the ticking continued. She sat up and frowned. "What?" she yelled.

"You're late for work," a muffled voice answered.

"Where are you?"

"Outside," Osgar yelled.

She went to the window in time to see Osgar toss another pebble at the glass. "Knock it off."

"Do you know what time it is?" He dusted his hands on his jeans.

"I don't care. I'm not coming in today." She opened the window. "I'm calling in sick." She'd earned a sick day after last night.

"Too much sex on your wedding night?"

"Fuck you, Osgar." She slammed the window shut and pulled the blinds. Before she turned back to the bed she opened the blinds and window. "I apologize. That was rude of me."

"I'll say. But you do sound like your husband." He looked up at her disappointed. "One night and you're already slipping."

Sofia ignored his comments in spite of the mix of emotions bubbling within. She had a husband. He was a vampire. Facts were facts. No sense in letting emotion muddle the mess.

She stared at Osgar. His face was scruffier than usual. "Don't you own a razor?"

"I do but when I'm working around the clock, it's hard to find a minute to shave. Besides, you're no longer available so impressing you has moved off my top ten list." He reached into his truck and pulled out a big black lunch box, the kind construction workers used in the 1950s.

"Why are you eating out there?" she asked, though truth be told she didn't want him in the house. She wanted to be left alone. She wanted time to sulk and be miserable. Then she would devise a plan of escape.

"My keys have been confiscated, and I've been ordered to remain outside the building." He bit into a giant sandwich and dripped mustard on his chin, which he did have the manners to use a napkin to clean.

"Did *he* do that?" *He* had no right to make decisions about her, her house, her friends, her life. "You can come in."

"He who? Fergus—yes. Jankin—yes to that one, too. Dragomir—no. He didn't seem so interested in whether or not I entered the house." He crunched a chip.

Dragomir wasn't interested in Osgar entering her house? Why not? Was he such a poor choice for a husband that he didn't know she shouldn't have other men in her bed? Was he so disinterested in her that he didn't *care* if other men came to her bed?

She scratched her head. "What time is it?"

"Noon." He cracked open a can of soda. "It's a good thing you're a friend of Jankin's. I hear that new employee relations lady is a real stickler about people showing up to work on time." He slurped his soda.

She frowned and shut the window. Four hours late for work. That damn vampire. She'd never been late for work, not once in her entire life. But this week alone she'd been late nearly every day. And today, she wasn't even going in. Her first sick call, too.

A week of firsts. Tardy, absent, marriage, learning to speak werewolf, being bitten by a vampire. Oh, and let's not forget our all-time favorite—sexual activity at the office with a vampire in front of an audience. A more impressive list of firsts could not exist.

She groaned and found her phone.

She called Fergus, got his voicemail and left a curt message about not feeling well and not coming in. Then she stared at herself in the mirror.

She looked like her usual self. She didn't even have the red, puffy eyes she expected to see from her evening of crying over her own stupidity. And the hideous bruise on her neck was gone. There wasn't even a mark from where…

She swallowed and watched her throat move, studying every inch of her skin. Maybe he hadn't bitten her. Maybe she'd imagined the incident. Could it have been a dream?

Sofia shook her head. No, not a dream. She drank vampire blood last night. Apparently, it hadn't been her first time either. But last night she licked it off his skin and then sucked it from the slice in his hard chest muscle. She squeezed her eyes shut against the memory only to have it play out behind closed eyelids.

She smacked her lips. She still tasted him. Hadn't she brushed her teeth last night? Why could she still taste him? Sweet and meaty. How was that possible? Weren't they opposite flavors or something? She grabbed her toothbrush and loaded a glob of minty freshness on the end then scrubbed with gusto.

Wait a minute. If she drank his blood, did that mean she was becoming a vampire? Her eyes widened. She curled her lips back to see if fangs had formed in her top jaw. Foamy toothpaste dribbled down her chin. Her perfectly straight teeth looked the same as always. She spit and rinsed, then ran to the window.

"Am I turning into a vampire?" She didn't see Osgar. "Osgar! Where are you?" She leaned out and looked toward the back of the house. "Am I becoming a vampire?"

"I'm right here."

She looked down as Osgar stepped off the porch below her.

"Am I? I drank his blood. Am I turning into one of them?"

He grinned. "Didn't he explain anything to you?" He held a bag of chips in his hand.

"We didn't really have a lot of time to discuss the particulars last night. Just tell me. Did I agree to become like him?" Sofia's heart nearly stopped as she held her breath waiting for the answer.

"No. It's not that easy. I don't know the exact steps but he'd have to drink most of you and then you drink most of him back and then, poof, you're a vampire. Well, by the next day, anyway." He munched a couple chips. "It's a lot more complicated than becoming a wolf, which you're no longer able to do."

Complicated was good. That meant it hadn't happened. She hadn't accidentally missed something and condemned herself to blood cocktails for eternity.

"Not that I want to be a wolf or a vampire, for that matter, but why can't I become a wolf?" She knelt down and crossed her arms against the cool October air.

"Once a human is bound to a vampire they can't be made werewolf. It's got something to do with the vampire blood. Besides, there isn't a wolf crazy enough to try to turn a master's mate. That's a slow and painful death wish."

"Okay. Thanks for the info." She closed the window.

Her stomach growled. *No more blood.* Funny, she didn't even have the slightest craving for blood, not that she'd had it last night either.

In a few hours he'd rise. He'd probably show up here, expecting her to put out, or at least put out a vein for him. He wasn't getting another drop from her or another moment near her body.

Why should he? Just because she'd made a flip decision did not mean she would be at his beck and call for eternity. Absolutely not. She'd lay the ground rules. Yes. A few simple rules and this arrangement might not be as bad as it seemed, or at the very least it might be tolerable.

She pulled on a pair of jeans and a burgundy sweater over a gold cami, stuffed her feet into fuzzy socks, and then laced her hiking boots. She combed her hair up into a ponytail. After a cup of tea, a peanut butter and honey sandwich, a handful of grapes, a bag of chips, and two chocolate bars she was ready to write her expectations.

First, no touching. Number two, no entering the house, her office, or any other room she was in without advance permission and an escort capable of physically restraining him. Third, no discussing the marriage with her or anyone else. Number four, no looking at her in ways that made her limbs useless. This might be the most important rule as it seemed to be the item that got her into the most trouble. It paved the way for everything else to happen. It gave him cause to touch her. Lastly, she wanted a different trainer, someone who could teach her to defend herself against him.

Dragomir had said she needed to train, so she would, but she'd do it on her own terms. It might be time to seriously consider werewolf training.

The doorbell rang.

"What is it, Osgar?" she yelled from the kitchen table.

The bell rang again. "Flowers," a stranger called.

She glanced out the window and saw the Flowers by Judy truck parked in her driveway. A young kid stood on her porch holding a giant arrangement of roses and looking terribly uncomfortable. He stared upward, his mouth hanging open.

She sighed and opened the door to find Osgar towering over the delivery boy looking as though he might throttle the poor kid. "I didn't order flowers." She didn't recognize the delivery boy either. Sofia had worked for Judy all through high school and college. She'd continued to do seasonal work with Judy and her sister Ilene up until the fire last year. Since Judy and Ilene had died, the business was sold, and Sofia hadn't gone back to the farm.

"No ma'am. They're from a..." The young man turned the card. "...D... Dra...Drag, something Pet...rescue. Oh, they're from the Dragmit Pet Rescue."

Osgar snickered.

Sofia glared.

"That's not right? I'm sorry. It's a weird name." He pushed the vase at Sofia.

"I can't wait to hear what he's written." Osgar reached for the card.

Sofia backed into the house, shooting a warning glare at Osgar. "Just a minute." She struggled to place the arrangement on the table. It was heavier than she'd expected. She reached for her handbag, but it wasn't in its usual spot on the chair by the table. "Where's my purse?"

"Here." Osgar handed the kid a couple bucks. "Beat it, Opie."

The delivery boy scampered to his truck like a rabbit fleeing the hunt.

"Did I leave it at work?" Sofia ran up the stairs, checked the bedroom, and came back. "In the car?" She dashed out to the Camry and stopped short.

The Camry gleamed. It had been washed and waxed. The inside even looked like it had been vacuumed. The windows were clean. In the backseat on the floor sat a crate with windshield wiper fluid, some paper towels and car wax. Her handbag sat on the front seat with her lunch bag and a note. "Get a tune-up and a brake job. Steering realignment. If not done today, Cader mechanics complete tasks tonight. D."

Was he telling her what to do? She read the note again. "Are these orders?"

"I thought your car looked awfully clean." Osgar read the note over her shoulder. "I'm not surprised you need an alignment. You gunned this car into a ditch. It's a Camry." He rapped his knuckles on the roof. "Sensible. Not remotely daring. Definitely can't take a ditch without sustaining wear and tear." He kicked a tire.

"My car is always clean." She carried her bags back to the house. "I'm not getting a tune-up and my brakes are fine." It was her car. She'd decide if it needed maintenance, not him.

Osgar stopped the front door from closing and pushed it completely open. "You need both." He sat on the top step of the porch.

"What do you know?" Sofia lugged the flowers to the coffee table in full view of the back glass sliding door and front picture window.

"I know your brakes are worn enough that metal is hitting metal in the rear and the shocks are worn, too." He sat back on his elbows, stretched his legs down the steps, and raised his face to the sun.

Sofia snatched the card from the arrangement. It was addressed to Sofia Engle Petrescu. She crumpled the tiny envelop in her fist. Who did he think he was? She contemplated ripping the little card to shreds then throwing the flowers in the driveway and backing her car over them as she recklessly sped away.

But curiosity niggled within her. Had he sent her flowers because he actually cared? She ripped the envelope open and read the card.

*To Sofia, May our love last an eternity. Dragomir.*

She rolled her eyes. "Is he kidding?" Love? Were vampires so far removed from emotions they no longer understood love?

"Tell me what it says. Please?" Osgar stood in the doorway, holding on to the doorframe and leaning on a nearly forty-five-degree angle into her living room.

"I thought you weren't supposed to come in."

"The order was not to set one foot in the house. Look. No feet." He nodded toward the floor. "Tell me what it says."

She shook her head. She'd never been a girl to kiss and tell, and she wasn't about to start now in spite of a wild desire to rant about her situation. She needed to find a girlfriend, someone she could trust. She needed time with someone rational, normal, human.

Sofia's shoulders slumped. Her three best girlfriends were off in the world doing their own things.

So far Sofia'd had no luck making friends at work. No surprise there. She always tried to remain professional, never cross the line, which meant no one ever relaxed around her. She was the person people liked as long as she did what they wanted, like interviews and hiring more warriors for their battle, but the moment she challenged or questioned she became Cader's most hated.

She examined the extravagant arrangement. There had to be at least three dozen roses clustered together in a short, round crystal vase. Each flower was exquisite, absolutely perfect. She could barely distinguish where one ended and the next began.

No one had ever sent her flowers like this. Sure she'd received small arrangements, even a dozen roses once or twice, but nothing the likes of this.

She turned the arrangement to view it from all sides. Prisms of sunlight reflected off the crystal vase onto the wall. The vase alone must have cost a mint. She couldn't even imagine what the roses cost.

An olive branch? Was Dragomir trying to win her over? Was this his attempt to show he cared?

Sofia bent to smell one and was mesmerized. The moment she touched it, it opened into full bloom. Petal after petal stretched wide and ended with a slight curl at the tip. Even wide open there were so many petals she couldn't see the actual center of the flower. She touched another and another. Each one blossomed.

The ruby petals had the appearance of plush velvet. The ones closest to the heart of each flower grew redder and redder to a nearly black shade of crimson. They were fuller than the petals of any roses she'd ever seen. They weren't paper-thin, like normal roses. They had body.

"These are gorgeous. So different. So plump." She stroked a finger over a flower and as it spread wide its perfume puffed into the air. "Whoever took over Judy's has an unbelievable gift with roses."

The sweet fragrance permeated the room. They smelled delicious, edible even. She'd never enjoyed the scent of roses so much. She pressed her face into the bouquet and as each one opened soft petals tickled her skin.

She giggled. "Roses."

"Are you all right?" Osgar swayed to the doorway, watching Sofia. He looked confused and trapped. His mouth hung open below furrowed brows, and it appeared he was trying to step in, but couldn't get his foot across some invisible barrier.

"Yep." Sofia nodded and shoved her nose into the heart of the bouquet. The sound of her loud inhale made her laugh. She tossed her head back, laughing so hard she didn't make a sound. She dropped onto the floor and knelt beside the coffee table. Holding the vase with two hands, she buried her face into the flowers.

"You are not," Osgar said.

"Uh-hun." Sofia plucked a rose from the arrangement. "I want to eat this one." She laughed. "It's so beautiful. Do you see the red?" She held the flower toward Osgar. "Look at it."

"I see it. What's wrong with you?"

She lay back on the floor between the sofa and coffee table, holding the rose to her face. "I want to eat this flower." She held it above her, twirling the stem between her thumb and forefinger. Thorns pricked her skin like tiny barbs.

"Don't eat that." Osgar stood on tiptoes to see her.

"I won't." Sofia bolted up, her eyebrows scrunched together. *What is wrong with me?* Her mind was foggy. It was the same feeling she'd had when she woke up from having her wisdom teeth pulled, like she was under some sort of heavy sedation.

She studied her fingers. Little red dots speckled her skin. "Why would I eat a rose?" She put the flower on the table and sucked her fingers.

"You wouldn't. So don't." Osgar banged the door. "Come outside."

The scent of roses swirled in the room so heavily she could see the path it took, winding around her, zigzagging back and forth between her and Osgar. When she studied the mist of rose essence, she realized it had formed a thin barrier between them. She'd have pointed it out, but the fragrance beckoned her to move closer to the source. She leaned into the flowers, inhaled and smiled. "These are so pretty. I can't believe he sent me flowers."

"Well, he did. Put that rose down and come out here. I'm getting tired of standing in the doorway."

Sofia glanced up at Osgar, having to concentrate on his face to see him through the haze of rose fragrance. "I should do something nice for him." She giggled and replaced the rose in the bouquet, fussing to make it fit perfectly with the others. "Osgar, I need your help."

"With what?" He watched her jump up from the table and dash into the kitchen.

She grabbed some cookies and two bottles of soda. "You want a snack?" She held out the bag of double chocolate chip cookies and walked to the porch swing.

Osgar pulled the door shut behind her.

"Did you just lock that?" She asked.

He walked toward the bench. "Homemade?"

"Yup." Sofia glanced at the door then back at Osgar.

He nodded and sat down.

"Soda?" Sofia sat in the corner of the bench. She smiled at the flowers through the picture window.

Osgar took the bottle and twisted the top off. "Lime? Wouldn't have been my first choice."

"It's made down the road." Sofia read the label. "You know the Gregsons over in Exeter own that tiny restaurant. They make this soda, too. It's good." She took a swig. She babbled on for another minute about Mr. Gregson's mother owning the place and having the affair with Mr. Hanson and how everyone always wondered if Parker really was a Gregson because he looked so much like a Hanson.

The crisp autumn breeze blew. She inhaled. Cool, clean air filled her lungs. The October sun heated her skin. The fuzziness clouding her mind began to clear. *What the hell did I just say?* "I'm sorry Osgar. I didn't mean to gossip like that."

Osgar shook his head and gulped a couple mouthfuls. "This soda's not bad. Still not my first choice."

She sat quiet for a couple minutes almost afraid to open her mouth. Each time Osgar finished a cookie she'd offer him another.

"If I didn't know better, I'd say you were trying to bribe me." He looked down at her, a sly grin on his lips.

She shook her head. "Why would I do that?"

"I don't know anything, if that's what you want help with."

She put her half-empty soda bottle on the porch and held open the bag of cookies. "You want another?"

"I'm good. Thanks." He cocked his head to the side and watched her.

"What?"

"What are you up to?" He brushed crumbs off his shirt.

She smiled. "Nothing. Can't we just sit outside together?"

"No. You're giving off some sort of I-want-to-trick-Osgar-into-something vibe. Out with it. What do you want?" He turned sideways, bending his leg between them.

"It's not that I want something. It's just that I thought maybe you could show me some moves or teach me a little bit about fighting. That's all. I don't *want* anything." Sofia shook her head and gazed at her roses.

Osgar squinted and nodded. "Let me get this straight. You want me to train you. After Dragomir already agreed to train you, you want me to take over. That's what you're getting at, isn't it?"

She shook her head in an up and down, side-to-side sort of circle.

His eyebrows rose. "What does that mean?"

"Please? Just show me a few things. You wouldn't have to take over. You'd just be preparing me for training with Dragomir." She scooted closer. "So that I'm not unprepared. So I don't get hurt." Sofia smiled and glanced toward the window. The perfumed air practically formed a hand waving her back into the house. She walked to the window and stared at her flowers.

"You'd rather I get hurt than you."

"What? No, of course not." Sofia froze in her tracks, confused by what to do next. She wanted Osgar's help, but she wanted her flowers, too.

The autumn breeze shifted. The scent of burning brush came to her, clearing away the scent of the roses. She shook her head to think more clearly. "Just show me a couple moves."

She descended the stairs and walked several feet out to the yard.

"First, that's Dragomir's job on so many different levels. Second, what do you think, I'm going to demo and you're going to instantly be prepared for battle?" He followed her off the porch.

She crouched in front of him like a wrestler waiting for her opponent to attack.

"You look ridiculous."

She stood up and sighed.

He swept her feet out from under her and she landed on her back. "First—anticipate. Second—never take your eyes off your attacker. Third—always pay attention to what's going on around you." His voice came from behind the truck.

Sofia spun to face him in time to see him lunge for her and take her down to the ground in a rolling attack. They rolled some ten feet before he let her go to continue the momentum of rolling into the forest edge.

She bounced to her feet, not willing to admit he'd scared her or that she hadn't been prepared. Was a window open? She'd have sworn she could still smell her roses. She shook off the thought of her flowers and concentrated on Osgar, waiting for his next move.

He circled Sofia, grinning like a wolf.

She turned with him, never taking her eyes off him. When he moved three steps forward, she scooted back five, ensuring a good measure of distance between them.

"You planning to take off running or you gonna stand and fight?" He shuffled a couple steps forward, his arms up and ready to grab her.

She wasn't sure. She stepped back. Then she stepped forward and moved to the side. After that she stepped backward over a short hedge lining the driveway.

Osgar stopped moving. "You're kidding me, right? This is how you fight? We're not ballroom dancing."

She peered at the picture window and was nearly entranced by the bouquet. "Do you smell the roses?"

"Forget those damn roses. You planning on offering flowers to an attacker? That's not gonna save you in a fight." Osgar's voice held the sharp edge of annoyance.

Sofia focused on him. "I don't really want to fight. I just want to escape." Truer words were never spoken. Sofia wanted to escape her life, all of it. "Can you teach me to do that?"

"You want me to teach you to run away? You're making me nuts." Osgar scratched his head. "Dragomir was right. You need to learn to defend yourself. Running is not an option."

He leaned over the hedge, picked Sofia up, and plopped her back in the grass. "Now, kick me."

She stared at him. "Why?"

"Kick me."

"No. Do you think I'm going to just walk up to people and kick them? Is that my defense?" She pursed her lips and shook her head. "That's stupid."

"Kick me." This time he said the words through clenched teeth. "Now."

She kicked him. In the shin and then backed up over the hedge.

He didn't flinch. "You have got to be kidding. You didn't even kick me in the nads. What is wrong with you?" He yanked her forward. "Stay in the arena. You step over those hedges one more time and you're going to be digging them up and doing push-ups in their place. You got it?"

Sofia nodded, staring over her shoulder at the flowers in the window.

"You want to be trained. We're going to train." He turned her chin so they were face to face. "And if you look at those flowers once more, I'll call Dragomir and tell him you're so obsessed with his gift all you can do is ogle them. You're like a teenage girl staring at her first valentine. Knock it off!" Osgar held his hand up by his head. "Kick my hand."

"Too high," she snapped.

"Now!"

She knew she'd never do it. She'd never in her life put her foot that high over her head.

Osgar glared. Sofia stepped forward and kicked up, missing his hand, and pulling her other leg out from under her. She landed on her ass.

"Again."

She scrambled to her feet, set up, and missed again.

"Allow me to demonstrate. See the low branch?" Osgar pointed to a branch from the oak tree at the far end of the driveway, then he lunged forward and brought his foot up sideways to kick the branch. The tree creaked. "That's what I want to see. Your foot up to the side, power through your legs. Let's go." His hand came up again.

Sofia practiced kicking for the next hour. When she mastered kicking with her right foot, he made her do it with her left. She learned not only how to kick without sustaining the impact, but how to aim and place a kick for a specific outcome. She learned to block kicks as well. Then she stepped over the hedge and stared at her flowers. That's when she found herself holding a shovel.

"Get digging."

She dug up the hedge and did push-ups in the dirt. About forty minutes into it she whined about wanting to take a break.

"You'll take a break when I decide." Osgar stood over her. "Those are lame-ass push-ups." His hand landed on her back and he shoved her down into the soil. "That's more like it."

When she finished with the push-ups, they moved on to defensive posturing.

The sun set and darkness began to fall, but Sofia didn't notice. She was too busy kicking Osgar all over the yard and blocking his return kicks.

She landed a kick to Osgar's chest and knocked him, winded, onto the ground. Exhausted, she dropped beside him. "I'm not defenseless."

# CHAPTER TWENTY-FOUR

Only the moon and stars lit the yard. The sensor triggering the front light wasn't working. Dragomir stood on the porch with Sofia and Osgar, watching his mate grow angrier by the second and worrying about how she'd respond when he forcibly removed her to Cader. She stood between them, huffing, arms folded over her chest, foot tapping furiously.

"Just who do you think you are telling me I can't go in my own house?" Her hands flew to her hips.

Osgar leaned on the doorframe acting like a goalie at a hockey game. He'd already bounced her back to Dragomir three times.

Dragomir kept one eye trained on the flowers and one on his fuming mate. She had already demonstrated tremendous strength and flexibility by snapping her porch swing from its hinges and hurling it across the porch only to race past it to stop it from crashing through her window.

"Well, if you didn't send them, then who did?" She pointed at the flowers. "I should have known they didn't come from you. Why would a vampire send flowers? That's like expecting a serial killer to send a condolence card." She raised her chin and huffed again.

The flowers glowed in the moonlight. Red petals blazed above black hearts. Each flower pulsed and the sickeningly sweet aroma seeped into the night.

"My guess is Kiernan. Was there no card?" Dragomir studied Sofia. Her mood had gone from pleading to absolute confusion to rage in less than four blinks of her eyes.

The poisonous flowers were certainly doing their job. She was hardly in control of herself and more than a minor challenge to contain.

She plastered herself against the window, drawn to the flowers like a child to a candy store. "It was signed from you." Her breath fogged the glass.

Dragomir looked at Osgar and raised an eyebrow.

"Now you can understand why I agreed to train her." Osgar shook his head. "She's better in the fresh air. This close she's somewhat obsessed."

Dragomir nodded. "She only touched them, no consumption. Is that correct?"

"Yeah, but she wanted to eat them."

"I'm right here." She glared over her shoulder. "They smell so good." She smiled and licked her lips then turned back to the window, pressing her forehead to the glass. "I'll share them." She sang the offer, batting her eyes at the flowers.

"Who delivered them?" Dragomir peeled Sofia off the window and pulled her to the edge of the porch.

"Flowers by Judy." Sofia tried to wiggle free.

He tightened his grip.

"Let me go." She pushed on his chest. "I want to go into my house. Let me go!" She glared at him. Her dark green eyes held more than the usual contempt.

"You cannot enter the house. The flowers know you. They want you." Dragomir held on to Sofia's hand while picking up the bag he'd brought. Swords and stakes clanged when he slung the strap across his chest. "We go back to Cader." He pulled her along the porch. "Osgar, I'll return with reinforcements."

"Okay." Osgar leaned against the house. "Good luck getting her back to the hospital."

"I'm not going there. You can't just drag me off because of some flowers." She dug her feet in, using all her weight in an attempt to remain planted where she stood.

Dragomir pulled her down the stairs, yanking her hand harder with each step she resisted. His grip tightened around her wrist, trying to keep hold of her without breaking any bones. Focusing on not hurting her, he didn't anticipate her next move. She swung her foot out, tangling her right leg between his and sending him flying down the last two steps. She sailed over his head, tumbling to a stop in the rut that had once been her hedges.

Bolting to her feet she made a run for the back deck.

"She trained easily. And she's a bit sneaky, too." Osgar chuckled. "Maybe I should have warned you earlier."

Dragomir caught Sofia well before she reached the first step. What he didn't expect was an all-out attack.

She spun to her left, planted her left foot hard, and kicked him in the chest with her right. He flew backwards, landing on his back. She sprinted up the stairs to the landing. Dragomir leapt onto the deck, blocking her path to the door.

Sofia hunched as though she planned to plow straight through him. Her eyes narrowed and she curled back her lips. "Get out of my way, vampire." Her voice dropped, making her sound possessed.

Dragomir did not move. He watched Sofia. Her eyes darted between him, the flowers, and the stairs. She panted. Sweat beaded on her upper lip. Her hands trembled.

"You have been marked. Black Magic Roses are deadly. Kiernan has sent an open threat. He means to kill you." Dragomir shifted his weight. "I know you hate Cader after sundown, but that is the safest place for you." He stepped toward her.

Her breathing came fast and hard. She edged back from him, glancing to the sides. "I'm not safe there. And you know it."

He had to admire her efforts. Obvious as she was, she looked for a way to stop him, an escape. But he'd not let her get away. She would not elude his protection.

"Killing you would be a tremendous blow to The Alliance," Dragomir said. He took a measured step to the right, cutting off her path to the stairs but allowing her a view of the flowers.

She stared at the roses. "Why? Because there'd be no one to write policies?" she hissed. Her eyes glazed and she stood up straight, dropping her arms and stepping toward the sliding glass door as though hypnotized.

Dragomir was familiar with the effects of Black Magic Roses. He'd seen vampires succumb to their poison. Even at this distance Sofia was helpless against their magic. One drop of their venom and she'd be lost forever.

Dragomir darted in front of her, pulling her against his body. "You are special to Jankin and you are my mate. To lose you would be painful for us both." He caught her chin and brought her gaze to his. "In spite of what you think, I care about you." He bent his head to hers, his mouth barely brushing her lips. "You're mine to protect. My heart is yours."

She didn't react, simply leaned against him. He didn't wait for her to protest. He picked her up and carried her down the stairs to the forest edge.

"Osgar, let us deliver Sofia back to Cader. We will visit Flowers by Judy tonight. There's a delivery boy with some information we need."

A gust of wind blew. The scent of the roses was carried in the opposite direction.

Sofia snapped out of her lethargy and squirmed like a puppy trying to break free. Dragomir lost his hold and she landed with a thud on her ass. "I'm coming." She stood up. "I'm not going to Cader. I'm coming with you."

"No." Dragomir caught her elbow and ushered her into the woods.

To his dismay, she flipped backward out of his grip. "Listen, you Neanderthal, you are not telling me what to do. In the past four weeks I've tolerated an awful lot from werewolves, Dr. MacDuff, and *you*. I have officially hit my limit."

Osgar joined them in the woods, looking from one to the other, though he didn't say a word, just watched their interaction.

"You're either taking me willingly or I'm coming on my own. You don't own me. I will not be forced to do one more thing against my will." She stalked back toward the driveway. "Tolerating violent wolves. Drinking vampire blood. *Marrying a vampire*. Magic roses." She turned around. "That's it." She threw her hands in the air. "Not one more thing. That's the threshold. One more thing and

I swear to God someone is going to die." She climbed into Osgar's truck. "And I'm riding shotgun."

Dragomir and Osgar looked at each other. Osgar's shoulders rose and dropped. "Do we take her?" he whispered.

"I can hear you!" she yelled. "Let's go!" She clicked her seatbelt.

Dragomir sighed and led the way back to the truck. "This is a very bad—"

"Zip it, Vlad." She crossed her arms over her chest and one leg over the other. Her foot tapped.

Osgar backed the truck out of the driveway.

"Sofia," Dragomir began.

She spun around in the seat, finger pointed at him. "Do not even think about telling me I'm staying in the truck. I've…" Her mouth dropped.

Dragomir sat watching her, silent, not breathing, still as the night. But he knew what she saw. He was ready for battle, ready to defend, ready to kill. His eyes blazed. He'd hoped to warn her about what she'd see before she turned around, but instead she, of course, had something to say.

If he hadn't experienced a similar event the other night, he'd have been just as surprised as Sofia. His vision had faded to black and white the moment he acquiesced to her demand to accompany them. He'd instinctively gone into battle mode, ready to defend her to the death. It was usually safe and comfortable. But with Sofia all that had changed.

Everything he saw was in black and white except Sofia. She remained in full, vibrant color.

She swallowed.

"May I speak?" His voice was low, calculated.

She nodded.

"As you insist on participating, tonight's mission will be just to gather information. We will not confront anyone. Do you understand?" He watched her face, waiting to see if her mouth dropped a quarter inch and if she averted her eyes for a split second, both telltale signs that she would agree. He knew her well enough to know when she was weighing her risks. If she agreed too soon, he'd take her back to Cader, probably bound and gagged and needing Osgar to help get her that way.

"But, what if the delivery boy is there?" Her eyes darted down and her mouth opened a touch then she bit her lip and looked back at Dragomir.

"We watch him. Nothing more." Dragomir concentrated on not smiling.

"But…"

"Then we return to Cader. Tonight you learn to use your arms and hands in a fight." Warmth rolled through Dragomir. The idea of teaching his mate to spar excited him. He'd trained many a soldier, but never one whose very existence was tied to his. "You've learned well with Osgar today."

"And no lessons before. Impressive," Osgar said. He turned the truck down Route 102 and took the left past Gregson's.

"My dad showed me a few moves when I was a kid. That's all." Sofia faced forward.

"I thought your dad had been sick. How was he showing you fighting moves?" Osgar slowed the truck, looking for the side street that led out to Wolf Run Road.

"I don't know. I guess he wasn't always weak. When I was a teenager, he couldn't do as much. But when I was younger we practiced and raced and stuff." She looked out the window. "It's the next right."

Osgar took the next turn and slowed.

"How do you know the farm?" Dragomir asked.

"I knew Judy and Ilene for a long time. Judy was my first boss. They were like family." Sofia turned to Dragomir. "They weren't really killed in a fire, were they?"

He shook his head. The Alliance had made up the story. Last Christmas Judy and her sister became two more dead victims of Bas Dubh.

Osgar drove by the farm without changing speed. Dragomir noted five cars parked in the back, one a limo. He cracked the window and inhaled. The musky scent of wolves blew into the truck. Wolves and the unmistakable scent of poisonous roses.

Sofia's head turned toward the farm and she inhaled loudly.

Dragomir didn't smell the vampires, but he felt their power coming from the building. He couldn't be sure which vampires were present, but there were at least three masters somewhere on the property.

Osgar drove to the end of the road and took a left. "I don't think we should make another pass. Too much power to risk it."

"Agreed. To Cader with a report." Dragomir held the window button and the glass slid back into place. "After our report you will show me all you can do, Sofia."

She glanced back and nodded.

Her agreement nearly confused Dragomir. He'd expected her to argue that she'd decide if and when she'd train with him. He was glad to be seated behind her in the dark where she couldn't see him. "You will learn the knife and the stake. When the times comes, you will be prepared to kill."

# CHAPTER TWENTY-FIVE

Sofia sat on the couch in Dr. MacDuff's office while Osgar and Dragomir gave a report on the events from the past twelve hours. She'd been in this office twice before. Both times Dr. MacDuff had left her waiting for him, giving her plenty of time to snoop. She was well aware of his "Sofia shelf" and his pictorial family tree that spread across three of the four walls.

"The roses are being grown on the farm, not twenty miles from here," Dragomir said.

Fergus and Dr. MacDuff nodded, occasionally asking a question, but otherwise they simply listened.

"He hasn't used Black Magic since the deaths of Ralston and Maria Campbell in 1898." Dr. MacDuff faced the portraits of Maria and Ralston. When he turned to face them, Sofia noticed he looked tired, older even.

"This time the flowers were much more potent. Fuller, petals like pockets of fluid." Dragomir stood to Sofia's left. "Almost like mutant roses."

"Sofia succumbed within a few minutes of their arrival," Osgar said. "I'd never seen them before. If I'd known what they were, I wouldn't have allowed that kid to deliver them." Osgar frowned and raked his fingers through his hair.

"You didn't know, lad. You weren't even born the last time we encountered them." Dr. MacDuff sat back. "I doubt you'd have been able to stop the delivery. Black Magic Roses are grown specifically for each victim. Sofia would not have allowed you to send them away. The roses wouldn't have allowed you to interfere." His eyes widened a touch.

"How were they grown for me?" Sofia asked. The roses *had* known her. They called to her by name.

"The poison is created from your DNA then fed to the roses as they grow. Someone has been working on this project for years," Dr. MacDuff answered.

"Bas Dubh has known about me that long? They've wanted me dead? They don't even know me." This was just great. She really was a target of some group of psychos. In the back of her mind she wondered how many of them she might have fired or disciplined at other jobs.

"Aye. They've known." Dr. MacDuff pulled out a binder from the shelf, flipped open a page to an article cut from the Mid-State Bulletin. The headline read: Football Team State Champs. He pointed to the picture below the caption. Sofia sat in the stands. "Do you see the man sitting two rows behind you, the one staring at you?"

It was a grainy shot, but she could easily see him staring at her. The expression on his face gave her the creeps. "I remember this. Dad was very upset by it. He looks like a pedophile. But I never even noticed him." She remembered her father not letting her leave the house unattended for several weeks after the photo made the paper.

"That is Kiernan. He could have easily swiped you away that day. Right under our noses he sat within an arm's reach of you." Dr. MacDuff closed the book. "He's been planning for a long time. He probably took a few locks of your hair that afternoon."

"Why do you suppose he didn't just take me then?"

"Kiernan is a patient man. Devious. Dramatic. Losing you on that day would have been painful. But watching you suffer the effects of the roses would have been far worse." Jankin's presence moved around Sofia like a warm blanket wrapping around her shoulders.

Sofia hadn't realized how close she'd come to her own demise before today. "He could have found my hair or DNA anywhere on that farm. Back then I worked two afternoons and Saturday mornings for Judy."

"Black Magic poison is a slow moving poison. The victim begins with an obsession about the flowers. The need to consume them overtakes her. She will stop at nothing, even killing to have them." Dr. MacDuff replaced the book on the shelf.

Sofia shivered. Dr. MacDuff was right. She had wanted those roses. She'd have killed for them. She glanced up at Dragomir. She had contemplated using his own sword to cut his head off.

"Once the victim consumes the poison, she falls prey to Kiernan's commands. And his main goal is to destroy The Alliance and bring civilized humanity to its knees."

This world was far too violent for her. What was she becoming?

"Why? Why would I be the target?" Sofia looked from Dr. MacDuff to Dragomir.

"It had to be your connection with me," Jankin answered. He watched Sofia with an expression of guilt. "I tried to be careful and keep hidden my friendship with your parents. But my efforts were not good enough."

"What do you mean?" His explanation confused her.

"I can only assume Kiernan saw an opportunity in our connection. His goal would have been for you to be under his command, but closely aligned with me." Jankin and Dragomir looked at each other as if a secret message had passed between them.

"And with you mated to me, Kiernan would have known I'd train you to fight." Dragomir's hand rested on Sofia's back. "He'd have commanded you to kill Jankin."

Sofia's mouth dropped open. "I couldn't do that. Wouldn't do it."

"You'd have had no choice," Dragomir said.

"I knew something wasn't right. The moment that truck pulled up I knew I should stop that kid. But I didn't." Osgar looked up at Fergus then back at the floor after only a second.

Fergus placed a hand on Osgar's shoulder. "Don't. You could not have stopped this delivery alone."

The moment they touched an invisible link connected Fergus and Osgar, and Sofia couldn't help but sense the current flowing between them.

"I didn't want her upset." Osgar's voice dropped to a mumble. "I should have killed that kid. I failed her."

"No, Osgar. You didn't." Sofia reached for Osgar's hand. "Don't think that. You helped me. I'd have eaten one of those stupid flowers. It's insane, but I wanted to eat roses today."

"Osgar, you did right by Sofia." Dragomir sat on the couch beside her. "Keeping her out of the house saved her. Rigorous activity flushed the poisonous vapors from her system."

"If you'd been there, you could have helped. You'd have been able to stop the spell before it started," Osgar said. His shoulders slumped.

"If she'd allowed me." Dragomir glanced at Sofia. His dark gaze moved over her face, and her heart sped.

"What do you mean?" She had the desire to touch him. It was almost as strong as her desire to eat poisonous flowers.

"To break the spell would have required physical contact, intimate physical contact of one sort or another." He licked his lips.

Heat rose up Sofia's neck to her cheeks. Her stomach knotted, and she thanked God she was seated because her arms and legs suddenly had that familiar feel of gelatin bones. She didn't want to look away. She wanted to be able to hold his gaze, not flinch. But she couldn't. Parts of her that shouldn't warm up were heating straight to her core.

She let her gaze drop to his chest.

"Well." Dr. MacDuff stood. "It seems we have a leak within our ranks. Sofia Engle-Petrescu?" He shook his head. "I'm not a fan of the hyphenated name. A bit old fashioned, I'll admit." He glanced at Sofia and Dragomir. "None the less, that information had not been shared until late this afternoon. Only we five, Meg and Jamieson knew last night. Our security plan needs an upgrade."

"Word of our mating seems to have spread with haste. Dice knew," Dragomir said.

"I released the announcement to The Alliance just before you and I met earlier. In fact, I sent the message as you walked into this office." Dr. MacDuff looked at Fergus. "You're sure none of the wolves breeched the information?"

"Aye. They were all given the command to remain silent in this matter."

"I'm not sure if the threat to Sofia was targeted solely at you, Jankin. It's quite possible Kiernan could have seen an opportunity to defeat us both. Whatever the case, Sofia needs better protection," Dragomir said.

Sofia nodded. "I'm ready to train. I concede. There may be a need for more physical responses in certain situations not related to employment where people have to defend themselves against attackers who can't be reasoned with."

All four men looked at her.

"Of course, I mean quickly reasoned with. No sense in getting killed because you launch into a long dissertation about human rights or mutual respect with a hungry vampire or rabid wolf. Do werewolves get rabies? I don't know. Either way, I'll train."

All four of them wore the same look—eyebrows raised, mouths hanging open.

"Sorry. Some things just don't change. I can't see hurting someone for no reason. I'm not going to walk around hitting or kicking everything that moves. There is a limit to my... Why are you all looking at me like that?" She sat up straight and glanced from one face to the next.

"I'm glad to hear you recognize the need for physical responses to certain situations." Dr. MacDuff sat on the edge of his desk. "However, I think we need to circle the wagons for a bit."

"Agreed," the other three men echoed.

"What wagons?" Sofia asked. That feeling like some sort of impending doom was looming just beyond the door hung in the air. She was fairly certain they weren't talking about Radio Flyers.

"For the time being it would be best if you resided at Cader," Dr. MacDuff answered.

She did a double take from him to Dragomir and back. "Here? No."

"Your home is off-limits until we find a way to safely remove the roses." Dr. MacDuff folded his arms over his chest. "If that's possible."

"I'll go to a hotel. Not here. That's a terrible idea. I'll even buy a gun. I'll shoot anyone who attacks. There's no need to stay here." She couldn't stay here. As it was, her skin had been jumping from the moment she set foot in the building. She felt like she'd shuffled across a shag carpet in a lightning storm while rubbing balloons on her hair. If she were any more tingly, she'd be able to stick a light bulb in her mouth and illuminate the room.

"There is not a safe hotel anywhere in this state," Dragomir said. His jaw was set as if he'd made up his mind for both of them.

"I'll take a guard. Two or three, if you want." She looked at Dr. MacDuff, not even bothering to try to sway Dragomir whose penetrating gaze practically burned a hole into her head.

"Sofia, child, I cannot spare the guards. Two or three will not keep you safe. Kiernan will send enough men to overpower them. Cader is the best place for you."

"No. I'm not staying." She stood up.

"No one will harm you here," Dr. MacDuff said.

"Oh, that's easy for you to say. No one zaps you every time you enter a room or leers at you like you might be dinner. And you don't live in fear of witnessing vampire lunch breaks." She marched to door. "I'm not staying."

"Sofia." Dragomir's hand covered hers on the doorknob. "I promise you none of those things will happen. You have my word as your mate and as a member of The Board of Masters for The Alliance. I will keep you safe here."

The familiar smooth flow of Dragomir's power moved along Sofia's skin, enveloping her in a calm she only ever felt when he touched her. That irritating tingling ceased. Her heart no longer felt like someone had jump-started it during a code blue. Her muscles relaxed.

"You can't stay glued to my side every second." She watched his fingers curl around her hand.

"We'll work it out," he said.

She sighed. The fact was she didn't want to be at Cader, but she didn't want to be outside of Cader. Now she was afraid of vampires who were on her side, werewolves who hated her, being tricked by roses and wimpy little delivery boys from the farm not ten miles from her house. She really had no choice but to accept Dragomir's offer.

She nodded and mumbled, "Okay." Was this the best she could hope for?

Dr. MacDuff sighed and a tension seemed to drain from the room. His face was much more relaxed than before, eyes clearer, jaw no longer locked. His shoulders lowered an inch or two.

"I'll take you to my quarters then speak to Dice," Dragomir said. "I'll only be gone a short while and you'll be safest there." His hand rested on Sofia's shoulder.

She thought to argue, but Dr. MacDuff beat her to it.

"Dragomir, take your mate and care for her. Tonight we leave you to get acquainted. I'll question Dice myself."

Sofia's eyes widened. Dragomir nodded. Osgar grinned and winked at her. *Oh God!*

# CHAPTER TWENTY-SIX

Dragomir had known Sofia had it in her. She was, after all, his mate. She drank from him. His drive to fight flowed in her veins. It took two hours of gut-wrenching assaults to get her to unleash it, but he finally unlocked the power.

She was amazing, blocking his blows with the ability he'd only ever seen in other vampires, anticipating his attacks like a seasoned warrior, and finally coming at him like a born killer. She was a true vampire mate.

They stood at opposite ends of his gym. Her breath came fast and ragged. Her eyes narrowed as she tracked his every move.

Dragomir felt her studying him, noting every muscle twitch, every intake of his breath. She stepped to the side toward his swords.

*Not so fast, lovely.* She was fast, but not vampire speed. He darted between her and the rack of weapons.

Her jaw clenched and a low growl escaped her.

He smiled.

She grabbed a nearby bo and came at him swinging the stick with the skill of a Japanese fighter.

Aimed for his head, the bo came down. Dragomir's hand shot up. He caught the end of the weapon, twisted to the left to pry it from Sofia's hands, and sent her flying twenty feet backward with a kick to her chest.

She slammed against a rack of bows and arrows, snarled and scrambled to her feet. Hunched across the room, her black hair hung in a mess past her shoulders and stuck to her glistening skin. Her green eyes were laser-sharp.

*Interesting.*

Dragomir circled her, holding the bo.

She'd stripped off her sweatshirt after he'd used it to hang her from the wall. She'd earned that by refusing to fight. Her sweater came off when he'd pinned her to the wall with the silver throwing stars when she tried to argue her way out of training. Her aversion to violence seemed to be waning. Especially when she feared for her own life.

Now she wore a tight little gold top. How she wore so damn many layers to begin with was beyond him.

To her credit she'd managed to destroy his shirt. She'd ripped it down the center and trapped his arms at the elbows. Amazingly durable fibers had nothing to do with how she'd managed to contain him. It was the way she stared into his eyes and rubbed her heated breasts to his chest that distracted him long enough for her to take his legs out from under him and send him hurtling into the weight rack.

She was cunning. He'd give her that.

"What are you waiting for?" She turned in a crouch, keeping him in her sights.

"I'll say I knew you were capable of some sort of defense. I just didn't expect it to be battle worthy skill." Dragomir lowered the bo. With a whoosh it smacked down only a hair away from her toe.

She didn't flinch.

"I've always known what I could do, too." She lunged but not for Dragomir. Instead she jumped at the bo. The force of her attack dragged him to the left. To keep hold of the weapon he allowed her to flip him backward.

They landed on the ground, Sofia straddling him, both holding the bo above his head.

"I've always wondered if you'd prefer the top." He licked his lips and smiled.

She glared, released the bo, and brought her elbow down on his chest with such force ribs cracked.

Dragomir let go of the stick, shoved her off him, and rolled onto his side, coughing and cradling his chest. Pain radiated from the ribs above his heart. He spit blood onto the floor. His own rapid gurgling breaths sounded louder every time he inhaled. He coughed and blood sprayed the floor. One final wheeze, a shudder, and he fell silent.

"Dragomir!" Sofia grabbed his shoulder and pulled him onto his back. "Dragomir!" Her voice shot up several octaves. "Oh, my God." She placed her hand on his chest.

His heart did not beat. He did not breathe.

"Oh my God. CPR. CPR. CPR. Oh my God." She pressed her mouth to his and blew.

His chest rose and fell but he did not breathe.

"I broke his ribs. Do I still press on them? Do I just breathe?" She pressed her mouth to his again and blew with the same result.

She stood up and paced the floor. "I killed him. Oh my God. Oh my God." Her hands went to her head. "I killed my mate. How do I explain this?"

He couldn't resist any longer. With her back turned he moved, coming right behind her like a shadow. He jerked her body against his, and holding her wrists in one hand pinned to her waist, knotted her hair in his other hand. His mouth lowered to her neck.

"Did I not explain the only ways to kill a vampire?" His fangs scraped her skin.

Her heart thundered. Shallow breaths rattled from her. She barely nodded.

He licked her skin. Salty and sweet. She tasted as good as she smelled. "Tell me."

"Decapitation. Staking the heart." Her voice shook.

"What is the punishment for being caught?" His mouth sealed over her skin.

She leaned back into him and moaned. "Push-ups."

His tongue swirled over her neck and her legs buckled. He grinned. "Hit the mat." He held her until she'd regained her footing. When she was stable, he stepped back and pointed to the floor.

She dropped and began counting out loud with each rise.

"You must trust no one. Everyone is your enemy." Dragomir's voice rose over hers. "Two hundred. Meet me in the kitchen when you're done. And you don't have to count so loud. I'll hear you just fine."

He left her on the mat, swearing between numbers.

The sight of her on the floor, lowering and rising in perfectly even rhythm, was almost more than he could stand. He was punishing her for worrying she might have killed him but not actually accomplishing the task.

He grinned. She had worried about him.

When Sofia met him in the kitchen sweat dripped from her skin. He handed her a bottle of water. "You did well, but not well enough."

"Obviously." She sat on a stool at the counter and held her hair up off her neck. "I never wanted to do that."

"Don't lose sight of what I teach you. It may save your life someday." Dragomir sipped his water.

"My dad sparred with me like that when I was young." She drank her bottle of water then replaced the cap.

Dragomir held another bottle to her. "Would you like another?"

She shook her head. "I'm the reason he couldn't do things when he got older. I broke his back when I was ten." The plastic bottle crackled when she squeezed it. "I haven't trained since."

Dragomir felt his mate's emotions, felt them like someone stabbed a knife into his side and twisted. Her eyes darkened and guilt riddled her face.

"He told me a girl needed to know how to fight." She met Dragomir's gaze. "'Sofia, you need to be prepared, be able to defend yourself. You never know when you'll need the skills.'" She imitated a male voice and shook her head. "If the poor guy ever knew how my life was turning out…"

He remained still for a moment. This was just one more detail he'd get cleared up for her. *Damn Jankin.*

"I've always known I was different. And until I met you, I'd been able to hide it even from Dr. MacDuff and Osgar. But not you." She met his gaze. A cold hard stare full of angst and confusion, anger and disappointment bore into him. "You've just brought out the beast in me."

# CHAPTER TWENTY-SEVEN

"You got anything stronger?" Sofia tossed the empty bottle into the trash.

"Vodka, whiskey."

"Either one." She used her sweatshirt to wipe her face and neck.

"No preference?" Dragomir grabbed two short glasses from the cabinet.

"No. I never drink hard liquor straight, wouldn't know which to choose."

"Never?" He dipped his head and looked her up and down. "Not even a little rum?" A sly smile flickered on his lips.

She winced and dropped her sweatshirt on the stool at the end of the counter. "Well, no. I mean the other night was the first time. I'd never done that before. Clearly. I mean I never did what we did before either."

He really was a terrible influence. She frowned at him. Handsome as the devil and equally as crafty. Now she was drinking, fighting, and screwing. Sort of screwing, anyway.

"You mean you're a virgin?" Dragomir's eyes bulged. He looked from her to the vodka and tossed back a shot then slammed the bottle on the counter.

She jumped. "No." My God what did he want? A whore for a mate? Not that they were getting into bed anytime soon. But he didn't have to sound so damn disappointed. "I don't live in a bubble. I just meant I—"

"What did you mean?" He slid a glass of vodka to her, sloshing liquor on the counter. "How many? Is there someone now?" Dragomir's cheek tensed.

Her mouth dropped open. "What? Now you think I'm a whore?"

Dragomir looked up to the ceiling then back to her. His dark blue eyes softened.

If her heart rate had dropped after their workout, she couldn't tell. Her skin felt like it was burning.

"I'm sorry. I didn't mean to imply anything." He wiped the counter then topped off her drink.

Sofia sipped her vodka and squeezed her eyes shut against the burn running down her throat.

"It's straight from Russia. I brought it back on my last trip. Ten years ago now." Dragomir sipped it, swishing a mouthful before swallowing. "Not bad," he said, watching the alcohol swirl in his glass.

"You drink vodka?"

He raised his eyebrows. "Among other things."

She looked at her drink, though kept her attention focused on her periphery, watching him.

Dragomir chuckled. "You're far too nervous around me, Sofia." He stepped back from the counter. "I won't bite you. Not unless you'd like me to."

The smile on his face made her shiver. She crossed her arms over her chest and rubbed her shoulders. She wasn't cold, but she knew her breasts were sending a message she didn't want him to receive.

He grabbed the ice container from the freezer.

His feet were bare as was his chest. All he wore were his jeans. His hair was tied back allowing for an unobscured view of his chiseled face. Midnight blue eyes watched her above red lips, redder than hers.

"Do you eat food, too?" She pushed her hair behind her ear, and a blade of grass fell in her lap.

"Sometimes. I haven't in many years, but I can, if that's what you're asking." He leaned against the counter and plucked the blade from her leg, twirling it between his fingers. "We'll have to get some groceries tomorrow. I'm afraid my cupboards are as bare as Old Mother Hubbard's." He dropped the grass on the counter, bent over, and opened a couple cabinets. "Empty."

"It's okay. I can eat in the cafeteria upstairs." She sipped her vodka and looked around the kitchen. There wasn't one item on the walls. No shopping list on the fridge. No out-of-place mail stacked on the countertop.

"I know you can. But we should still have food in our quarters."

Our quarters. The term sounded foreign to Sofia. First, she'd never considered her own home to be her quarters. Second, *our?* The idea of sharing was strange, yet exciting.

She glanced toward the living room and shifted on her chair. "Two." She gulped a mouthful of vodka then opened her mouth and exhaled loudly.

"Two what?" Dragomir poured more vodka into their glasses.

"Men. Two men. That's it." She looked everywhere but at him. "Not a whole heck of a lot going on from that angle." He might as well know. She wasn't the most experienced lover. She was fairly certain she could find her way around his body. She just wasn't a hundred percent sure he'd enjoy it that much.

He nodded. His eyebrows dropped, one eye squinted. As he watched her she felt like a specimen under a microscope.

She cleared her throat and rolled her glass between her fingers.

He took another swallow of vodka.

"What about you?" She finally looked up at him.

Dragomir choked. He spit the mouthful of vodka into the drain and stood gasping over the sink.

"Are you all right?" Sofia went to his side, firmly patting him on the back.

He wheezed and coughed and gripped the counter as though he were holding on for dear life.

"It's best if you put your hands above your head." She grabbed his right arm, shoved him away from the sink and stood in front of him, thrusting both his arms up over his head. "Don't look at me. Look up. It will help."

Dragomir stared at Sofia. Her fingers squeezed his triceps as she forced his arms over his head. She nodded as she ordered him to look up.

"I'm—" Dragomir coughed again.

"Head up!" She let go of an arm and tilted his chin up toward the ceiling. "I'm telling you, it will help." She rested her hand on his chest. His heart pounded like a drum.

He gasped then took a deep breath and swallowed. His heart slowed.

She grinned up at him. "Better?"

"Yes. Surprisingly." He dipped his head toward hers and inhaled. His eyes closed for a second. When he opened them, they were the bluest she'd ever seen them. Still dark, but clearly blue. And they focused on her as though he was looking into her.

Heat rose up her neck and she ducked out from under his arm. "Told you." She walked back to her seat. "So I take it that means it's a high number."

Dragomir rubbed the muscles at the back of his neck.

Sofia held her glass close to her mouth and waited. He'd been around for a while so she could only imagine what he was going to say.

"I am nearly eight hundred years a vampire and a man for twenty-five years before that."

"I'm older than you?" Her glass clinked the counter. "I never intended to marry anyone younger than me." She was a cradle robber. She'd robbed a vampire cradle. *Great. An eternity married to someone younger than me.*

"I'd hardly call you older, darling."

She inhaled and her mouth opened to say something, but she didn't. He was right. He was older—sort of.

"Nonetheless, I have been with more than two women."

She nodded. "I thought so." She looked away, cheek pinched between her teeth. Her fingers combed through her hair, working to smooth the disheveled tresses. Several more blades of grass dropped to the floor.

"A lot more?" She was sure she didn't want to know but curiosity made her ask.

He nodded. "Let's not discuss this. I can't even think of a number to tell you. Eight hundred years is a long time."

"Like one a night?" She knew it was foolish to persist. The answer wouldn't please her but she couldn't stop herself. "More than that?" She looked down, hoping he wouldn't notice her worrying. With that much experience he would have certain expectations. He'd notice when she didn't know what in the hell she was doing.

Two lovers. Neither particularly adept at loving. And nothing about either experience was worth remembering. Oh, they'd both tried and tried and she'd tried, too, but as the saying goes *close only counts in horseshoes.*

"None since arriving in the States." He tilted her chin to him. "In eight hundred years I've never met a woman the likes of you, Sofia. Not one could compare."

She couldn't stop the silly smile from appearing or the warm flush that spread from her neck to her cheeks and chest.

"You should know. I was married before, when I was human." Dragomir leaned his hip on the counter and rested on his elbow. "She was the only woman I ever loved."

"What happened?" The giddy sensation tumbling inside her vanished. Now Sofia felt such sadness tears welled in her eyes. Dragomir seemed lost in a memory.

"She died. Our children died of illness, plague or something and she died of a broken heart." His gaze dropped to the floor. "Her name was Elena."

"I'm sorry." Sofia swiped the tear trickling down her cheek. "Were you married long?" How could she possibly feel such grief for not being his first wife? Good Lord, had she already had too much to drink?

"Ten or so years, maybe a bit more." He sighed. "I did not intend to make you cry tonight. You did enough of that last night." He caught a tear rolling down her face. "I forgot this happens."

"Tears? Vampires don't cry?" Sofia sniffled.

He smiled. "No. I forgot about the emotions of mates. We feel each other's emotions." He brushed his fingers along her cheek. "For so long I've tried not to think about too many details from my life. It hurt too much. And now you've made me remember. Here you shed tears I've refused to acknowledge."

"How many children?" Sofia's voice was soft, interested but guarded. She didn't want to make him feel worse, but she wanted to know about his life. Who he was, what he did, and how he became a vampire.

"Three. Two boys. One girl." Dragomir smiled.

The zing of pride sizzled inside Sofia. Hot, happy pride.

"Energetic. Beautiful. So full of life. Inquisitive, every one of them." He seemed lost in the memories. "Two like their mother. The boys." He chuckled. "My girl, like me, only pretty."

Sofia watched him, her head tilted to the side. She enjoyed the warm feeling of happiness. She doubted he'd felt it in quite a while. "They sound wonderful."

"They were." He drained his glass.

"When did *this* happen?" She waved her hand at him. "The vampire situation."

"Ah, the vampire situation." He chuckled. "Interesting reference."

Sofia's stomach growled.

They both looked down and Sofia's hands pressed to her abdomen.

"I might have something somewhere." Dragomir opened cupboards. Each door he opened revealed it was truly empty except the cupboards to the right of the sink. Those held glasses, plates, and bowls.

"I'm fine. Really. The vodka is plenty." Her stomach growled even louder, and she squirmed in her seat.

"You're hungry."

"Honestly, Dragomir, I'm fine." She poured more vodka into her glass then filled his. "You're avoiding the question."

He bent to look under the sink. "No. I'm trying to keep you comfortable. You're my mate, remember?" He walked past her to the pantry. "My job is to care for you." He unlocked the door and stepped inside.

"I can take care of myself," Sofia called after him. "The cafeteria is open."

"Here. These are for you." He placed a box of Thin Mints on the counter in front of her.

She stared at the box for a moment and then giggled. "For me? You bought these with me in mind?"

"Not exactly," he mumbled. "Do cookies last long? I bought these in March." He picked them up and turned them around. "Shouldn't there be a date on here somewhere?"

"I thought you'd only been in the States a few days?"

"I was here for a board meeting to discuss hiring an Employee Relations Manager." One eyebrow rose. "For the record I was against it. Crazy to put a human in danger." He pushed her hair off her shoulder. "But look what I'd have missed if I'd won my argument."

Sofia didn't know whether to scream ah-ha or to let the flicker of excitement grow. She'd known he thought her job was foolish but now they were married. He didn't expect her to quit working, did he?

"I don't intend to sit around unemployed," she said.

"I have no doubt you plan to continue your crusade of doing away with violence in our world. I just hope you'll be much more realistic in your expectations." He handed her the box of cookies and stood behind her picking grass from her hair. "Eat your dinner."

"Why do you have a box of Girl Scout Cookies?" She leaned into his touch and Dragomir's stomach grumbled.

He reached around and tore open the box.

Sofia squirmed. "You're mushy!" She giggled. "Tell me. Why did you buy them?"

"Who are you calling mushy?" He dumped the box on the counter and two sleeves of cookies tumbled out.

"You. Tough guy."

"I like to support the local youth."

She laughed. "Liar."

He smiled. "I am not." He ripped open the bag and held it for Sofia to take a cookie. "I do like to support the local youth, especially blue-eyed, toothless-grinning little girls in brown uniforms."

"Ah, a weakness for women in uniform." She bit into the chocolate-covered biscuit. "Try one. You might like it."

He held up a little round disc covered in chocolate, turned it around, and studied it from all angles. Then he sniffed it.

"It's a chocolate mint cookie, not a poisonous flower. Just put it in your mouth." She nudged his hand.

He licked the rim, rubbing his tongue back and forth over one spot. Then he sucked his tongue.

Sofia suddenly felt hotter. She knew full and well his actions had been tactical in nature—understand the cookie, not make Sofia hot and bothered. But his tongue slowly rubbing back and forth over the cookie had just that effect.

She adjusted the straps and neckline of her cami, opened another bottle of water and chugged it.

"When did you run into a Girl Scout? I didn't know they sold cookies in the woods." She tossed the empty bottle into the trash. "No wait, wait." She waved her hands in front of her. "I know. They were selling door-to-door in the Lower Level, right? I wonder what badge they'd earn for that. Definitely survival." She tossed her head back and laughed. "I can just see them knocking on a door and coming face to face with The Board." She was near hysterics, holding on to the counter. "A little troop of Girl Scouts pulling wagons of cookies. Ha!" She dabbed the corners of her eyes with her fingers. "Can you imagine the shock on everyone's faces?"

Dragomir smirked. "Why do you think I lied?" He bit the edge of the cookie. "It's not bad." He broke off another small piece.

"I could feel it." Sofia sniffed and sighed.

Dragomir handed her a paper towel.

She blew her nose. "You were all warm and gooey and then you got all hard and cold." She shrugged her shoulders. "Sounds weird but that's the best I can explain."

He nodded and licked the chocolate off his lips. "I'll have to remember that."

She popped a whole cookie into her mouth and crunched for a bit. "Right. No lying. Your wife will find out."

"I can tell when you aren't being truthful as well." He watched her.

She licked her lips. "When?" She inhaled then held the breath deep in her lungs before glancing up at him. She'd been lying quite a bit around him. From the first moment she laid eyes on him. He couldn't have possibly known all this time. She picked up the box and pretended to read the ingredients.

"You were afraid of Rick. Even though you said you weren't."

"Yeah. I lied." Well, if that was all he offered, she wasn't digging for more on this topic.

Her stomach growled.

"I knew you were hungry even when you said you weren't."

She smiled. "You still haven't answered my questions. I know what you're doing."

If he thought he'd managed to evade her, he was in for a surprise. She didn't give up anything that easily.

"We'll start slow. Tell me how you ended up with Girl Scout cookies."

His smile made her knees weak. She looked right at him, straight into his eyes. For once she wasn't afraid he'd somehow turn the tables. She knew she had him running.

"I needed juice and a few other necessities so I went to the grocery store on a Saturday early one evening. The little buggers had a table. They asked me if I wanted to buy some. I couldn't say no."

She beamed. "So little girls can wrap you around their fingers with just a box of cookies." She held up the Thin Mints.

He leaned on the counter only inches from her face. "Big girls can, too."

She blinked. He pulled the box from her hand and set it on the counter. Then he slid the edge of a cookie along her lips. The smile on his face was absolutely devilish. "Open."

She did and the cookie touched her tongue. She bit down, and he pulled the remainder of the cookie away, grinning. Then he ate the rest.

"You seem to like cookies," he said.

She felt his excitement. Wow, but he was good. Well, with enough vodka two could play at this game. She poured another shot. "I like it when you feed me." She pressed the glass to her lips and sipped. The cool liquid ran down her throat. She slid her tongue over her lips slowly.

He smiled and picked up another cookie. "For a woman with so few lovers you're quite a flirt." He touched the cookie to her lip. When she opened her mouth, he pulled it away and bit it.

She watched him wide-eyed. "I do what it takes to get what I want. How did you become a vampire?"

"Really?" He offered the cookie to her, watching her like she might bite him. Sofia opened her mouth and the minty biscuit slid in. His fingers brushed her lips.

She blinked up at him.

Dragomir poured them each more vodka. "After Elena's death the solitude made me crazy. I searched for trouble. Every chance I got I jumped at the opportunity to meet my death. When I finally thought I'd meet my maker, it didn't turn out as I'd hoped. Andrei gave me death. Then gave me life. And every day and night since I've relived that moment." He placed the bottle on the counter.

Sofia sat silently. The heat from only moments ago dissipated, replaced by a cold loneliness. "I'm sorry. I didn't mean to make you feel badly." She squeezed his hand. "I only wanted to know how it happened."

"And now you do." He brushed his thumb over her fingers.

She came around the counter to stand in front of him. "At least you know where you came from. Parts of me are still a mystery." She laced her fingers around his neck.

He pulled her up into his arms. "One I wouldn't mind unraveling."

# CHAPTER TWENTY-EIGHT

The anticipation of kissing Sofia was almost more than Dragomir could stand. He pressed his lips to her mouth, and she kissed him with such force he thought she'd consume him. Her tongue danced with his, gliding along his, delving into him with no inhibition.

He carried her to the sleeping chamber and placed her on the bed. The floral woodsy scent of their union perfumed the air.

He tugged her top down without breaking the kiss. Her hands flew to the button of his jeans and she unbuttoned and unzipped them without hesitation. Before she reached inside and took hold of him, he caught her hand. "Slow. There's no hurry." He whispered the words against her ear, making sure he breathed along her skin and enjoying the shiver that rocked through her.

"Don't you want me to touch you?" She panted.

"Yes, of course. But no rush." Dragomir wasn't surprised by her rush to touch him. She'd only had two lovers and it didn't sound like they'd been magnificent. "There is such a thing as foreplay in spite of what you may have been told." He nibbled her ear.

"Oh." She swallowed loudly. "You want to do that?" Her body tensed. "I should probably shower first."

Dragomir pulled back from her and smiled.

"I'm sweaty so it's probably best if we just…you know…call it quits for a bit." She wiggled out from under him. "The shower?"

Dragomir pointed toward the bathroom and watched her scurry off to the shower. He rolled onto his back and lay spread across his bed listening to the water run. She had no clothes to put on when she finished and he loved that fact. He waited three more minutes then went to his mate.

The whole room was steamed. He could barely make out the outline of her body inside the glass stall. Her arms were raised above her head working shampoo into her hair. Full round breasts came in and out of focus with the flow of the steam. Shapely hips turned to reveal her lovely round ass.

He dropped his jeans to the floor and opened the glass door.

Sofia gasped when he stepped inside. "What—"

"I worked out, too. A shower seems like a very good idea." He crowded his way under the stream of water and watched Sofia watch him.

Suds bubbled in her hair. They sluiced down her chest, foamy waves gliding between her breasts to be captured in the dark curls between her legs. Her mouth formed a perfect O and she blinked wide eyes at him. She lowered her hands to cover her breasts.

Dragomir shampooed his hair, then rinsed, keeping his back to the glass door and Sofia in front of him. He lathered his chest and underarms then slid soapy hands downward.

Sofia's attention followed his hands and one eyebrow arched as she watched his cock harden with every foamy stroke. He took great care to linger with each stroke and enjoyed the way her breasts rose and fell as she watched.

She sucked in a fast breath. "My eyes." She reached out for the water, eyes closed against the suds trailing from her hair.

Dragomir stepped aside and maneuvered her under the water. He tucked his fingers into her hair, working the suds clean and rinsing them from her face. "Better?"

She blinked up and nodded.

He turned her back to him and began soaping her body. First her neck, slow gentle swirls massaging her skin, then he worked his way to her ass.

His hand slid around her waist and he pulled her back against him, wedging his erection between her cheeks.

She gasped and jumped forward but he held her tight to him.

"Easy Sofia," he whispered against her ear as his free hand slid soap along her breasts and down to her belly.

Her head rested against his chest.

He replaced the soap on its rack and ran a filmy palm over her skin, cupping her breast. Sofia's heartbeat picked up, pounding through her breast so quickly he felt it vibrating against his palm. Her breaths became rapid though shallow. Dragomir's lips traced her ear and moved lower.

"Sofia."

She looked over her shoulder at him, water dripping from long lashes.

His lips came to hers. He held her full breast in one hand and let the other hand slide lower to work its way through the nest of curls.

Her mouth opened and she kissed him. Her hand came up to his neck, holding him to her. She was hungry. He could tell by the soft moans, the way her body molded against his and the scent of her need.

She parted her legs and tilted her hips into him. Her other hand clung to his wrist, nails digging into his skin. He worked her soft wet clit, gently pressing his finger over and over, small circles that made her hips rock.

Her ass pressed against his cock and he moaned into her mouth. He held her tight against him, nearly lifting her from the floor. She pressed herself into his hand and wiggled against his fingers.

Two fingers worked quicker circles over the sensitive area. He squeezed her breast, wanting nothing more than to take it into his mouth and suck. He wanted to drop to his knees and trail his tongue from her nipple to her clit, lapping the water from her skin and driving her over the edge.

She broke their kiss and cried out as her body arched against his. His fingers moved faster until her hand slid down to his and she tried to pull his fingers away.

But he didn't release her. Instead his fingers slid between her legs. Her hand moved back to his wrist. His fingers slipped inside her. Hot and wet, she was ready. He bent a little lower. His mouth came to her neck and he licked his way from her earlobe to her shoulder and back, slowly lapping at the water mixed with salty sweat.

Her release perfumed the shower making him harder. He had to taste her, all of her. When he removed his fingers, she whimpered.

He turned her to face him and pulled her up into his arms. Her mouth came to his, eagerly searching for more. She locked her arms around his neck, and as he picked her up, she fastened her legs around his hips. He backed her against the wall and she lurched into his chest.

"Cold." She relaxed back against the tile.

He groaned when her hot, wet center bore down on him. "Now?" she asked and nodded. "Yes," she answered her own question, positioning herself just above his tip.

"Yes." He smiled and pushed up as she lowered herself onto him.

She held her breath and stared at him until he was firmly buried deep within her. Then she gasped. "You're big."

He couldn't stop smiling. "Yes." He raised her up an inch or two and lowered her.

She exhaled, bit her lip, and let her head fall back against the wall. "Again."

He was more than happy to oblige her breathy demand and raised her up a little further then lowered her more slowly, intensifying her pleasure.

"Again," she whispered. Her eyes closed. Her hands gripped his shoulders. She held him, but not firmly enough to support herself. She was letting Dragomir support her, care for her, please her.

His mouth came to her neck and he kissed her over and over as he slowly raised her up so that only the tip of his cock stayed inside her then he lowered her down to take all of him inside.

Her breathing began to match his movements. Heavy exhales with each plunge into her and long inhales with every ride up. She moaned and ground herself down onto him each time he thrust into her.

She bit her lip so hard she drew blood.

He sucked her lip and it drove him crazy. He pushed into her faster, breaking his slow rhythm.

She cried out and ground herself onto him with such force she nearly slipped from his hands. Her arms wrapped around his shoulders in a grip so tight he knew if he let go, she'd stay in place. Sofia rode him hard. Her thighs squeezed his hips so tightly she was bound to be bruised.

"Harder. Please Dragomir. Please."

Who was he not to give his mate what she needed? He kept one arm firmly around her hips. The other hand hit the wall above them, bracing them in place. He drove into her, matching the fast rocking pace she'd set.

She screamed. Her breasts pressed to his chest. Her head tilted back. Water streamed between them. "Take me. Take all of me. I know you want to."

He did. He wanted to taste every inch of her. He wanted to mark her during lovemaking the way a mate claims what's his.

But he could not. He couldn't do it without knowing for sure she understood.

"Sofia."

"You don't want me?" She looked at him and the beautiful expression of ecstasy left her face. She appeared as though she might cry.

"Why do you think that?" He kissed her lips. "What have I done that leads you to think I don't want you?" Dragomir held her firmly, ignoring her attempts to wiggle free. "Tell me."

"You said we could die soon." She put her chin on his shoulder and tried to lower her legs.

"You were sobbing hysterically, love. I was trying to please you." He kissed her cheek. "And I was trying not to blubber with you." He kissed her again and pressed her against the wall, squeezing her thighs in his hands.

Sofia wrapped her legs around him again. "What do you mean?"

"We feel each other's emotions, remember? I was tempted to drive the car off the nearest bridge, then stake myself." He waited for her to look at him.

When finally she did, her eyes shined with unshed tears.

"I've loved you from the moment I saw you, Sofia."

"You have?" She batted her eyelashes at him and looked down at his neck again.

He tilted her face to his. "Yes. I never thought I'd love again, never wanted to. But I won't live without you. I can't. I can't stand the thought of losing you."

"Then why won't you bite me?"

He smiled. "Because I want you to know what you're offering before I take it." His heart sped. Now he would review the union of true mates. He'd explain it so she understood. If she chose to leave, he'd have no choice but to live away from her, to try not to go mad until her natural death.

She rocked her hips. "I already know our lives are tied to each other."

Whether it was her rhythmic movements or the way she blinked those green eyes, Dragomir couldn't say, but his cock hardened again.

He gripped her hips, stopping her from distracting him. He had to ensure she knew before she drove him too far.

"Our lives will become as one. This is not the place for us to discuss this, not like this." Dragomir untangled them, lifted her up and off him, and placed her on her feet in front of him much to both their disappointments.

"I'm not getting out of the shower," she said. "You explain it here. I was having a good time." Her hands went to her hips.

He shook his head. He'd been having a good time, too as was clearly evidenced by his still throbbing erection.

"If we drink from each other while making love, we will seal our union. At this moment you can still walk away. It won't be comfortable, but you could live apart from me." Dragomir positioned Sofia back under the water when he saw goose bumps rise on her skin. "To consummate our joining will force you to be with me. You won't be able to leave. Your freedom to walk away, to have a life without me ends. You will need me."

"We both drink?" Her nose twitched.

# CHAPTER TWENTY-NINE

"Yes. We must both drink." Dragomir's gaze on Sofia was unyielding.

She stepped forward to allow the water to drill into her back, which suddenly tensed as though she'd been the one holding him up for the last twenty minutes. "We already did that."

"The true bond is formed during the act of love, when we give ourselves to each other completely with no reservations, with no threats or worries."

He was nervous. Sofia felt it. His emotions were jumbled. Excited, happy, frightened, worried. She'd never noticed so many things before, not even in herself. She didn't like seeing him worry.

"I cannot allow you to enter into this without fully understanding." He shivered.

Sofia pulled him under the water. "Tell me then." She held his hands and looked up at him. There were so many things she needed to know. She just wished they could have found another moment to discuss them.

"The bond of true mates is more powerful than anything else. It transcends life, death, the afterlife. You would be swearing yourself to me, agreeing to be at my side, to take my place in all matters, even battles."

Sofia reached for the knob this time. Maybe this really wasn't the best place for the discussion. "But I'm not a vampire. I'm not even half as strong as you, and I'm no warrior. I don't understand any of the vampire rules." She turned off the water and stepped out of the shower into the towel Dragomir held for her.

"The laws, I can teach you over time. There's no need to understand them all now. It's the commitment you must acknowledge." He stood in front of her naked, gingerly rubbing a towel over her hair.

She couldn't help but notice his arousal. The desire to touch him crept back over her. If she didn't have so many questions, she wouldn't have been able to keep her hands off him.

"I thought we were already trapped together?" She forced her gaze up.

"Yes to an extent. But you could still choose to be away from me."

"Or you from me?"

"Yes, but that is not going to happen. I've made my decision. I've given my heart to you freely." He stopped massaging her hair.

"I did the same."

"You threw yourself between me and a stake. I believe it was a promise made under duress." He pulled a comb through her tangled hair, gently working out the knots. "You did it to avoid a violent outcome."

"I would do it again." She unwrapped the towel from around her and dried Dragomir's chest. "I can't explain why I feel this way. I just know as sure as I'm standing here that I would do it again and as plain as day I feel a connection with you all the way into my soul."

"You will never remove the violence of my world, Sofia." His hands caught the towel as she began to rub his belly. "You must accept that you live in a different world than before, one where you will be tested. You will be required to defend yourself and possibly to strike first."

"I know." She could barely think the words aloud. Actually hearing them come out of her mouth was nearly a shock. But she said them, staring up into his eyes. "I know this world is different. I don't understand it all. I know it's not Disneyland. But if this is where you are, it's where I want to be."

The tingling began in Sofia's neck. It traveled down her abdomen, to her toes and out to her fingertips. Her head tingled as though every strand of hair was energized. Dragomir's woodsy-soapy scent came to her. Only now it was perfumed with something sweet, flowery. She breathed in the aroma, wanting to hold it inside her forever.

Dragomir inhaled a slow breath. "Do you see it? Our bond holds us together."

She didn't see it. She felt it. Just as she felt the connections the wolves had, she recognized her bond to Dragomir. As two energies flowed together into each other she felt them merge to one, stronger together than alone, bound by some metaphysical force. Warm, hot even, but cool to the touch. Comforting and strong. Powerful yet soft. It wrapped around them and Sofia couldn't help but fall into it.

She sighed. "I feel it. I feel you, your love. Take mine. Keep it in your heart forever." She pressed her hands to his chest.

Dragomir gasped and threw back his head. He jerked Sofia into his embrace, holding her tight against him, and moaned loudly.

She licked her way across his chest, catching one of his nipples between her teeth and sucking.

"Ah. Sofia." He drew out her name and shuddered. His hands held her in place. His head rested on hers.

After a moment of listening to his ragged breathing Sofia giggled.

His hands came to her neck and he cupped her face. "You surprise me at every turn, my love."

She smiled. "Well, who knew that could happen?" She certainly had no idea she could give him an orgasm just by touching his chest. That had never happened to her before. "Must be an erogenous zone." She traced circles over his heart.

"I had heard of such things. Just never experienced…" He grinned and his voice dropped to a low, throaty growl. Then he yanked the towel from between them and picked her up, peppering her cheeks and neck with kisses. "Let me show you what I can do."

# CHAPTER THIRTY

Sofia lay panting beside Dragomir. He drew a lazy zigzag pattern up and down the inside of her thigh and she shuddered, nearly into convulsions. He fought to hide a surge of pride. Her head rolled toward him and her eyes fluttered open. "Stop that. You've done quite enough for one night."

"Hardly." He turned her on her side and cuddled her in the curve of his body. Her hair fanned out on the pillow above them. He nestled into it, willing to let her rest, but ready to take her again.

He'd pleased her quite well. Her limp body was testament to that. Those big doe eyes that had stared up at him when he first brought her to the bed had morphed into the most seductive pair of bedroom eyes he'd ever seen. She'd hardly needed any prompting to unleash her inner vixen.

She wasn't skilled and hadn't seen a lot. Two facts that pleased him more than he could ever explain. The thought of another man's hands, lips, or any other part on Sofia made Dragomir's vision fade to black and white. He'd gladly kill anyone who even thought about touching her.

Sofia sighed and snuggled further under the blanket. She yanked the pillow down under her chin, rolling it into a ball to fit in the curve of her neck. "Good night," she mumbled.

"Good night, love." He kissed her cheek and placed his head on the tiny corner of the pillow she hadn't claimed. Maybe he wouldn't get another. He certainly didn't mind sharing. He couldn't have been more comfortable with her in his bed. He tightened his hold.

He planned to keep her in bed for a few days. Food. He'd need to order some food for her. If he hadn't been so damn comfortable, he'd have gotten up then to get it, but there was no way he'd leave her side the first night he had her, not even to acquire items to please her.

He watched the glittering cloud swirl above them. Their bond. He grinned. She was his and he, hers. Given freely to each other. Soon that faint cloud shimmering in the night would illuminate their quarters. It would be all the light they'd need. And even when the bond was sealed so tightly no one else could see it, they'd still be able to call upon it to guide them.

He replayed her soft pleas in his mind. "Take from me. Seal us together. Forever." She'd tilted her head back, offering the tender flesh of her neck. But he'd already marked her there.

When he'd shaken his head, she gasped, eyes flooding so quickly Dragomir almost bit her to stop the tears. "Why?" All the seduction drained from her voice, leaving only hurt and worry. "Not there." He kissed his way to her breast, sucked the nipple into his mouth. "Not here, either."

The so recent memory of the most perfect moments of his existence made him hard. He lay behind her solid as a rock and wanting very much to wake her with a good hard orgasm. But he restrained himself, replaying the moment in his head. "Where?" A breathier whisper filled with desire had never been spoken. He'd kissed her belly, suckled her hips, poised his open mouth on her inner thighs and grinned. Her heart raced. Her sweet scent filled the air. He followed it to the source. "Here." He licked her clit then dove lower, sliding his tongue inside her so fast she bucked into him.

He watched her back arch, breasts pointed to the ceiling. Her hands bunched in his hair. She tried to wrap her legs around him, but he pinned them open, wanting to see every move she made.

Sofia had screamed his name when his tongue found the spot that brought her to come. Her sweet juices flowed and he drank her, like a drunken man he drank. When she began to relax and he knew she thought he was finished, he bit and sent her spiraling into her next round of orgasms. This time she cried. Tears rolled down her temples, and she begged him never to leave her, never to stop. "Promise you'll always love me."

The demand brought him up to kiss her lips. "Always. Until the end of days."

"Let me drink from you again." Another demand holding more than just possession. Love.

He pulled a knife from his bedside table and pierced the skin over his heart. "No. Your neck."

He brought the blade to his throat. "Why? Why not near my heart?"

"I want everyone to see you're mine." She wrapped her hand over his and nodded.

Dragomir sliced into his skin. Sofia pushed him down, pinned him beneath her, and drank from him. As the slash began to heal she bit into his neck, clamping her blunt teeth around the wound. Pain seared into him until she sucked it away.

Just the memory of her taking from him, claiming him as her own brought him too close to the edge. He nuzzled her neck. "Sofia. Wake up, love. I want you again."

"So soon?" She started to roll toward him.

"Stay. I want you now." He hooked his hand under her thigh and pulled her top leg up then slid into her, burying himself as far as he could.

"Oh." The surprised moan didn't help to contain him.

"Don't say anything else. I'll never last."

She didn't, but the soft giggle unleashed him and he roared as he held her against him and pumped into her, stroking, kissing, squeezing, praying he'd be able to hold on for long enough. It was a miracle they were so well matched. If she'd lasted any longer, he'd have ended in misery for not pleasing her.

"You're insatiable." She panted and pushed her hair away from her face and neck.

"Only when it comes to you." His leg draped over hers.

She was right. He was insatiable. The moment he pulled out of her he wanted to be inside her again or tasting her or kissing her. He hadn't experienced this feeling of excitement and unbridled desire since his transformation. It was very much like being a new vampire. Lustful, hungry, needy. Wild emotions colliding with common sense.

He'd need to get a hold of himself, if he wanted to keep her happy and not hurt.

"Dragomir?" Sofia twisted around to face him.

He raised his leg so she didn't struggle, but lowered it right down the moment she stopped moving.

"Tell me when you did it first." Her fingers played in the hair on his chest.

He wasn't sure he could remember that far back. It was with Elena. Of that he was certain. . "Well, on my wedding night—"

"Not that." She smoothed her hand over his cheek and onto his jawbone. "The first time you gave me your blood. Why don't I remember?"

Apparently, there were topics that could dampen his desire. He sighed and rolled onto his back.

*****

Twenty minutes later she sat on the couch in one of his shirts, seething. "So our whole marriage is built on a lie?"

"No." He placed a glass of juice on a coaster on the coffee table in front of her.

"Oh, yes it is. You lied." She glared at him. "I married you because I believed you."

"You married me because Fergus and Jankin were going to execute me." He drained his bottle of cherry juice. "Drink your juice. You're pale."

"Weren't they? You were in that predicament because you lied." She gulped from her glass. "And if I'm pale, it's your fault."

"Yes, Fergus would have. And I would not have stopped him." Dragomir stood across the room. He almost couldn't look at her. The return of her disgust of him was so painful. It hurt to think she hated him. But there it was written all over her face.

"So, I should have just let them stab you with that stake? Is that what you're saying?" She slammed her glass onto the coaster.

He didn't respond. Part of him thought it might have been better for her if she'd just let him die. Living without him, without truly experiencing love, might have been better than living with someone she wouldn't trust. But then she'd never know the truth and she deserved that much.

"No. I'm not saying that at all. I'm grateful for what you did."

"Well, of course you are. You're alive and fucking me." She stared right through him. If looks could kill she'd redefine the word violent.

"I lied to protect you—"

"Protect me? Protect me?" She bolted off the couch. "By fucking me?"

"You and Jankin."

"What?" She looked around as though she might be scavenging for a weapon. Little did she know the only weapon she needed against him was that look of disgust. He'd stake himself to avoid seeing it ever again.

"You drank from Jankin, not me." He hadn't wanted to be the one to tell her, but he wouldn't allow her to believe a lie. "When you were born, Jankin saved your life."

Her mouth hung open. She clutched her chest. "He delivered me," she whispered. "A preemie."

"You would not have survived without him." Dragomir stepped toward her. "Your father begged him to help."

"Don't touch me." She backed toward the sleep chamber. "You're all liars. Every last one of you." She ran from the room and slammed a door shut.

# Chapter Thirty-One

Sofia lay in bed, weeping. Where were her parents when she needed them? Dead. Why hadn't Dr. MacDuff sought to save *their* lives? He'd stood at both their bedsides when they passed. His eyes had glistened with unshed tears.

"What an actor."

He hadn't cared about them. Or her. If he had, he'd have never let her lose them both.

Now she was swept up in a world that didn't belong to her, eternally bound to a stranger. She looked around the room. The bedside lamp cast a dim light.

The foolish cloud floating in the atmosphere of the room pooled around her like a metaphysical blanket. It draped over the bed and wrapped across her shoulders. She brushed it away, trying to separate herself from the bond.

"Stupid thing." She hopped off the bed to pace, sending brilliantly sparkling particles scattering only to reform like a cape covering her shoulders and trailing behind her. When she reached the wall, she turned back and charged through the damn cloud, sending it tumbling aside before it reformed around her.

She gave up and ignored the gem-like nebula.

Nothing hung on the walls. No carpet warmed the hard floor. No windows opened to bright sunshine.

Sofia didn't even know the time. She wanted to go home, back to her house with her own things, sleep in her own bed, enjoy sunlight on her face.

Instead, she sat on the edge of a huge bed in a basement, hiding from the rest of the world.

She sniffled. There was no going home until this rose situation was fixed. She'd been put in danger by a maniac trying to send a message to Dr. MacDuff and Dragomir. They had put her life at risk. If she'd never met them, never had to know them, she'd be living in blissful ignorance and probably still working at her old job.

Her parents had begged him? Had they known what they were asking? Had they known she'd be sucked into this other world? They never mentioned what he'd done, never even hinted of something so absurd.

She needed to go home and scour the house for clues. Her mother must have known. She must have left some hint of what to do.

Her number one priority would be to go home. Get rid of the roses. Get the hell out of Cader. Then she'd find a new job. She'd move on with her life.

The cloud tumbled around her. Its colors jumbled with each other, no longer forming pretty waves. Instead, they crashed into each other in a frenzy of crystallized dust.

"If they want to beat the hell out of each other, so be it. Why should I care?" She waved her hands in front of her and barreled through the torrent of sparkling nonsense. "What do I care if they all kill each other? I don't. Let them live with no rules or policies or humanity."

The damn specks reorganized and clung to Sofia. Tears spilled down her cheeks. "Get off me!" She shook the weightless dots off and padded to the bathroom to blow her nose, slamming the door before any of them reached her.

She pressed a cool compress to her face and neck. "I'm leaving," she called to the cloud. "Don't touch me. Don't follow me. Don't even look at me."

Ten minutes later Sofia emerged from Dragomir's bedroom dressed in a pair of his dress slacks, belted at the waist and cuffed so she didn't trip over the ankles, and a black t-shirt underneath his button down, sleeves rolled to her wrists.

She was nothing if not annoyed that he'd tossed her clothes with his in the washer when he'd gone to get drinks for them between lovemaking sessions. "Sex sessions. Whore," she snapped. She'd been duped into bed by yet another man. He wasn't the first, but he'd be the last. She wasn't falling for anyone telling her he cared about her. Not ever again.

"I'm leaving." She stomped up the hallway barefoot. "Where are my shoes? Get off me!" She whipped her hands at the air surrounding her, sending sparkles spinning out of control. "Dragomir?"

He didn't bother to rise from the sofa or turn to face her. "Before you go you should speak to Jankin."

He wasn't stopping her? Why? This was too easy. "Fine. I'll let him know I'm leaving. Where is he?"

"Here, Sofia." Dr. MacDuff walked in from the kitchen holding Sofia's shoes. "But before you try to leave. It's time I told you the truth."

Sofia nodded once. "Yeah. It is." Her hands fisted. Of all the things she hadn't expected, the urge to punch Dr. MacDuff's lights out was high up there. She breathed heavily, trying to calm the brewing anger. She wanted to kick the crap out of someone, and he was the perfect target. He started all this. He should pay.

*Why do I want to hit him?* The question didn't stay unanswered for long. *Dragomir. This is all his doing.*

Crystals hovered between Sofia and Dragomir.

*That damn bond.* She swatted at the cloud. When that did nothing to disperse the glittery fuzz, Sofia glared at Dr. MacDuff.

For the first time in all the years she'd known him, Dr. MacDuff seemed weak. The pallor of his skin was not clear, not smooth. He appeared ill. His eyes were no longer green. They were darker, nearly black. "Come. Sit."

For a brief second she believed she could pummel him into the ground, just beat him to a pulp and then be free. Dragomir had said he wouldn't force her to stay. She wouldn't have to try to escape him. He'd let her walk out.

"Sit, Sofia. Your rage at Jankin or me will only make you less safe. Do not react foolishly." Dragomir wore only the pants he'd pulled on when they'd begun arguing. A multitude of crystal particles coated him.

"Don't tell me about my rage. You have no idea what I'm feeling. Even with this…stupid…" She waved her arms around her. "…thing surrounding me."

Jankin smirked.

"Don't laugh at me." Sofia snatched her shoes from Dr. MacDuff's hands, dropped them to the floor, and crammed her feet into them.

"I am not laughing at you. I'm simply admiring your bond." He motioned to the aura encircling Sofia and Dragomir.

"Yeah, well, I'm not taking this with me when I leave." She swatted at the cloud.

"Oh, you should get acquainted with it. It's a permanent bond, as your mate has explained." Dr. MacDuff sat in the chair across from Dragomir, leaving only the couch for Sofia.

She marched around the back and sat on the arm.

The space between Dragomir and Sofia filled with millions of sparkling flecks, leaving only a thin layer surrounding either of them. It was like having a third person sitting between them.

Dr. MacDuff smiled. "It's a very strong bond."

"Just get on with it. What lies have you fed me?" Sofia did her best to ignore the calm aura pulsing beside her. The damn thing was trying to influence her. It behaved like a low, soothing essence. It apparently had no idea how angry it was making her. The more it tried to calm her, the more she wanted to grab a vacuum and suck the damn thing into it.

"As you know your father was a good friend of mine. Your mother's pregnancy was very unexpected and very much desired." Dr. MacDuff smiled. "I helped your father paint the nursery."

Sofia threw her hand in the air. "That didn't give you any right to make me drink vampire blood." She scowled.

"Six weeks earlier than intended." He stared at the floor. "My best friend begged me to save his baby. Your mother offered her own life for yours." He folded his hands in his lap. "She bargained. If one life had to end, she begged me to take hers and spare you."

When he lifted his face, tears ran from his eyes. "I did wrong. I broke our most sacred law to save you. I loved your parents like my own family. The moment I saw you I loved you like my own child. We couldn't lose you."

Sofia swallowed back tears, remembering her mother telling her how special she was, how much she was loved. Her mother's voice played in her mind over and over. "Uncle Jankin loves you. You're special to him." Then the warning—" Only go to Cader with me or Daddy or Uncle. Never alone."

"You should never have done it," Sofia whispered and swiped at tears trickling down her cheeks. "No good deed goes unpunished, Uncle."

Jankin nodded.

"If she'd known what would happen to me, she'd have never allowed it."

"Child, if you believe that, you didn't know your mother very well." Jankin removed a handkerchief from his breast pocket and wiped his eyes. "If your mother ever saw the bond you've created with Dragomir, she'd have thanked The Heavens for vampires."

Sofia hated that he was right. She hated that he'd known her parents so well. Ever the romantic, Sofia's mom would have been dazzled by the damn entity billowing between her and Dragomir. "How long had they known you were *this?*"

"I met your father when he was a boy, befriended him in the woods behind your home. He was a smart boy. He figured me out or maybe I let him." Jankin sighed as though lost in an old memory. "We told your mother shortly after your parents became engaged."

"Did you bite them?" Sofia leaned forward, eager to hear if he'd fed from her parents. She'd kill him herself.

His eyes faded to green. "Not once, though they both offered. I respected them both, Sofia. I never betrayed that."

"No." She laughed harshly. "You think this..." She waved through the aura beside her. "...was not a betrayal? You're sadly mistaken. This was the ultimate betrayal."

"Your mother would disagree." Jankin's attention fell on the center of the couch. He regarded the aura with a slight smile. "She wanted nothing more than for you to find love. She wanted you to know what she had with your father. This is exactly what she had in mind."

Sofia glanced at the sparkling wave then through to the vampire on the other side. Dragomir couldn't have looked more miserable if he was waiting for a root canal. He stared ahead, not making eye contact with either her or Jankin. His jaw was set and his eyes were darker than she'd ever seen.

"She would not have approved of the way it was made." She cast a sideways glance at Jankin.

"She would have known—" Jankin began.

"Why did you let him lie?" Sofia pointed toward Dragomir, disturbing the gently rolling wave between them.

"If I had not and the truth was known, you'd never be safe, not even here," Jankin answered.

"That brings us to fate. I was not supposed to live. You are not God. You had no right." She could hardly believe she was saying she should die, but that was the reality. She hadn't been meant to live.

"I don't believe one's fate is cast in stone. Every decision affords a new opportunity."

Sofia stared at Jankin without any sense of how she felt. She'd gone past rage, to heartbreak, to incredulity, to not feeling a damn thing. "And now death waits for me just outside Cader. Poisonous roses grown just for me." She shook her head, realizing how difficult this situation had become. "Now more people than you or Dragomir or my parents must offer your lives to save me. I can't let that happen."

She stood to leave.

"I knew the moment I introduced you to Dragomir you belonged together. If not for that, I'd have never allowed him to bear this burden. You are his true mate. There is none other for him. Nor for you."

Another lie. Sofia was sure of it. She couldn't live a life of lies.

"If that's true, then we weren't meant to have love." She walked out the door.

# CHAPTER THIRTY-TWO

The cafeteria was empty, which was just as well. Sofia was in no mood to hide her feelings and put on a professional face. She really wanted to break something.

"You did not honestly think you'd make it out of the building. Did you?" Noelle opened another chart and skimmed a patient's record.

Sofia bit the spoon as she pulled it out of her mouth, letting her teeth slide along the metal. She'd gotten as far as the stairwell leading up to the ground floor before Fergus caught her. She'd had no choice but to agree to stay with Noelle until the Black Magic Roses had been cleared out of her house and the greenhouse behind the farm.

Apparently, being a mate meant you could be the bossiest prick on the planet and it was acceptable. She'd stood in the stairwell arguing about whether she should or shouldn't leave Cader with Fergus, Jankin, and Osgar for twenty minutes before Dragomir made an appearance.

"I forbid you to leave the building," was all he said, then he rushed past her, up the stairs and out onto the ground floor, his black duster flapping in his wake.

Sofia had marched up the stairs demanding to know just who he thought he was but he'd left the building before she'd made it to the top step and out of the fake supply closet. When she'd tried to exit the building the damn sparkles attacked, surrounding her and holding her captive.

"What the—?" She was held suspended a half-foot off the ground until she stopped fighting.

Of course, once her feet hit the floor she tried to leave again and had the same experience. And, stubborn as she was she kept trying to find a way past the damn bond.

It was Noelle who finally tired of the situation and carried her back downstairs. "Come on. Let's get you some decent clothes."

So here she sat across from Noelle in the Cader cafeteria wearing borrowed clothes and eating split pea soup at midnight with a swirly-twirly-sparkly dust cloud encasing her.

"It actually seems happy with itself," Sofia complained.

"Oh, it is. It's keeping you safely where your mate wants you." Noelle didn't bother to look up from the chart.

"I'm irritated."

"No kidding. Not a soul in the house could have figured that out." Noelle stacked the chart in the finished pile.

Sofia huffed.

"They'll be back shortly." Noelle sat back and smiled. "Ah, these don't look so bad." She tapped the charts. "The nurses are doing a fine job with documentation. I am doing a great job with this group."

*Not too smug, are you?* Sofia tried to keep a straight face. "How do you know?"

"About the charts or the return of the team sent to deal with your roses?" Noelle shuffled the charts around, placing them in alphabetical order.

"The team." Strained calm coated Sofia's answer.

"With Dragomir and Jankin and the four wolves there's no way it will take long to clean out the house."

"What about the farm?" Sofia wondered if she could possibly get lucky enough to have this whole episode end in one night.

"Jankin sent a contingency to the farm. They'll wait for the others to finish the task at your house then together they will deal with whatever's happening on the farm." Noelle smiled. "Not to worry. Dragomir will be fine."

"I'm not worried about him," Sofia lied.

The cloud clung to her. It was like being hugged by a giant glitter storm. Sofia sighed.

"You're a terrible liar."

"Do vampires have radar for that?" Sofia dropped her spoon on her tray.

"Why? Heard it before?" Noelle smiled. "Your bond knows what you need. It's comforting you. I like to see it work." She tilted her head. "I've only ever gotten to see a bond like this once before when Jade and Dice first came back from their honeymoon. And I only saw it for a few minutes—the length of time it took him to carry her from the car to their quarters." She grinned.

"Did it ever occur to you that I might be agitated over being stuck here and then strapped to a vampire for eternity?" Sofia balled her napkin and threw it on the tray, too.

"Did it ever occur to you that everyone in this building might be worried about you? Or that everyone here cares for you and your mate? Or that Cader is actually where you belong and not in some unprotected little house by yourself where Jankin and Dragomir can do nothing but worry about you?" Her eyebrows pulled together, and she drummed her long fingers on the stack of files.

Sofia frowned. So now it was her fault they worried about her? She'd never asked for this, never once. It hadn't occurred to her to request a supernatural husband from the underworld. She rolled her eyes and stared at the parking lot.

"Your uncle and mate are the two highest ranking vampires in this branch of The Alliance. Their heads should be in the game not up your ass," Noelle hissed. She leaned over the stack of files. "Listen up. We're all tolerating a lot of bullshit with this no violence in the workplace crap. We've tried to play nice in the sandbox with you. And for the most part we like you. But if you think allowing your mate to sacrifice himself to please you is acceptable to anyone, you are sadly mistaken."

"What are you talking about?"

"If the right players are at the farm, Dragomir will make a trade tonight. Him for your safety." Noelle's eyes widened as her brows flicked up for a split second. "How's that for true love?"

"Why didn't he tell me?" Sofia leaned forward. "That's a horrible idea." She gripped the table with the sudden urge to toss it through the window.

Little pulses flowed over her skin and she huffed at the bond.

"Yeah, well that's what happens when you bind yourself or at least when you love the person you're bound to. You make sacrifices to please her." Noelle stood and gathered her stack of files. "Get your shit. We're going below."

Sofia cleared away her tray and followed Noelle to the security office.

"Any word Ray-Ray?" Noelle asked as they walked by the night vampire guard.

"Nothing yet. Should be soon. Can't take long for Jankin to torch the—" he stopped short.

Noelle glared.

"Torch the what?" Sofia asked.

"Never mind. Let's go." Noelle led the way to the Lower Level.

"Torch what?" Sofia repeated.

Ray-Ray looked from Noelle to Sofia. "Um…"

"Zip it, Ray-Ray," Noelle snapped from the stairs. "Let's go, Sofia."

Ray-Ray turned his back to Sofia and from the cold wall he presented she knew not to bother with any more questions.

"You'd better just tell me." Sofia jogged to keep up with Noelle. They went down the same corridor that led in the direction of Dragomir's place, but took a left and two right turns instead of following it to the end.

"In." Noelle held open the door and Sofia stepped over the threshold.

Noelle's place was much cozier than Dragomir's. Pictures hung on the walls. A fish tank bubbled in one corner. She had chairs and pillows and area rugs. She even had a TV, which she flipped on.

"You might as well get comfy. You're not going anywhere any time soon."

"I thought you said they'd be back shortly." Sofia sat on the overstuffed sofa.

"They will. But then they'll meet with the rest of The Board and decide what to do next. That's if Dragomir comes back. If he's already offered himself, then it's done and Jankin will meet with you to get you set up alone." Noelle kicked off her shoes and plopped into the reclining chair angled toward the TV. "Course, if that happens, you probably shouldn't come back to work here." She pointed the remote at the tube and surfed the channels. "It's a pity you don't love your mate. Most women would die for what you have. I know I sure would."

Sofia gulped. She'd wanted a friend. Someone to talk to, to spend some time with, but this wasn't what she'd had in mind. She'd hoped for someone who liked her.

"I never said I didn't love him." Sofia wasn't sure she'd ever said she did. But after the revelation from Jankin, she wasn't quite sure how she felt about anything.

"Well, if this is your display of love, I'd hate to see what over-the-top joy looks like." Noelle tossed her legs over the side of the chair.

Sofia pulled her feet under her and sat cross-legged. "This is all new for me."

"What? Caring for someone? Letting someone know you care? Or is it giving a damn about anything other than your policies and letting the wrong people have every opportunity to get away with shit?" Noelle dropped the remote in her lap and glanced toward Sofia. "Maybe you'd like to allow Kiernan to explain himself before we kick ass."

"I'm not sure I know what we're talking about."

"We're talking about you and Dragomir. Mates are a fated pairing." She gave Sofia a once-over. "Most spend years, sometimes centuries searching for one another. And most times they don't find each other. But you were pulled back from death, snatched right out of its hand and tenderly guarded, although Jankin certainly did not know how precious you were." She pointed the remote at Sofia. "If I could, I'd change your channels so you'd get a better picture. Dragomir will offer himself in your stead. Essentially, he'll be a prisoner until your natural death so that you can live a happy little existence without him."

Sofia's head pounded with the worst headache she ever remembered having. Her heart thumped erratically. The thought of Dragomir imprisoned because of her was too dreadful.

"Yeah, happy, happy Sofia. Then when you die, you can bet his death will be a long and drawn out, merciless slaying. Oh, fuck Dragomir. He's only your mate, right?" Noelle swept out of the room like she was racing to a fire. "I'm not sure I can even stand to look at you."

Sofia ran after Noelle. "It's not like that. I don't want—" A door slammed in her face. She didn't bother with the knob. She kicked the door and smashed it to the wall.

Noelle glanced up from her bed. She lay on her side, cuddling a gray kitten. "You're scaring my cat."

Sofia caught the door as it swung back toward her after slamming into the wall. "I don't want him to die or be tortured. I never asked him to do this. I want him to be happy and safe."

"Strange way of showing it." Noelle cooed at the kitten then kissed him between his ears. The cat purred happily.

"What do I need to do?"

"Well, you can't leave. He's forbidden it." Noelle glanced toward her. "Used your bond as it was meant—to bind you." She nuzzled the kitten. "A powerful thing, that glittery fuzzy cloud. You wouldn't expect it to have such far-reaching power."

Sofia studied the specks surrounding her. They swirled away with a push from her breath then resettled in their place. There were fewer now than when she was at Dragomir's. Only about half as many.

"Does that bossy prick move work from both sides?" she asked.

Noelle grinned and nodded.

# CHAPTER THIRTY-THREE

Sofia sat at her desk reading the training plan written by Rick and approved by Osgar. For the most part it seemed acceptable. Aside from the three references to inadequacies due to weakness, fear, and "plain stupidity" she thought it would work.

She rewrote the Workplace Violence Policy to include the training plan as outlined in the new addendum, edited the training plan to include language allowing for secondary placements for wolves not possessing the necessary skills to join the front lines, and scheduled a meeting for the next afternoon to discuss the new policy.

She glanced at the clock. Three-forty. It couldn't possibly take much longer. Patience was a virtue, just not one she'd ever possessed. "Practice makes perfect," she told herself.

"You can say that again," Noelle called from the conference room down the hall.

Sofia rubbed her neck. She'd never get used to vampires being able to hear everything. "If I'd known you were going to eavesdrop I'd have closed the door."

Noelle laughed. "I assumed you were speaking to me since we're the only people up here."

"I was just talking to myself." Sofia tapped her pen.

"You shouldn't do that too often," Noelle teased. Her voice carried down the hall and Sofia stared at the door half expecting to see her appear. "People will think you're crazy." She laughed again.

Sofia turned back to her computer, figuring that idea had already taken root.

When Dragomir arrived she'd talk with him, bargain with him, and then with Jankin. If they were truly meant to be together, they'd be equal partners in this bond. There'd be no more caveman moves from Dragomir, and he'd need to control his emotions. Sofia needed to figure out whether she was truly drawn to him or if she simply felt his desires. And Jankin would need to stay out of their relationship.

After reviewing three more policies and at least ten more job applications, she felt the team return. The wolves thundered across the land moving quickly on the trail of sleek and terrifying power. They followed Jankin, racing back to the stronghold with solid determination. But it was the shimmering aura that triggered her awareness of Dragomir. It practically did cartwheels when he set foot on Alliance soil.

Everywhere it touched her, Sofia tingled to the point of feeling jittery. "Stop that. You're making it much harder," Sofia ground out. She was absolutely determined to control this situation, not to be the weaker of the two, not to let him take charge. She'd ordered him back to Cader. She'd face the angry warrior's wrath. But it would be a lot easier if she didn't feel like she sat on pins and needles.

After an hour-long wait, Jankin knocked on her doorframe.

"You don't still need me so I'm heading down." Noelle peeked past Jankin with a slight smile. "Good luck, Sofia."

"Thanks."

"May I come in?" Jankin asked.

"Sure." Sofia closed the folder holding the applications. "Where is he?" Her mate was clearly in the building.

"In your quarters." Jankin leaned in the doorway. Dark, unruly curls crowned his head. Reddish stubble shadowed his chin.

"Growing a beard?"

He gave the slightest shake of his head. "You've never seen me so late in the night. I believe you'd call this a five o'clock shadow." He rubbed his palm over his chin. "He's not pleased."

"Why? Because I figured out what he was up to or because I learned how to control this?" She waved her arms out at her sides and light reflected off the sparkling wave.

"I surmise he's agitated over both pieces of information, though I think being commanded back to Cader was the most disturbing." He closed the door.

"Two can play at this game. I'm not living with the guilt of him being imprisoned while I live a decent life." Sofia tapped a red pen on the pack of sticky notes she'd been using.

Jankin sat in the chair across the desk. "Have you ever been in love? Real love."

Sofia shrugged. "What does it matter?"

Jankin folded his arms over his chest and regarded her. "Love so powerful it hurt to be away from him?"

"I don't see where you're going with this." She dropped the pen into the coffee mug beside the computer monitor where it joined several others.

"I'm wondering if you have anything for comparison. Any relationship that could help define the measurement of a mating bond."

Sofia hadn't been in love. She'd dated several men, liked many of them, not enough to continue dating them but she'd had relationships. She'd thought she loved the two men she allowed into bed but that proved to be incorrect. Though she'd liked them better than most of the others.

She shook her head. Why try to lie? He already knew the truth.

"Dragomir finds himself in a very unfamiliar position." Jankin leaned forward, resting his elbows on his knees. "For some six hundred plus years Dragomir's first thought has been his allegiance to The Alliance. He'd gladly lie down and die for this organization, if that would help its cause." Jankin glanced toward the floor then directly into Sofia's eyes. "Tonight he abandoned all logic and thought only to please his mate."

Sofia wanted to hold Jankin's gaze but she couldn't. The power behind his eyes was more than she'd ever realized. She glanced at the keyboard.

"He prepared to offer himself in order for you to be able to live without having to hide and without having to be with him." Jankin sat back. "He was prepared to bargain to ensure he was not killed during the duration of your natural lifetime. He had a strategy. He always has a strategy."

Sofia still couldn't look up. The tone of Jankin's voice told her she'd foiled Dragomir's plan and the disruption hadn't been well received.

"I never asked him to do that."

"He cannot help but love you. For him there was no other option."

"There's always another option," Sofia said.

"Not for true mates. There is only happiness for each other." Jankin crossed his ankles. "You love him, too."

Sofia's back stiffened.

"Don't try to deny it. You've been able to scent him from the moment he arrived." He raised an eyebrow. "You can't fool me. Oh, you fooled him, but he's blinded by love and all its overwhelming sensations. I see the truth." He sat silently and waited for her to say something.

Sofia rubbed her head, not really knowing what to tell him.

"You've been avoiding the *dead* employees, acting as though you're afraid. But it's not the vampires you fear. It's just one particular man and only because he calls to you in a way no one ever has."

She bit her lip. There was nothing in the world like having an old vampire call you out on being in love. He eyed her with all the confidence of an oracle.

"Come now. Admit it."

Sofia sighed. "Yes. I noticed Dragomir's scent immediately. The moment I opened my car door the morning after he arrived I smelled him. Even from the Lower Level I could smell him all the way outside. I'll never forget that moment. It was the very second all my senses came alive. Like I'd just awakened from a deep sleep." She brought her hands to her face and inhaled. She still smelled of him hours later.

Jankin nodded. "Can't get enough of him?"

Sofia shook her head and stared at her hands. She couldn't. She'd faked not loving Dragomir so well she'd even started to believe it. But now having Jankin ask made it impossible to pretend anymore. She needed Dragomir, would die without him. She loved him so deeply her whole body ached. It was then she realized the crystals clung to her like millions of little fingers, massaging her pained body.

"You've obviously done some work toward your bond," Jankin said. "Most couples don't leave their bedroom until the bond is sealed. He smiled.

Sofia's cheeks heated. She was not comfortable with discussions about her private life. She'd struggled telling Dragomir about her past, never mind having everyone know what they'd started but not finished.

"Do you know how ridiculous a master vampire looks when he stutters mid-sentence while he tries to bargain for his mate's happiness?" Jankin snorted.

Sofia's head jerked up to find Jankin bent over, holding his side and laughing. After several moments, his loud chuckles shifted to silent belly-shaking laughter, and then on to teary gasps for air.

"Oh. Oh. You had to see his face." He banged his fist on the desk and howled. "If I never see another funny thing in all my existence, I won't care. I'll cherish this memory forever." He finally sat back into the chair, dabbing his face with his handkerchief. "Oh, Sofia. You are without a doubt his true mate. No one else could have accomplished that. The moment you commanded him back to Cader he froze and stumbled." Jankin took a deep breath and sighed. "The bond gripped him so tightly he winced." He chuckled again.

Jankin reclined in the seat, his legs out straight and arms hanging over the armrests. He continued laughing. Though he looked toward Sofia, he did not seem to notice her. It was the puffy, glittery cloud that captured his attention. "Once your bond with him is strong enough it will dissipate. No one but you and Dragomir will be able to see it. Well, for the most part. The rest of us will notice it on occasion, when something happens, high emotions and the like. It will reappear to others when it's needed."

"I had wondered if I'd have this ridiculous sparkling shadow riding on my back for the rest of my life." She peered at her shoulder.

"Well, that's the other thing." Jankin laughed again. "A glitter-covered warrior marching up the front steps of the farm, moonlight glinting off him. I think he was more deadly than usual because he was sparkling. You left him no choice but to finish his mission in record speed." Jankin could barely get the words out through the peals of laughter. "Oh, Sofia. You have to put him out of his misery."

# CHAPTER THIRTY-FOUR

The door was unlocked. Not one light was lit, though Dragomir was very easy to find. Above the couch his half of the bond churned like a tidal wave. He reclined on the sofa, bare feet hanging over one arm while his head propped against the other. One hand rested on his chest. The other clung to a vodka bottle. A stake lay on the coffee table.

"I've already selected the weapon." He raised the bottle toward the stake. "There you go, love. Come take your freedom." He tipped the bottle toward his lips and swallowed several mouthfuls.

Sofia walked to the table and sat beside the stake.

"What's the wait? Get on with it. Let's be free." Much faster than Sofia could follow, Dragomir sat up, pressed the stake into her hand and lay back, bringing the point to his heart. "Right here. Raise up and thrust down with all your might. I won't fight you." He nodded. "Come on. Time's wasting."

Sofia wrestled her hand from his and replaced the stake on the table. "I don't want you to die."

"Right. I told you if one of us dies the other lives in misery. It's a sad truth, but you'll have a few weeks, months maybe of unaffected freedom. Our union's not that strong. You might even have a full year." He grabbed the stake and shoved it back into her hand. "Take it, love. It's the best you're going to get. Now finish me."

Sofia threw the stake over the couch. "I don't want you to die because I love you, not because I'm afraid to die."

"Love me?" He drained the last third of the vodka from the bottle. "Is that what that was?'" He swatted at the rapidly circling glitter above him. "Love. I'd have never guessed it."

Sofia moved to the couch, pulled the empty vodka bottle from Dragomir's hand and placed it on the coffee table. "It's not as though I've had a lot of experience with love. And certainly never with this sort of thing." She wove her hands through the air above the couch and sent the illuminated cloud dancing. "I shouldn't be condemned without being given an opportunity to explain." She rested her hand on his chest.

Dragomir stared up at her unblinking. Sofia suddenly felt hollow, as though a pit had opened in her belly. She wished he'd say something. But he didn't. He just stared at her. Every so often he'd take a breath.

What seemed like an eternity passed between them. Sofia bit her lip and fidgeted with the buttons on his shirt, not daring to look past his lips.

"Do you plan to explain tonight?" His tone was cold, disinterested. "If not, get the stake."

"Well, I..." Now she didn't know what to say. It seemed so simple when she admitted to Jankin she loved Dragomir. Jankin seemed pleased to hear it. Dragomir looked like he'd rather be staked. His dark eyes stared through her. The muscles of his jaw ticked.

"I loved you the moment you arrived at Cader. Even when I said I didn't like you. Even when I told you to go away. And when I said I didn't need you, I lied." She turned away. "I did call you back to Cader to teach you a lesson. At first. I wanted you to know not to order me around."

She tried to stand, but Dragomir's arm came across her lap. "Stay put."

Sofia gritted her teeth. "You have no respect for me. I just told you I don't want you to order me around and you did it again. If you want to be separate from me, fine." When she tried to stand, his arms locked around her.

"I never said I wanted to be separated from you. Not once." He flipped her down onto the couch and easily maneuvered around so she lay beneath him. "I want you with me forever." His mouth came to hers and he whispered against her lips. "Above all else I want you to be happy. Preferably with me." He kissed her tenderly at first, but when she responded, holding him to her, his lips pressed more firmly.

The hard wall of emotion she'd met coming in the door melted away to be replaced by heated desire and need. How quickly his focus went from anger with her to removing her clothes.

Sofia had to turn her head to breathe. "Don't ever make a decision that impacts us both without consulting me first." She panted. "I'm not one of the rank and file. I'm your wife."

Dragomir smiled. "Yes, you are. And I believe you have some wifely duties to attend to." He tugged her shirt up over her head.

"Is this all you think about?" Sofia unbuttoned his jeans.

"Lately, yes."

"We're not through with this discussion." She ripped open his shirt.

"No, we're not. And that's the fourth shirt to be destroyed since I met you." He sat up, legs on either side of hers, and shrugged out of the ruined fabric.

"Stop wearing them and this won't happen." Sofia wiggled out of her jeans, careful not to lift a knee too high and put a major kink in what was turning out to be a nice end to their fight. She struggled with the ankles. Dragomir reached back and jerked the jeans clear away.

His mouth was back on hers in no time.

Sofia's hands moved up and down his back, squeezing and clawing. She was ready now. No need to delay. No need for foreplay. She lifted her hips. "Can we get straight to it?" She nipped his lips. "Please?" She pressed into Dragomir.

He growled. "I said I only want to please you." He thrust forward and the glow of their union lit the room as if the sun shined down on them.

Sofia had never seen anything like it. She could barely think of words to describe what she saw. Every color of the rainbow and so much emotion. Warmth.

Reflection. Memory. Love. Comfort. Protection. Need. Trust. Hope. Unity. The entity rising above them encompassed everything she could ever need or want. She watched it swirl above them in awe.

The light expanded until the brightness was too much for her eyes and she tucked her head into Dragomir's shoulder. His breath came ragged against her ear.

Her body moved with his like they were made for each other. Each working to please the other. Even with the pleasure of his skin against hers she couldn't help but watch the glittering beauty dancing above them.

"Love, that pretty cloud will be here for several days. There's no need to ignore me." He stopped moving and flipped them around so Sofia straddled him. Then he pushed her up to a seated position. "Now you can just focus on me." He smiled.

With rhythmic movements he pushed in and out and she met his pace, riding him until she was overcome by ecstasy. Even with her eyes closed she saw the light brighten. Beneath her she heard Dragomir's moan. His fingers dug into her flesh and his body became rigid.

When he relaxed, he pulled her down onto him and sighed. "I haven't lain in the sun in almost a thousand years." He tucked a hand under his head and used the other to rub Sofia's back. "You are the light to my darkness." He kissed her head.

She curled into his arms, wanting nothing more than to be his forever.

# CHAPTER THIRTY-FIVE

Four days later a visit from Jankin made it clear Dragomir had little choice but to leave Sofia and their quarters. The call to duty clashed with his desire to stay with his mate and finish sealing their bond, but he knew well avoiding the impending war could have far worse consequences than delaying his time with Sofia. After they had gone to the farm and thwarted Bas Dubh's attempt to kill Sofia, Kiernan ordered a larger scale attack.

The fastest high school track stars were turning up missing all across the state. Local colleges reported their biggest football players quit the team and dropped out of school, and several state police officers had called in sick for the last four days.

Jankin was certain none of it was coincidental. "The troops from the British Isles arrived last night. Vampires and wolves. Thank God for Rowan. But we need leadership in the field."

Sofia stood in the doorway leading from the gym into the living room. Sweat dripped down her neck and back. Her muscles vibrated from the grueling workout she'd just had. "What about the interrogators? Weren't they able to ascertain anything from the wolves?"

Jankin had interrupted Dragomir's training session with Sofia. She was becoming the world's greatest lover and fighter all in less than a week. The reward for fighting was always a nice makeup session. It was fantastic motivation, if he did say so himself.

"Aye. We know Kiernan himself orchestrated the fire at the farm last year. His primary goal had been capturing Sofia. He'd made arrangements for Judy and her sister to trap Sofia. But his plan backfired when Judy was killed by the flames," Jankin said. He paced the floor as though he was mulling the information. "He has sworn to use the power of the roses against us."

"Then his attack is personal." Dragomir handed Sofia a glass of juice. "But for which of us, you or me, Jankin?" He caressed Sofia's chin. The urge to reward her efforts in the gym surged.

She blinked up and smiled that coy grin that had a way of distracting him.

"It was a clear threat to both, planned for many years and certainly he's up on his Alliance gossip. He knew of your mating before most everyone else." Jankin paced. "Dice heard about the mating from Orion who'd heard it in the field. It seems you announced it yourselves after you left Cader but before you were sealed." Jankin motioned toward the crystal wave flowing between Sofia and Dragomir.

Sofia dropped her head forward with a groan. "That damn glitter cloud gave us away. I never even noticed it until we…" She waved toward Dragomir. "You know."

He smiled and grasped her hand. "Nor did I."

Sparkles continued to zoom around them, though the number of visible flecks had diminished considerably.

"You had a lot on your minds as it were. And apparently Bas Dubh agents have been lurking closer than we'd realized." Jankin continued pacing. "Sofia, I must take Dragomir away for a bit. This assault on innocents must be ended."

"Of course. At this point I might—"

"No." Dragomir and Jankin echoed each other, their voices booming.

"You'll be safest here in the stronghold," Jankin answered.

Sofia frowned. "With all this training I thought I'd offer." She twined her fingers with Dragomir's. "Just be careful."

Dragomir kissed her neck. "Always. There's plenty of food in the fridge. I'll be back as soon as I can. You'll have Internet access on the computer. We'll look into a TV when I return."

"You don't think I'm staying down here, do you?" Sofia asked. She squeezed his hand. "I'm going to work. I have things to do. Policies to write. Employees to meet with. I have a job." She took the empty glass from Dragomir's hand and headed for the kitchen. "I won't leave the building. But I'm not staying in the basement."

"She'll be the death of me," Dragomir said.

"Let's shower and change so we can go to work." She crossed the living room and stopped short before the hallway. "I need more clothes, business appropriate clothes." She stepped toward the door. "I'll borrow something from Noelle until this is settled."

Dragomir knew she was debating the idea of home. She'd mentioned it several times over the past few days. He'd managed to dodge the conversation in spite of wanting to settle it outright. Sofia had been through enough and he wanted her to enjoy a few days before they had to decide where to live. He wanted to enjoy her before having to choose between her or The Alliance.

"Then I'll go home for my stuff." Sofia bit her lip.

Dragomir stole a look at Jankin. The Master appeared as worried as he felt.

Dragomir wasn't accustomed to having someone glance at him and so easily know what he felt. Sofia practically read his mind. He'd have found it utterly disturbing, if he didn't love her so damn much. But as it was, he wasn't fast enough at covering his reaction to her statement.

She wasn't even looking at them, but she knew something was up. "Out with it." She turned to face them.

"She's your mate," Jankin said. "I don't want to interfere."

"Such a close relationship with her family. You've known her since birth. Far be it for me to trump that," Dragomir said.

The two men stared at each other.

"Are you both wimping out? This is rich. You're more afraid of me than Bas Dubh?" Sofia smirked.

"Not afraid." Dragomir shook his head.

"No. No. Not fear," Jankin agreed. "Not sure what you'd call it, but it's not fear."

"Let's shower. You have Noelle's clothes. We'll dress and I'll take you up to your office." Dragomir turned Sofia toward the bathroom, looked at Jankin, and nodded toward the door.

"Yes. I'll see you at the board meeting." Jankin made a hasty exit.

Sofia watched Jankin leave. "You're up to something."

"Love, I don't have much time. I need to attend the meeting so let's not delay." Dragomir stripped down and jumped into the shower, leaving Sofia trailing after him. He managed to shower and exit the bathroom before she'd even shampooed her hair. And as painful as it was to tear his gaze from the silhouette of her naked body in the shower, he did. Anything to avoid upsetting her. He waited in the living room.

Sofia emerged smelling of a combination of perfumed soaps, fruity flowers, and crisp autumn air. "What kind of soap is that? Coast?"

"No. It's Romanian. The old women in my village make it."

"Huh." She nodded. "I like it."

It took all the fortitude Dragomir could muster to escort her to her office and leave her there while he went to the board meeting. And for longer than he'd ever hoped to have to endure, he sat through the meeting, listening, debating, and planning all the while wanting to be with his mate.

Two hours later Dragomir and Jankin went to Sofia's office to try to explain why she no longer owned a home. From the look on her face it was clear she wasn't pleased with the information.

She held the inside of her cheek between her teeth. Her eyes narrowed and she barely blinked. It was the exact expression she'd had when she lectured Dragomir about sexual harassment.

Streamers of the union connecting Sofia and Dragomir raced between them. Considering her stance on workplace violence, she hadn't responded as well as he and Jankin had hoped. He would have stood closer in hopes it would ease Sofia's acceptance of the information, but he didn't want her to hit him again. His chin still hurt.

She'd taken quite well to his lessons on fighting. And when he was foolish enough to remind her of her Workplace Violence Policy, she'd coldcocked him. At that moment he was more than pleased to have heeded Dice's advice on waiting to teach her how to dispatch a vampire.

"So let me understand. You torched my house." She stared from Dragomir to Jankin and back.

"It was the only way." When Sofia stood up, Dragomir stepped back. "You said you'd remain seated."

One eye narrowed while the opposite eyebrow shot up. It was the expression that played on her face whenever she was deciding her strategy for attack. Dragomir had been able to predict her movements in practice because of the obvious signs she exhibited. Eventually he'd have to teach her not to show them, but for now he braced himself.

"My family home. You burned my family's home."

"The flowers had already rooted into the house. The entire living area was covered in thorns. The perfume of the roses made it near impossible for the wolves to enter. They had to wear masks." Jankin leaned forward. "Sofia, the roses had tasted you. They had to have come in contact with your blood. It's the only explanation for what they did in that building."

"My home." Her eyes glistened. "All my parents' things. Every memory. All the mementoes. Gone." She cleared her throat.

"No, love. We salvaged as much as we could from the top floor before the fire." Dragomir reached for her and she leaned into him, wrapping her arms around his waist. "The boxes are in receiving. We'll get them down to our quarters soon." He rubbed her back and wanted nothing more than to take her to retrieve her things then sit back with a glass of wine and watch her unpack herself into his quarters.

If she was set on remaining in Rhode Island, he would. He'd go wherever she wanted. He'd do his duty for The Alliance from whatever location made her happy. But, if she was willing, he'd take her to Romania and show her his home, his land, his world. She would light his castle like no one ever had.

"My mother's things," she whispered. "That's all I had left of her."

Dragomir squeezed her tight. "I'm sorry, love." He sighed and glanced at Jankin.

"Sofia, did you touch the roses, remove them from the vase?" Jankin's voice was strained as though he was trying not to demand the answer.

"One. I held it by the stem." She sniffled. "Then I put it back in the arrangement."

"Were there thorns?" Jankin asked.

"Yes. Quite a few. I pricked my fingers several times." She dabbed at her eyes.

"Hmm. That's why the roses took hold so quickly. They tasted you." Jankin nodded. "I thought the scent of the roses at the farm was much stronger than usual. He's perfected his poison." Jankin removed his cell phone and sent a text message.

"It would seem so. That's only a few drops of her blood over a twenty-four hour period." Dragomir kept his arm around Sofia. "Love, the entire first floor was overrun with pulsing rose vines. They'd begun to creep up the stairs." He tilted her chin up and placed a soft kiss to her lips. "We had no choice."

She nodded, though tears flooded her eyes again. "It's just that was my parents' home, and my dad grew up there. It's the only home I've ever really had."

Dragomir's heart ached. To see his mate distraught was worse than any other punishment. His vision faded to black and white. He closed his eyes. Kiernan would pay for hurting her.

The phone in Dragomir's breast pocket vibrated when the text Jankin sent to The Board arrived. *Eventide. Moontide.*

The wolves would succumb to the poison of the roses much easier than the vampires, especially if the roses recognized any of them. The eventide meant the first wave of the attack would be the vampires. The wolves would follow. "I'll lead the assault," Dragomir said. "She is my wife. I want to ensure Kiernan gets the message."

"We go together. She is my family." Jankin stroked Sofia's cheek. "I'll be in the war room." With a curt nod he left Dragomir alone with Sofia.

"Where are you going? I thought you took care of the farm." Sofia reached for a tissue on her desk.

"There seems to be a camp within twenty miles. We go to destroy it and take prisoners." Dragomir picked up his coat. Though it was weighted down with several stakes, silver throwing stars, and four knives he slipped into it with ease.

"That's a lot of stakes for prisoners." She sniffled.

"I like to be prepared." He smiled. "I'll be back before dawn. There's no need for you to stay up all night." Dragomir placed a small skeleton key in Sofia's hand. "This will unlock the first lock on the door to our quarters."

"I'll wait. I have a lot of work to catch up on." Sofia pointed to the stack of envelopes piled on her desk.

"Yes, but you are not a vampire. You need sleep." He curled her fingers around the key. "You don't have to remain awake."

"As if I could sleep with you and Jankin and everyone else out there." Sofia looked toward the darkened window.

"Do your best. When I get back, I'll want you well rested." He nuzzled her neck. "We'll be fine. After using the key, place your left hand flat above the knob and the second lock will release."

"Just come back." Sofia wrapped her arms around his neck.

"I will always come back to you."

# CHAPTER THIRTY-SIX

The troops left the stronghold just after midnight. Sofia watched them go from her darkened office. She was no help in a battle, and in all truthfulness, she was frightened. She hadn't bothered to offer to go even though she wanted to mete out some sort of vengeance for her family. There would have been no point to attempting the argument. Plus, she knew her presence would simply be a distraction to everyone.

When the last of the team disappeared into the woods, Sofia wandered downstairs to the inpatient units. She still hadn't met all the staff and figured now was as good a time as any. The highlight of being in the employee relations position was getting to know people when they weren't in trouble.

It was a slower than usual night on the second floor. Of the sixteen beds only four were occupied. A nurse sat behind the desk and one walked the floor.

"Can I help you?" the pretty redheaded vampire seated at the desk asked with a toothy smile. She clicked a couple keys on the computer and the screen went blank.

"I'm Sofia Engle, the Employee Relations Manager," Sofia answered. "I just came by to say hello and introduce myself."

"Engle or Petrescu?" The blond coming up the hall asked. Her fangs were descended and her blue eyes glowed.

"I haven't quite decided…shouldn't you put those away?" Sofia knew very well the Professional Appearance Policy required everyone to always appear human with no traces of supernatural presentation. Fangs and glowing eyes certainly did not work.

The blond frowned and let her fangs slide under her gums. "So sorry. I'm Rachel. This is Lisa." As she extended her hand her eyes became crystal blue.

The gleam in her stare stood as a warning and Sofia suspected the vampire would break another important rule, the one about unleashing even a flicker of vampire power on humans.

Sofia braced herself then grasped Rachel's hand. A mild sizzle of power hummed up Sofia's arm. "I'm fairly certain that's unacceptable as well," she said.

"Is it? I hadn't realized we couldn't be ourselves in front of you." Rachel released Sofia's hand. "It's a pity. We had hoped you'd be fun." She leaned on the counter beside Sofia. "We get so few visitors up here at night. It'll be especially boring tonight with everyone out."

Sofia noticed a monitor on the desk showing two flat lines. "Are those monitoring the patients?"

Lisa followed Sofia's gaze. "Oh, yeah. But they're fine." Lisa stuck a pencil under her cap and scratched her head.

"Nothing to worry about," Rachel said. "I was just down there. They're all set, tucked in for the night." She tugged at the collar of her white uniform.

"Where's the nursing assistant?" Sofia asked. It was odd that the nursing assistant was nowhere to be seen with so few patients. She focused on the floor, trying to sense any vampires or wolves that might be present. Though the two nurses stood in front of her, Sofia registered none of their energy. But down the hall she sensed a young vampire. And she knew from the aching energy the vampire was in distress.

The two nurses glanced at each other.

"Break," Rachel finally said. "Be back in a bit."

"The census is low tonight. So what's the caseload like?" Sofia asked. She waited to hear if either nurse could give her any idea of what the patients' needs were.

They glanced at each other again.

"We don't want to bore you with medical mumbo jumbo." Lisa walked around the desk and reached beneath. "Flower?" She pushed a bouquet of roses into Sofia's face.

The moment the flowers touched Sofia's skin they sprang to life, puffing an unnaturally fragrant aroma into the air.

Sofia gasped and backed away.

"Come here, girl." Rachel jumped over the counter and barreled toward Sofia. The front of her white uniform was covered in blood from her waist to her feet. "We've been waiting for you all night." Her fangs descended beneath amber glowing eyes.

"He said it would be easy. I just can't believe they really left you here alone." Lisa held up the bouquet of roses. "Taste one. They're delish." She made a show of licking her lips.

Sofia roundhouse kicked Rachel and the vampire flew backward over the counter into Lisa. She didn't wait to see if she'd done any damage. She bolted down the hall and into a patient room only to come face to face with the nursing assistant. She was strapped to the bed in silver. The smell of burning flesh stunned Sofia.

"Help me. Let me up. Please. Please. My skin." The poor girl's skin bubbled and blistered. Puss and blood oozed where the silver touched her.

Sofia covered her mouth and peeled away the silver, trying not to lose the contents of her stomach all over the girl. "I'm so sorry." She tried to be as gentle as she could.

"Just hurry. They're coming." She staggered to her feet and pulled up her pant leg to remove a stake from a shin strap above her calf. "I knew there was something wrong with them. They've been awfully happy these past couple nights. When they arrived tonight they were practically giddy. They're usually so miserable. I can't stand them. Rotten wenches."

The nursing assistant tore a strip from the bed sheet and tied it around her neck. She did the same with her waist. "You're Dragomir's mate, right?"

She nodded. "Yes. Sofia."

"I'm Amy. I know you hate fighting, but you're going to have to help me. I might be able to handle one, but never two. Not like this." Her wounds had stopped bubbling but the oozing puss ran down her neck, hands, and scrubs.

"There's blood in the lab," Sofia said. "If we can get down there and—"

The door blasted in. "Come here, you." Rachel stood in the doorway. Blood oozed down her face and smeared across her cheeks. "You're going to pay for this." She held up a fang. "These don't grow back."

Lisa snorted behind her.

"I'm so sorry. I hadn't meant to hurt you." Sofia stepped backward.

"No? What did you think kicking me in the face would do?" Rachel sneered. Blood dripped from the spot where her fang should have been. "You're mine. If he thinks I'm bringing you in, he's crazy after that move."

"You don't have to do this," Sofia said.

"Yes I do." Rachel licked the gap created by her missing fang. The look of hatred on her face said it all. Sofia would pay with her life.

Sofia remembered what Dragomir taught her. *Stake through the heart.*

"You're going to wish you'd never heard of vampires when I'm through."

Sofia grabbed the IV pole beside the bed and hurled it like a javelin just like she'd seen Melanie Andrews do in the Emergency Room.

Rachel's voice silenced. A high-pitched keening cry sounded behind her. The bodies of both vampires dropped to the floor in the doorway. They landed on their knees, mouths open, eyes holding only vacant stares.

"That could not just be adrenaline," Amy said. She slumped back onto the bed still gripping her stake. "If I hadn't seen that with my own eyes, I'd never believe it could happen. Man I wish I'd gotten it on video."

Sofia's hands shook. She'd killed someone. Two people. "They were going to kill me. It was the right thing to do." Her voice quaked. She couldn't catch her breath. Her heart pounded so loudly it was all she heard. Amy's lips moved, but Sofia couldn't hear a thing. The room began to spin and darken until finally all was quiet.

*****

Something cool rested on Sofia's forehead. "Open your eyes, love."

Sofia whimpered.

"You're fine. Wake up." Dragomir's voice was steady, but it didn't hide the emotion behind it.

Sofia felt his concern and something else. She couldn't quite recognize the other feeling. It was powerful and edgy and coursed through him like raging water. After several minutes studying the feeling she understood. Dragomir fought to hide his fear and worry and anger.

She opened her eyes. His face was the first thing she saw. Dark hair hung above her just barely tickling her skin. Midnight blue eyes gazed at her above a smile to melt her heart. That edgy power ebbed, receding until finally it disappeared. Sofia tried to smile, though her head throbbed.

"You did quite well." He kissed her forehead and she winced. "Put a nice knot on your head when you passed out, too." He placed an icy gel pack on the sore spot.

"When did you get back?" She tried to sit up but the room tumbled. "Uuh."

"Just lie still and rest." Dragomir pressed her back into the pillow.

The large room was barely lit, but she could see IV poles and metal trays holding instruments. There was a monitor beside the bed where she lay and beds on either side of hers. Across the room was another row of beds, some of which were occupied, though Sofia didn't know who lay in them.

"This isn't the ER," she said.

"No, it's the infirmary. We're in the Lower Level." Dragomir straightened the sheet covering Sofia. "It's noon. I couldn't leave you upstairs." He smiled.

"What happened in your fight?" She remembered quite vividly what occurred with the nurses. For some reason the squishing sound of the IV pole stabbing into both vampires played in her mind. She swallowed hard. "Wait. Who were those nurses?"

"Rachel and Lisa were Bas Dubh informants. They'd gone over to the other side shortly after you started here." Dragomir held Sofia's hand. His skin was cool against hers.

She nodded. "I killed them." She looked up at him. She'd never killed anything bigger than a stinkbug before last night. Her stomach twisted and she looked at her hands. Killer's hands.

"So much for nonviolent responses." Dragomir watched her. She felt him sizing her up, waiting for her reaction.

"It was one of those necessary moments. A me or them situation." Even though she said the words and knew them to be the truth, she still fought to keep the tears from her eyes.

"Hey." He turned her chin toward him. "It was the right thing. They had lost all sense of reason and moved to the other side."

She nodded.

"Sofia, they'd have killed many more people, first humans and eventually, when they were strong enough, vampires and werewolves. Your act was a justice for society. Don't forget that. Don't let your feelings about the action cloud your judgment."

Squeaky wheels and clanging trays drew Sofia's attention. Osgar and Rick pushed a table with a giant potted plant. A multitude of slender spikes covered in small spiky yellow flowers spiraling up the stems waved with the motion of the table.

"The mignonette," Dragomir said. The word rolled off his tongue and Sofia smiled.

"My favorite flower. How did you know?"

"I did not. But this is the fragrance I smell whenever I'm near you." He turned to face both Sofia and the flowers. "One greenhouse held several of these spiky little things." He slipped a stem of flowers through his palm then smelled his skin and smiled. "The Little Darling."

"Oh, so you know about flowers, do you?"

"Just my little darling." The smile on his face widened.

Sofia blushed.

Osgar groaned. "Okay. There'll be plenty of time for that when you're home." He plopped onto the bed, yanking the file folder out from under his arm. "You'll be pleased to know we have edited, approved, signed, and posted the new Workplace Violence Policy." He opened the file and held it for Sofia to read.

She sat up. "Wait. Edited? Edited? How? Which draft is this? Posted? I haven't signed anything." She pulled the paper toward her.

Dragomir turned on the light above the bed and Sofia squinted against the brightness. As her eyes became accustomed to the light she read the draft. It was clearly the one she had written, edited, reedited, rewritten, and nearly given up hope for getting approved. But here it was signed by Fergus and Osgar. Two empty lines remained. One for her signature and one for Dr. MacDuff.

"Here." Rick pointed to a paragraph on the second page. "Wolves and vampires not suitable for front line positions will be reassigned to other duties within the stronghold." A slight smile curved his lips but vanished before anyone could have tried to prove it happened.

"So Louis?"

"He's learning how to understand the monitoring system for now. Eventually, he'll go back to college, probably become an engineer and find himself a nice job at Cader." Rick handed Sofia a pen. "Your turn."

"Wait a minute." She closed the folder and turned to Dragomir. "Jefferson? What about him?"

"You'll have your chance to meet with him. Guarded, of course." Dragomir's eyebrow crept up and his lips pulled into a tight line.

She squared her shoulders, knowing full and well guarded meant with him plastered to her side and probably Noelle, Osgar, and Rick restraining Jefferson. But it was a start. "I knew you'd see it my way."

"I'll admit I didn't believe you when you included the line 'Deadly force will only be used in extreme situations involving imminent danger and clear threat of death,' but then you killed those two bitches. Now I have to believe you're a woman of your word." This time the smile on Rick's face was unmistakable.

Sofia frowned and took the pen.

"Still coming to terms with what happened." Dragomir rubbed her back. "She'll get there."

"I'm not killing anyone else." Sofia made one minor edit and signed her name then closed the file on the policy.

"Well, she's awake." Noelle's voice came from behind Rick and Osgar. "You were a more difficult patient than most." She stepped between the men and handed Sofia a glass of juice. "Complaining about your head and telling me not to bother with you. Where's my husband? Go take care of Amy. Ah, Amy's fine." Noelle waved her hand at Sofia. "This is why I like the vamps and wolves better. They know better than to give me shit."

Amy sat up in the bed across from Sofia. "I'm fine. Who needs to sleep during the day when you're only twenty? Certainly not someone who was attacked and chained in silver by two of the most horrible coworkers a girl could have. Her curled red hair bounced all around her head. "And let me just say, they were not our best nurses." She flopped back onto her pillow. "I deserve a raise after last night."

"Go back to sleep, little one," Dragomir whispered the words and Amy stopped grumbling and sighed. Faint snores came from her bed.

Sofia looked at Dragomir in a quizzical way.

"She is mine." He raised his eyebrows. "Nice kid, but talks too much."

Sofia knew from the powerful rumble of energy entering the room Jankin and Fergus were headed toward them.

Jankin smiled, looking much less worried than he'd appeared in the past few days. His eyes were brighter, face gentler, shoulders relaxed. Sofia wasn't sure she'd seen him look this relaxed since she'd started at Cader.

"You're looking well," she said.

"As are you, Sofia. Thankfully, you're looking radiant." He admired the mignonette. "Yes, this is the one." He nodded to Dragomir and chuckled.

All around Sofia she felt powerful ribbons of energy coursing. The currents coming from her husband, Noelle, and Jankin were smooth as glass though fluid as water. The werewolf energy vibrated. In her mind's eye she pictured a lightning storm where brilliant bolts shot along the skyline one after another.

She wanted to ask about it but remembered the way Fergus had reacted when he learned Sofia could sense the wolves.

"What is it? You look confused," Noelle asked.

Sofia glanced at Dragomir. "I can tell when certain people are around but not others." She frowned, unsure of how to proceed.

"Do you mean the wolves?" Dragomir's voice lowered.

"And some vampires," she said.

"You will be able to sense anyone bound to me," Dragomir explained. "Our union gives you access to my progeny and any of my wolves. So you're now linked to Osgar and Amy and others."

Sofia nodded and briefly glanced toward Rick and Fergus and then looked away.

"Ah, the werewolf whispering. That's what troubles you." Jankin clapped a hand on Fergus's shoulder. "I've explained how I bound you to me when you started at Cader in order to ensure your loyalty to our cause. I apologize for not allowing you to remember the incident but it was for your own good."

Jankin gazed at Sofia and though his face remained expressionless Sofia felt him coaxing her into agreement. The hazel fleck in his green eyes sparkled and he appeared more like a mischievous college boy than a thousand-year-old vampire.

"Oh," was all she said.

"I believe there is a policy awaiting my signature." Jankin held out his hand.

Sofia handed over the file and pen.

"The prisoners are ready." Laurent strode into the infirmary. "I believe at least two of them can tell us about upcoming attacks and possibly know the whereabouts of Kiernan's lair."

"Very good. We use whatever force is necessary." Fergus cleared his throat. "They aren't employees. They're war criminals. Osgar, Rick, let's get going." He stepped aside to let them pass.

"See ya, Sofia." Osgar followed Rick. "Hey." He turned around and walked backward toward the door. "Before you come back to work, make me some more cookies." He grinned.

"Okay." She laughed.

"Dragomir, take care of your mate. Sofia, don't be so rough on him. We need you both." Fergus smiled. "I'll see you soon." He left the infirmary, getting the full report from Laurent as he went.

Jankin perused the policy. "Very well done, Sofia. It took some doing, but I think you might even be learning patience. It was never one of your strong points."

Sofia couldn't argue. She sighed.

"Plenty of time for learning patience, love." Dragomir stroked his fingers up and down her arm.

Jankin flipped to the signature page and smiled. "Congratulations, Dragomir." He signed the last empty line and handed the file back to Sofia. "Petrescu. It's a good last name. Strong. Very fitting for our Employee Relations Manager."

Dragomir's gaze met Sofia's. He couldn't quite stop the smile from appearing on his lips.

"Well, we are married," she said.

"That we are, love."

Thank you for reading Black Magic Rose, Book 1 in The Alliance Series. I hope you enjoyed it. If you did, help other people find my book by writing a review.

**Look for these other stories by Jordan, available on
Kindle, Nook and other eRetailers:**

The Demon Mistress, Book One in The Eva Prim Series

**The Eva Prim short story collection is available
on Kindle, Nook, and Kobo.**

Demons and Deep Dish Pizza
Demons and The Dark Roast
The Vampire Hand Guide: Myths, Tips & Advice
Choices. Anarchy. Hypocrisy.

**Also available in print and ebook from Amazon and Barnes & Noble:**

Perpetual Light

# ABOUT JORDAN

Jordan loves vampires. But if you know anything about Jordan, you already knew that detail. What you didn't know was it wasn't long ago that she began writing about them.

A few years back Jordan received a copy of a popular vampire story from her husband as part of an anniversary gift. Eight weeks and eighteen vampire books later the idea for her first book, Perpetual Light came to her followed very quickly by Eva Prim.

Jordan is a member of the national Romance Writers of America organization and several chapters.

When she's not writing about one vampire or another Jordan enjoys spending time with her husband, Ken and their lovable Labrador, Dino on the beautiful beaches of New England.

Sign up for my newsletter at *http://www.jordankrose.com/*

Follow her tweets. *https://twitter.com/#!/jordankrose*

Like her on Facebook. *https://www.facebook.com/pages/Jordan-K-Rose-Author/307285709309992*

Find her on Pinterest. *http://pinterest.com/jordankrose/boards/*